Meridian

TOOTH & CLAW

AURELIA T. EVANS

ENTWINED PUBLISHING

Tooth & Claw
ISBN # 978-1-80250-276-3
©Copyright Aurelia T. Evans 2025
Cover Art by Kelly Martin ©Copyright October 2025
Interior text design by Entwined Publishing
Published by Eternal, an Entwined Publishing imprint

Published in 2025 by Entwined Publishing, United Kingdom.

Entwined Publishing is a division of Totally Entwined Group Limited.

TOOTH & CLAW

Chapter One

The line out from Sordid didn't curve around the corner, but it was still ten o'clock before Rose made it to the front. However, once there, the bouncer immediately pulled back the velvet rope to let her in.

Becoming a vampire didn't make a person much more beautiful but for smoother, firmer skin and the healthiest of hair and nails, which continued to grow after undeath. However, vampires did tend to change humans who fit their ideal of beauty. They preferred not to forge deeper connections with humans, only the vampires they became, and, given their long lives in the dark, they almost always chose a lovely view.

She wouldn't have been the only lovely view in line for the historic downtown speakeasy, but the way she displayed that view certainly didn't hurt — nor the way the bouncer's neck scars stretched up from under his shirt collar as he turned.

Rose's gold heels were thin and high, but she didn't struggle on the steps down into the building's basement. Despite the dim red-tinged light — a staple for bars and clubs, but also a courtesy for Sordid's more nocturnal patrons — she could see the whole room clearly from its entrance.

She wasn't old enough to have attended speakeasies in their heyday, but she'd visited a number of dance and novelty clubs around Meridian since arriving a week ago, and already she liked Sordid better than most. A band at the front played low and slow, if not soft, with a torch singer whose voice was so sultry Rose wondered if her blood would taste of smoke.

In dance clubs, there was freedom in losing oneself to the music, to a rhythm so strong she thought her heart might be beating again, but it could also be so many flashing lights and sounds that she couldn't hear herself think even when she wanted to. Here, the bass provided a gentler pulse, the upright piano tingled emotion over her skin, while the singer's smoky alto thrummed something deeper, but she could also hear her own thoughts, and other people didn't have to shout to be heard. Sordid was not a place to discourage whispers or first or second thoughts. As the lights were dimmer for night eyes, the music was more tolerable for those with keen ears. Her senses all let out a sigh of relief as she stepped into the speakeasy.

There were roughly a hundred to a hundred twenty-five people in the relatively small basement, which was the reason for the line, although it was difficult to get a good count due to privacy curtains in the booths and a hallway that would lead to private rooms.

The speakeasy was strict about no money changing hands except between bouncer, bartender, or band. Everything else was barter, which was no different from any other venue that encouraged shallow carnality between its patrons.

She left the bar with a frosted glass of red to weave through the crowd.

One thing that set her apart from the rest was that she'd come alone. Most people in Sordid arrived in groups, from couples to packs, regardless of species. Safety in numbers meant safety for curiosity, with members of one group or couple sometimes breaking away to join another, mingling on the dance floor like tentative watercolors to the hypnotic, evocative, seductive music coming from the stage.

Rose was tempted to ask if the woman was a siren but decided to simply leave a good tip at the stage edge. The singer, with meticulously crafted finger curls, glistening red lips, and a glittering black dress, glanced down over her ribbon microphone and locked dark eyes with Rose. Then her gaze drifted down. Rose stood still, allowing the singer to take her time over the slinky liquid dress the color of pewter, loose enough that the thin straps threatened to fall away from her full breasts at the slightest provocation if Rose didn't know how to hold herself, or how to be perfectly, predatorially still. In Sordid, there was no reason to pretend she was anything but what she was.

She'd moved down to Texas because she'd wanted to finally enjoy solitude, and space, and rooftops, and beautiful windows that never slanted sunlight onto her bed but still brought daylight into her world. Yet she'd only been in Meridian alone for a week and already felt…lonely. A little over twenty years as human, a little over sixty as a vampire, she didn't think she'd ever been completely alone.

As a vampire of a vaunted and tight-knit family home, she hadn't been able to really choose her own company since she'd died—until she'd packed up all her beautiful things and signed away her right by blood to remain or return without going through the same channels as any outsider.

She didn't think she'd ever return.

That didn't mean there weren't things about her decision that were difficult, even frightening, although she was usually the creature in the dark that people feared.

The delicate titanium cuff on her ear and the oath in new ink around her wrist, however, indicated to those who knew what they meant that she was safer than most. And Sordid was an Alliance business. Not a demon club, where humans were victims, servants, slaves, or hunters trying to prove they were badass and unafraid. The Alliance was an agreement between vampires, werewolves, and hunters in Meridian that none would hunt the species of the others, as long as the hybrids were marked well enough for hunters to notice in the dark. Urban werewolf packs could run freely through city parks after dark, aiding the coyotes and bobcats in controlling the rodent, rabbit, and deer populations. Vampires could live peacefully off butcher blood and voluntary donors with a promise not to kill or turn. Hunters could focus their efforts on hybrids more inclined toward carnage.

The Alliance wasn't universally beloved, even among those who'd agreed to it, as evidenced by the occasional glower between the three camps coexisting within Sordid's walls. Sometimes mistakes were made or someone tried to use the Alliance to get away with murder. But the last twelve years had been a largely successful experiment, which was why Rose had moved to a completely different city in a completely different state, all by herself for the first time in decades.

And looking for someone who might make this freedom all the sweeter.

The torch singer was sweet indeed, and the shift of her body and cant of her hips suggested she thought the same about Rose in her evening gown, her inked oath and former family crest, her Art Deco diamond and emerald pendant—a gift from her sire long ago, chosen because of the way her cleavage framed it. The lower the singer sang, the more Rose wanted to draw her down to the dance floor and against her body so she could swallow the vibrations.

Rose sipped from her drink, unblinking, enjoying the music both close to the instruments and coming from the speakers and the waves of desire emanating from the singer, rising in something reminiscent of heat low in Rose's abdomen.

Large, hot hands smoothed over her shoulders, threatening the straps so carefully placed to keep herself as decent as a woman needed to be in a place like this. The man imposed but did not expose, trailed his palms down her arms before he pressed gently behind her.

"Beautiful woman like you shouldn't be alone." A subtle growl in the voice shivered like the singer's alto over and under Rose's skin. There was something so very alive in the stranger's heat and scent, heightened by the animal musk entwined with it. "I can see that you can take care of yourself, but you wouldn't have to with me."

Rose was tall in her heels, and the man still had to angle his head to rest his cheek on her shorn scalp, where his stubble was rougher than hers. She briefly leaned back in his hold, relishing his scent—all the vitality of a human and all the virility of a werewolf spilling from every pore and responding to the pheromones from hers. Perfumiers of her family home made colognes from both to sell to those who could afford not to ask the price.

He dragged his lips over her scalp and whispered in her ear, "Meet me there." He pointed to a booth currently occupied by another werewolf–vampire pair, both wearing titanium cuffs on their ears as well. The vampire was buried deep in the werewolf's shoulder. "I'm going to get myself a stiff drink, and you can get a *real* drink from me. Someone like you doesn't have to be alone for long."

Rose shrugged his hands off her arms, then stepped away from his furnace body. She didn't mind the ambient chill. "I already have a drink."

The werewolf's low rumbling growl of desire harshened. Rose didn't resent his upset. Werewolves were not renowned for their ability to conceal how they felt. Between human expression and werewolf volatility, emotions made themselves plain one way or another. Despite his disappointment, though, he drew away from her to seek satiation elsewhere.

It would not be unusual in Sordid to be approached out of interest for her bite. The vampire's thrall—a combination of mysticism, which vampires could control, and pheromone, which they could not—was addictive on both sides of any encounter, casual or long term. There were vampire clubs in Meridian, like the Slaughterhouse, designed to reel humans in like fish, but Sordid advertised itself through word of mouth as a place where people could satisfy the desire for a safer bite—one where they were guaranteed to make it through the night. There would inevitably be both the curious and the experienced from all factions allowed in the speakeasy.

As the band finished their set and headed to the bar for a break, stereotypically trance-like goth music filtered through the speakers — still not so loud that it would drown out conversation, whispers, the squeak of vinyl and soft moans, louder cries coming from behind closed doors. The speakeasy knew its patrons and what they came for, couldn't conceal the metallic tang of warmed blood on tap next to beer from local breweries, or the raw or lightly cooked meat that they provided from the kitchen. Most of the attendees were dressed in the gothic mode, much like the family many an evening within their sprawling house. Expectations were clear — not to mention detailed on their website and on a poster outside the building. It was a place for humans to safely visit, but it was *for* the vampires and werewolves, whether they embraced their costumes or not. As long as it wasn't some cheap Halloween ensemble, humans donning elements of vampire culture was considered both flattery and a certain amount of permission or invitation. The cultural expression was all a bit reductive — Rose had many more clothes than formalwear or gothic style — but sartorial expression was part of the ritual, like wearing Sunday best to church. She respected the effort and clearly made some of her own, as she had during feasts and parties in her own family home.

She joined the band at the bar with her drink and settled on a barstool a few seats away, waiting to see if the torch singer had merely been playing to her audience or was genuinely interested.

Twenty years ago, she would have just switched on the thrall and had the singer right there against the bar, leaving her faint or dead. There was an abundance of gutters here in Meridian in which to throw bodies. One of her new butchers had his own crematorium.

13

The singer glanced over her shoulder and met Rose's eyes. Then she slipped off her seat to bring her glass of prosecco over with her while the bassist and pianist grinned and returned to their discussion.

As the singer joined Rose on the next stool, she brushed her fingers over Rose's arm and leaned in. Rose was ready to kiss those lips, to smear the singer's red lipstick over her own makeup-free mouth like blood.

The singer shifted to the side to murmur in Rose's ear like the wolf. "No visible scars, but I flow freely in other places." She took Rose's hand and drew it under the slit in her skirt. She stopped Rose's fingers on her inner thigh, where smooth knots suggested she'd had teeth there many times before.

Rose kept her sigh to herself, but her lust went cold, like swimming through warm waters and hitting a pocket of fresh spring chill. She stroked over the scars with her nails, then pressed a kiss just under the singer's jaw, yearning for the pulse underneath and mourning the moan that arose. The singer's pleasure was just as pleasant as her music. Rose wished she could explore that more, perhaps in one of the private rooms. But she stroked the singer's cheek as she withdrew from her neck, from her thigh.

For a moment, the singer was stricken, but like the wolf, she accepted Rose's refusal with grace, despite confusion and frustration visible in the furrows beneath her finger curls.

Rose drank deeply from her glass, then left the bar again.

Searching.

Maybe this wasn't the place to find what she was looking for. Sordid was a venue where humans and werewolves wanted to get bitten by a vampire, where humans and vampires wanted sex with a less inhibited werewolf, where they all wanted to walk on the edge of a forest fire without getting burned. At its less aesthetic heart, it was a safe space for chasers.

Rose had had enough of that over the decades. So many humans had chased her into early graves. Werewolves had followed her into their own servitude.

But here she was, weary of arson and looking instead for a cozy little fire in a hearth.

She didn't think either the wolf or the singer would have trouble finding what they wanted, though, among the crowd of steadily introduced new blood as pairings and groups left the speakeasy—mutually satisfied or with the promise of a more private evening in softer, larger beds.

Rose's gaze finally fell on a cluster of werewolves gathered around a table piled with the chaos of cleared and partially cleared plates and assorted glasses of beer, wine, and bourbon.

As becoming a vampire smoothed and firmed skin, becoming a werewolf increased tone and tightness of muscle, bulky or lean as body type demanded, and they burned hotter than humans, which especially appealed to her sensitive sense of smell—sensitive everything, from heat-sensing that bordered on reptilian to the almost-taste of wolf musk emanating in a denser mist around them. Not to mention the scent of carefully prepared raw meat, designed for such patrons but also to keep health inspectors happy.

Among the friends gathered around the table, men and women met her eyes, angled toward her, and she knew she could hold out a hand and one or more might come with her. For an hour. For a few. There was knowledge in their consideration, in their quickening hearts, broadening desire, the intrigue of their attraction.

She stopped in front of the boy occupied with his plate of beef tartare. Stood in front of him until he noticed — or showed that he noticed. The larger cuff on his ear pushed through his long hair. When he looked up, the curtain of his hair fell away from his face. She expected it to be as casually scruffy as his hair was healthy and wild, loose around his shoulders and reaching halfway down his chest. But he was clean-shaven, with only a shadow of stubble from the end of day. His hair was brown in low light but gleamed with enough gold that sun likely made him blond — not that she could easily see that for herself. His eyes, too, seemed sun-bleached, piercingly blue, unsettlingly guileless.

Time would tell if those pale eyes, widening pupils, and wild hair could be trusted. In Rose's experience, beauty itself was suspicious, including her own. Many sharp things were wrapped in silk. But she liked what she saw. And there was no mistaking he did, too. Men had more trouble hiding that from her, werewolves even more so. That made them easier to manipulate, if she chose, but also less guileful by default.

The boy — everyone younger than her was 'boy', and as a vampire, she struggled to gauge ages, especially among the hyper-healthy werewolf population — lifted his plate of beef tartare to her like an offering. "Would you like some? I don't know if you can have it or not, but..."

Rose used her nail to gather a few pieces of beef. She didn't need anything other than blood, but she could appreciate animal protein as well as sugar. About the only foods she couldn't enjoy like she had so long ago that they seemed like dreams were vegetables and plain bread, although she adored chocolate cake.

She took the meat into her mouth and hummed around the bland shallots and hit of salt. Raw meat was better than cooked for her, too. She took his fork and gathered a larger bite, fought the urge to slither her tongue around the metal. She left the rest for his more voracious appetite, though she craved myoglobin.

A flush blooming over the boy's cheeks deepened the color in his lips. "So you *can* have things other than blood."

Now she wondered how young he really was, in the sense of how recently he'd been changed. All she knew was that, because he was here at all, he was old enough for her purposes.

"I like savory and sweet. What do you think runs through blood?" All blood tasted more or less the same to humans — that much she remembered — but vampire tongues discerned a thousand differences in the balance of what blood spread through a body to maintain it, from vitamins and minerals to fat, protein, and glucose. There was a mystical element to vampirism, of course. Nothing without a heartbeat should be able to live, move, breathe, speak, fuck, and yet they did. But in other ways they were just as biologically grounded as the werewolves.

She stole a slice of salmon from the sashimi plate and rested it on her tongue before drawing it in. Buttery, slick, rich, a little sweet, tender to bite.

In return for his hospitality, she held her drink out to him.

"Blood?" he asked.

"Does it smell like blood?"

A wolf could drink it if it were. He'd even enjoy it. He leaned in and put his lips where she'd put hers.

When she glimpsed his dark tongue, she tipped the glass to give him a taste. He smiled even as he swallowed.

"Sangria. Why choose cold around here when you can have hot?" he asked.

She took another drink. Macerated fruit mixed with red wine made her feel like a fruit bat trophy wife, but she loved it anyway. After just a week in Texas, she'd discovered sangria swirl margaritas and known she was going to have a problem, even though her body processed alcohol such that it had only the mildest effect.

Rose set her mostly finished glass on the table. She took the boy's hand instead, smiling when he shivered from her cold, wet skin. "Is that what you want me to do?"

"I asked you first."

"Dance with me?"

"Yes, ma'am."

"Boy, I know I moved south, but if you 'ma'am' me again, this evening's gonna end before it begins."

A charming grin stretched across his face. Fine folds suggested he was older than she'd initially thought. She still couldn't pinpoint a decade.

Rose stepped back until he had no choice but to stand to follow her. Standing took longer than expected. Everything about him was lankier than it appeared slouched back in his chair. His tunic-like shirt over fitted jeans accentuated the length of him, everything just a little too long.

Everything? part of her wondered, but that didn't distract her as much as the way he seemed to burst from his own clothes, shirtsleeves rolled up to keep from showing how his arms were too long for them, his jeans ripped from artistry rather than wear. His shoes were fashionable, buffed, and large.

She backed through the tables to the dance floor without having to look behind her. Either people got out of her way, she sensed their closeness, or she saw them through the werewolf's eyes — in their reflection or his concern.

On the dance floor, Rose guided his hand to her waist. He got the hint and joined it with his other, but he was still a gentleman, with space between their hips as they swayed to the rhythm of the pre-recorded music. Rose thought that was adorable, approaching perfect, and had to convince herself not to get her hopes up.

Even if he wasn't exactly what she was looking for, though, she'd already decided to give him the night, nice young man that he was.

"You're new around here," the wolf said.

"If that isn't just a line, how would you know?"

"I've never seen you in Sordid before. I would have noticed. I'm not cheesy enough to say you're the prettiest woman to walk through that door, but you're certainly striking. Also, your Alliance ink still smells wet."

He blushed again, but she drew an inch closer and smiled for him without letting her fangs slide down, although she caught him searching for them.

"Fresh. I mean it smells fresh," he said.

"Don't you mean ripe?" She sidled close enough now for her hips to brush against his.

He didn't pull away, just adjusted his arms to hold her better and encourage her to press closer, and she did. His natural heat wrapped around her like a good blanket in summer.

"I am new here," she finally replied. "To Sordid. To the city. I've been getting to know the nightlife. It's better than where I came from."

"It's not quite Vegas or New York, cities that never sleep. Meridian sleeps at least a few hours a night, but it has more stamina any other Texas city. Maybe because it's younger. Or maybe because the monsters don't stick to the shadows here like they do most every other place."

"You consider yourself a monster?" Cuff and oath aside, she wasn't interested in someone who would moralize her all the way to a Catholic confessional for something that had been done to her against her will sixty years ago.

She accepted her responsibility for most of the decisions she'd made since, but the fact was that she wasn't human anymore, wasn't subject to the same rules and laws. Just because she could eat meat and chocolate cake didn't mean she could live on anything other than blood. Not every city had sanguine butchers who happened to serve the vampire community without asking awkward questions about what they needed all that pig's blood for. And every vampire knew that human blood was better by multiple factors. It made the undead feel alive.

"Only in the traditional 'Universal Horror' sense," the wolf replied. "I've been told I look quite mild-mannered."

"Are you as laidback as you seem?"

He gave her that charming crooked grin again. He had dog teeth, unironically — both canines, which made him appear more like a vampire than her to the untrained eye. Long arms, long torso, long legs, long teeth. She'd bet he sprawled in chaotic directions on a bed.

"I guess you could say I'm slow to anger. I don't Hulk out into the werewolf or anything. But I've still got the wolf in me. Everyone does, even the ones who aren't tied to the moon. I might be more nervous with you if I were less in tune with mine."

Rose was entranced by how he didn't look away from her now, although he'd barely let himself look before she'd chosen him. If she hadn't known that werewolves had no intrinsic thrall beyond the animalistic quality of their pheromone, she'd think he was trying to hypnotize her.

"Wouldn't that put you more on edge, knowing what you could do if you lost control?" she asked.

"You may look one shake away from naked, new girl, but anyone who isn't a fool knows a vampire is dangerous. I'm not afraid of you, though, because I trust your new ink, and because I trust my wolf to protect me. You can't turn me, and I can't turn you, but we can do damage to each other if we need to."

"You're not afraid I can make you do whatever I want, if I chose? You're not afraid I'm doing that right now?" she asked, her breasts heavy against his chest and threatening even more to fall out of alignment with the dress, to expose her to him and anyone else watching out of curiosity or envy.

"I think the fact we're dancing like goth prom instead of me on my knees or in one of those booths or rooms, and you're not mixing my blood in with your sangria, suggests you're keeping your thrall to yourself. Not that I'm against any of those things, if that's where you see tonight going."

"Is that all you want from me?" Not plaintive or petulant. That he wanted her was academic. She needed to know if he was like the others. "My bite in exchange for your blood?"

"To be honest, I just come here for the food."

Rose burst out laughing into his shoulder.

"They have a good raw meat menu. More seasoned than rat or squirrel. And I like their music, and the way people look to be here. Everything's so casual in the pack. It's nice to have an excuse to get dressed up." He swayed into the music with more emphasis. "If all we do is dance, I'd still be happy."

Her fangs slid out of their own volition, mimicking the stiffening of his erection struggling against his jeans, against her. She wrangled her thrall back to just pheromones, but not before he curled his fingers into her waist and hips and fought a groan.

As the band headed back toward the stage, the pre-recorded music faded from the speakers. Rose and the boy stopped dancing.

She looked up at him and wondered if her gaze captivated him like his did to her. She knew what the rest of her looked like, but she hadn't seen her face in decades, so her memory of that was less clear. She remembered that her eyes used to be gray or blue, depending on the light, but being a vampire would have changed their quality, beyond the mercury reflection that moonlight flashed in the pupil. Werewolves flashed green.

"Have you ever been with a vampire before?"

"Do you mean have I ever danced with a vampire?" The teasing sparkle in his eyes had nothing to do with reflectivity. "I'll admit, dancing's all I've done."

"I won't ask if you've never had sex before." Whatever his age, he was old *enough*, and when werewolves got together, lived together, stripped down to nothing, they were as prone to indulge their sexual appetites as their more prosaic hungers. It was both vampires' and werewolves' natures to indulge—the nature of the beast, as it were.

"You looking for some young thing to corrupt?"

The torch singer resumed singing with her band, which did nothing to curtail Rose's lust. The slither of her tongue between her fangs tantalized the nerves in and around them, made her imagine his tongue between her folds.

"Is this corruption?" Rose slid her hand down between them and, without hesitation, underneath the waist of his jeans. It was a tight fit, and she moved slowly to give him a chance to stop her. But he didn't, not when she crossed the line, not when she found the hot shaft of his pulsing erection and wrapped her cold fingers around it—which did nothing to shrink or soften him. Quite the contrary.

And yes, *all* of him ran long.

A low growl mingled with his startled moan, a hot exhalation against her bare scalp. In his moment of hedonism, he drew her even closer, canted his hips to thrust against her hand, and rubbed his cheek against her head, which was when he discovered that her close-shorn hair was soft. His neck was mere inches from her aching fangs, which begged to sink into him slow and fill herself with his heat, but she held back, even as she stroked him as well as she could in the small space provided.

"The preachers say what they say," he finally replied, when he could think well enough to string words together, "but they're just threatened. Threatened by pleasure that isn't transcendental, celestial. Threatened by bodies. By the mess. They'll make you feel guilty about anything and everything if they can, by the fact that you're just an animal who can think it's something better. But we *are* animals, and animals don't care. They just…ah…do as they please, as they're created to do, and pleasure is good and pain is bad, unless it's also good and… God, your hand is cold, how does it even…?"

With her free hand, she guided his—with its long fingers—up from her waist to her breast, barely covered by the dress strap, then not, as she eased him underneath to cup her. She admired the way his hand looked while molded to her curve, then raised her head again. His pupils were dilated, and he panted, tongue wet behind sharper teeth, flushed lips licked.

"Would you like to come home with me tonight?"

"Is that a trick quest—?" The growl infiltrated his voice, deepening it, and to the shudder of the torch singer's vibrato, Rose tilted her head to capture the last of the growl and cut his reply short.

There was nothing she could do about her pheromones, or the effect of her fangs with direct contact, but at this point, the boy mostly knew what he was getting into. She wrapped her free arm around his neck to draw herself up on her toes and surge her breast into his hand. He squeezed, although not hard, teasing her taut nipple with his thumb and the webbing next to it.

She teased him just as much, making him gasp when she used her nails—just nails, not claws—to smooth his pre-cum over the head and shaft. Her hand burned from the heat he created.

And the rest of her threatened to go up in flames from how quickly he showed that he was *not* inexperienced with his kiss. Whatever meat he'd consumed earlier had done nothing to deter this different but just as carnal hunger, only heightened by the caress of her fangs against his lips, his tongue, which met hers before he succumbed to her.

They'd lost track of where they were on the dance floor. Rose slammed back against a table, which was fortunately bolted to the floor. Instead of shouting with indignance, the people at that table laughed and grabbed their glasses before the impact could topple them over. Which was good because Rose tightened her grip on both neck and cock and whirled the boy around to shove him against the table instead.

He broke from the kiss, gasping. Rose abruptly released his erection so he wouldn't come — or if he did, so her hand wouldn't get too messy yet. She trailed her touch back up over his tunic shirt and stopped where his heart beat faster than the bass.

He caught her nipple between fingers, pinching a little harder, but mostly he tried to control himself — not a wolf's natural state, though neither man nor beast would want to finish too soon.

Not that a werewolf was as limited as a man, and her thrall could extend the endurance of the quickest shot.

She admired his self-control, though, and his naked desire for her as he stared at her lips, her teeth, her eyes, her breasts — one bare now, the other barely covered and threatening to escape from the tenuous strap.

"My name is Rose, puppy. What's yours?"

He was still breathless when he replied, "Simon. But you can call me 'puppy' or anything you fucking like. *Fuck*."

She stepped back, her hand over his heart pinning him against the table still. With the other, she readjusted her dress, although what had been seen could not be unseen. She didn't much mind. Living so long half-demon meant that so many people had seen her without clothes, and many of them would live much longer knowing the sight. As long as it was her choice.

She curled her finger to beckon him as she started for the door. "Follow me."

"Anywhere."

Chapter Two

Out in the alley, she was struck again by all the scents of city — concrete, oil-slick water, sod, exhaust, metal, glass, pollution, and people. People. Among the enticing smell of restaurants, cooked meat, caramelized sugar, she got a double dose of delicious from the people still up and hot and heartbeating in the living center of Meridian.

Two people leaving Sordid meant two more could enter. There was still a line, and there would be until two in the morning when the doors would shut to new patrons, but there were others there in the alley's dark places, corners, nooks. On scent alone, they were either making out, having sex, or feeding. The alley was within the purview of the speakeasy, so the same Alliance rules applied, but even if they didn't, all the sounds penetrating conversation in the line suggested that no one was trying to kill anyone — not completely, anyway.

Before they could leave the alley, Rose grabbed Simon by the shoulder of his shirt and pushed him against the wall, front first. He grunted from the force she used — even those experienced with vampires could be unprepared for their less visible strength to make itself known. But despite any discomfort he might have experienced, he closed his eyes and bit his lip, which was how she knew she and Simon would get along just fine.

She stroked over his shoulders and upper arms, enjoying the more physically represented strength she found there. He hugged the brick and panted as she teased his exposed neck above his collar with the tips of her teeth, inciting a gasp with every thin, focused caress. She knew from experience that it was like lightning bolts of arousal from point of contact, then like a hard, violent climax from point of impact, insertion.

"Never had a vampire bite you before?" she asked. "Just a nice, polite dance?"

"It never seemed like a good idea, even with Alliance vampires," Simon replied. "I see humans and wolves coming back for more all the time, craving, isolating."

"Yet here you are."

"There's something different about the way you hunt." He glanced behind him, meeting her eyes. "You hold back. I can tell. It doesn't seem like hunting at all. I was curious. I *am* curious. Is that going to kill me?"

"Not too much. Do you have to return to your pack before sunrise?"

"We don't have a curfew, if that's what you mean."

"Good," she murmured in his ear before caressing it with her fang. The boy whimpered, struggling to keep his legs holding him up. "My place has little direct sunlight, and it's been a while for me. But before we go, I want you to stroke yourself off onto this wall."

"Oh, fuck." He pressed his forehead against the brick and closed his eyes, clenching his teeth, which set the tendons of his neck and the hollows of his cheekbones in relief. "I don't think that's going to take long."

"Make it last." She kissed his neck, lingering against the strongest pulse and the cologne of life that emanated from there, then retreated before she inadvertently made his stamina that much more difficult to maintain.

He unbuttoned the bottom buttons of his shirt to give himself some more room before undoing his jeans. He didn't seem to have any more problem exposing himself in dimly lit public spaces than she did.

Rose kept herself angled out of sight of his erection as he wrapped his fingers around his cock and clenched his eyes tight shut again with a groan. With his other hand, he braced himself against the wall, so that he was hunched over, his shoulders working under his shirt, straining against it like the beast that he was while he stroked, slow, luxurious pulls, although the way he twitched told her how much he wanted to rush and spill over.

"Imagine that it's my hand." She slid hers up his spine, but that was all. Just a touch through his shirt and her voice, although she let a little thrall creep in for effect, to wriggle her words through his ears and into his brain until all other sounds disappeared in insignificance. "I'm touching you, relishing the warmth of you. Your heat seeps into me, making me feel alive, until I heat around you and we're the same. You're hot enough for us both. Do you feel how you burn? Do you burn your own palm, thinking it's mine?"

"Damn, that's new." He quickened his strokes, his forearm a blur, but he forced himself to slow back down, reaching down to squeeze his balls, clenching his jaw as he worked to control himself. A wolf had to have some control, although the beast had less inclination for it in anything but the hunt.

Without eyes on her, though, he made himself vulnerable, which meant he was not the predator here, but prey.

But he didn't stop, didn't glance nervously back. He trusted her, trusted the way she'd shown her intentions, trusted — perhaps unwisely — that she wouldn't manipulate him into something he wouldn't otherwise do on his own. And she wouldn't. She had no desire to do anything except see what the puppy was capable of.

"Too much?" She walked her fingers along his back playfully.

"Just enough." He caught his breath, then released the death hold on his scrotum to stroke himself again.

"Good." She tucked herself against his hip, resting her cheek on the blade of his shoulder. His low growl was all the more evident so near its origin. "Now, instead of my hand, imagine it's me you're fucking. I'm against the wall, the dress fallen away from my breasts, my skirt over my hips so you can just push right in, hard, because I'm no delicate flower. I want every bit of your werewolf strength plunging into me."

"Fuck. Oh, fuck yes." His thrusts slowed, but he moved his hips with more intention, more force, pushing violently into his grip.

"Imagine how you want me moaning and shoving back against you, fucking myself with you, but you're harder than you've ever been and need to come so badly. Imagine how I sound on the other end of your desperation, crying out." She raised her head again and brought her chin to his lowered shoulder to make a breathy facsimile to how she would sound, wordless moans low in her throat, edging on groans, making her think of the torch singer singing a different kind of song.

"Oh my God, Rose, you need to stop that. I can't...*oh*."

She shuddered her moans into a laugh as his hips snapped hard enough against his hands to slap from the force of it. The wet addition of his pre-cum made her mouth water.

"Are you imagining it without the ecstasy-track?" she asked. "How I sound when I come? How much you need to, how much you want to come inside me, fill me with your feverish heat? Fill me, Simon. Fuck me, fill me, make me come with you here against this filthy wall. Make me filthy with you."

She insinuated her arm around him to gently stroke the head when he thrust his erection through his hand.

"Yes. Fuck, *yes*. Yes, *oh*... You absolute *bitch*."

From a werewolf, that was high praise indeed. She laughed again as his bracing arm buckled and he fell with his forehead on his forearm as he came. Semen gathered in hot strings over both their fingers and splattered the brick. He bucked into his fist, groaning and growling through gritted teeth, sharper than before. His hand on the wall was longer, too, and claw-tipped.

When he was finally finished, the galvanized tension through his back, shoulders, and arms loosened. He slumped, although he held his hips back so he wouldn't smear his clothes with the mix of semen and whatever city dirt from the brick now mingled with it.

Rose brought her slick hand to her lips. Not as good as blood, but it was yet another bodily fluid that sustained and imbued her with strength, power, life. She licked at her fingertips but was compelled to take as much of her hand into her mouth as she could to gather all of it at once. She wanted, needed, hungered for his blood, thrumming, pumping, and pulsing so close to her. Although it was hybrid blood, werewolves were close enough to human, and the magic that rushed through with their life was just as invigorating.

Simon caught the tail end of her with half her hand in her mouth and groaned again. He looked away, but not soon enough to keep arousal from quickening his heart once more.

"If you haven't yet, you should try for yourself," she said. "It's just another protein. You'll like it."

"Not my own before."

He turned around on the wall away from the wax-drip of cum down the porous brick, then licked broadly over his fingers and palm. His jeans were still open, but his shirt mostly covered his cock except for glimpses in the shadows. She was transfixed instead by the sight of his tongue and the harshening of his deeper growl, the glint of emerald in his eyes as she strode forward to displace his fingers with her tongue. She kissed him half-hard again until there wasn't anything left of his cum on either of their lips and she couldn't hold her fangs back anymore, which left him gasping, groaning, grasping at her dress, down to her ass and thighs.

"You're dangerous, aren't you?" he murmured against her mouth when she forced herself, shaking, out of the kiss. "I can see why people get addicted to this, and you haven't even bitten me yet."

"What if I promise I won't hurt you?" She framed his face, stroking the hair that brushed back from his temples. "Oh, I can't say anything for the integrity of your skin, and I'll sometimes feed, because it's so good when I do, for both parties. But I promise I won't *hurt* you. I won't make you want me, won't do anything but enhance what's already there. I won't force you, Simon. Do you trust that?"

"I believe you mean it. But it's not just addictive for the person who gets bitten. Things get twisted in wolf packs, too. You ever done something like this before, Rose?" He stared at her through the curtain of his long hair, with those big guileless pale eyes. He seemed like a man of simple pleasures, but it would be a mistake to assume that meant he was a simple man.

"You're right that I'm dangerous. I'm not going to sugarcoat that I only stopped killing people five years ago. Other than my own conscience, I'm never going to suffer any judgment for that."

That was a big part of the reason why hunters didn't like the Alliance. To them, it must have seemed like mass murderers pinkie-swearing to never kill again in return for immunity for all previous deaths. But hunters had blood on their hands, too, from assuming that the solution to demons and hybrids was indiscriminate slaughter just because they weren't human and therefore always evil all the time. The very existence of the Alliance should have suggested otherwise, but hunters tended not to see the shades between black and white.

She'd awakened five years ago to the idea that what she was doing wasn't just wrong but changeable. She'd back-slidden a few times since but also developed all kinds of strategies to change not only what she did but who she was.

She reveled in her power, in the way she could see so clearly in the dark, the way she *felt* the world. There was nothing wrong with being a vampire. She just had to find another way to be one so that she wasn't also a monster in more ways than what her fangs and claws made of her.

"But I can control myself because I don't *want* to hurt anyone," Rose continued. "Harm them, anyway. I think you'd be harder to break, but if it makes you feel better, that's not why I chose you."

"So you didn't forgo that singer just because you were worried what you might do to her? I wouldn't be offended by that. She was hot and we just met. Too soon to be jealous. That was one of the things I lost after…you know. Hard to get too jealous in a big pile of fur after a fight."

Rose smiled at the imagery. Without fur, vampire piles were less adorable by definition.

"To answer your question, Simon— No, I've never done this before. But I've wanted to for a while, and because of Meridian's Alliance, I'm able to try. If you're open to all the benefits of a vampire without the accompanying werewolf service, I'm your girl. I'm not proposing. Just…"

He brushed his thumb against her cheekbone, almost mirroring what she'd done to him. "Looking for a companion. Someone to run with. I understand that much, Miss Rose. And I think, if you're trustworthy, you'll be a new adventure. But you're beautiful and daring and have such a pretty smile and I like the way you treat people and treat me. I think I'll trust you a little."

She took his hand from her cheek but kept hold of it as she drew him away from the alley. He held his pants closed, didn't pause long enough to fasten them again. Her car was in a parking structure a few blocks away. She thought he'd enjoy her 2004 Mustang, and she thought he'd enjoy her new home—for the irony alone.

* * * *

Archie pulled into the empty space in front of the stairs after checking them in to the motel, so cheap that half the outside lights weren't working and the street sign had lost three-quarters of its bulbs and half the letters on the sign so that it was impossible to tell what any of it was trying to say except *motel* and *vacancy*.

No surprise to Lis that this motel had vacancies. It was in a low-traffic part of Meridian, on its southern edge, away from even the fringes of its vaunted nightlife — at least the kind they advertised with neon lights and bright colors.

There were very few colors where Archie had driven them. The motel sign was supposed to be red, but it had faded and flaked into an unappetizing shade of brown. Same with the motel doors. Night sapped the colors even more, rendering the world into etched charcoal grays. Lis was so used to a nocturnal existence that light and colors tended to hurt her eyes, so much so that she would slide on a pair of sunglasses whenever she had to endure one or the other.

The cheapness of the motel didn't matter. All that mattered was working air conditioning, and these days Archie could fix most units in a pinch. They would keep a Do Not Disturb sign on their door all the time, because what a maid would find inside would raise more questions than answers, and neither of them trusted housekeepers in places like this to properly wash anything. Between the two of them, they stripped the room and shoved the comforters, sheets, and pillows into the sliding-door closet, then deep-cleaned within their means. Only when the rat traps and roach motels were set up in corners and under the beds and the runes were painted over the window and door frames did they bring their life into the room.

Lis unpacked her clothes and put sheets on her bed while Archie did the same. Then she went in search of the closest places of business for necessities and the best routes to get to each. There was a diner near a laundromat across the street—although Lis suspected the laundromat was a front for something in the back room. Like the motel, these businesses seemed to primarily serve the unhoused or partially housed community in the mostly ignored Meridian neighborhood that locals and graffiti apparently called the Wastelands. Cemetery Grove, eight city blocks north, had most of the rest of the necessities — grocery, gas, convenience corner store, affordable restaurants — but a long, dark walk of intermittent streetlights, hollow eyes, and hungry mouths threatened in between.

She might look like a sleepwalking goth child to the untrained eye, but Lis was safer in the dark than anyone would suspect. No one bothered her on her way back through the Wastelands. Her stomach growled, craving burgers from the diner, but Archie hadn't sent her out with money, and she presently had none of her own. If he wanted to eat something fresh or warm for their next meal, he'd have to get it for them himself.

Her greater appetite never seemed satisfied while on Archie's schedule. She was much more active, burned too bright and hot beneath her dark clothes, behind her dark eyes. She kicked her covers off every time she slept to keep from overheating. At least she and Archie had agreed that the room they lived in should be cold. Given that Texas decided to run summer nine months out of the year, she always returned from the hunt sticky.

By the time she made it back to the motel, she was approaching that state once again, but air conditioning blasted her as soon as she stepped over the threshold into their room. In the corner, Archie had already set up a second mini-fridge, the hematology analyzer, and a slew of home test kits, from blood pressure, blood oxygen, cholesterol, and hemoglobin to hGC.

Lis was a biological machine. Like he did with air conditioning units, Archie regularly tested her to assess her condition and troubleshoot any issues before they affected her performance. He had notebooks full of tables and shorthand she didn't understand, but by the end of weekly testing, she knew if she was maintaining optimal performance, inside and out.

She drew Archie a rough map of the walkable area, not just of primary locations but of notable buildings along the way and sites she thought might be points of intersection between humans and the monsters Archie had brought her to Meridian to kill.

Without a word — so much of their communication was non-verbal these days, forged from endless repetition with the discipline of ritual — he pointed at one of the tent enclaves on the edge of the Wastelands. He warmed up a Hot Pocket for her while she prepared again to leave.

Then he locked her out.

Only Archie kept hold of the motel room keys. That way, if she turned, she couldn't lead anyone back to the room, then let others in to feed upon him.

He would work deep into the night, probably with the television or radio on low, scribbling notes or researching through ancient books he bought from online auctions and estate sales. She didn't know where he stored those books after he finished working on them. If he had a storage facility somewhere, she'd never been invited. The research wasn't important for her side of the job, though. All she needed to do was make sure her blades were sharp and her muscles loose and warm when she headed into the battlefield.

Archie had driven her all over Texas. She didn't think the state had a monopoly on monsters, but its many large cities acted as dinner bells for demons, and Archie knew the territory — born in Houston, moved to Dallas, then to Meridian. After sustaining an injury, he'd moved back to Dallas, where he'd found her, seven years old, next to her dad, who was dead in an alley — exsanguinated.

She'd been too young for a proper vendetta beyond *I want to hurt what hurt my daddy*. It'd since had time to grow.

But it wasn't really a vendetta anymore. Anger had burned out of her, as though she was too small to carry such big emotions *and* the weight of the world.

Now this was just what she did. Night in and night out, she brought the fight to the monsters, then slept all day, like them. Archie was obsessed with the idea of her becoming a better machine to fight monsters. They experimented with nutrition, training modules, even magic to level her up to a better hunter.

So much so that the little girl she'd been at ten years old — left alone again in an alley, this time with nothing but her knives and told to make it home in one piece — seemed like another person, another lifetime. Soft. She'd made it home, obviously, but she'd burst through the four locks on Archie's door, covered in blood from fourteen vampires as well as herself and crying as though she was at her own funeral, afraid cross-contamination would turn her. Back then, Archie had gathered her in his arms, staining his clothes, and praised her for surviving. He'd let her cry until the sobs had subsided, when he'd unwound from her and told her to clean herself off. Then, while he'd stitched her up, he'd reassured her that she wouldn't turn.

Next day, he'd done it all over again, and the day after that and the day after that, and he hadn't held her anymore — not until his field skills had been inadequate to her injuries and he'd had to take her to hospital at thirteen.

Anger — at monsters for existing, at her dad for being weak by dying at their hands and leaving her alone, at Archie for keeping her in this world, even if he'd equipped her to handle it — had petered out somewhere around fifteen. Not feeling anything at all was better. Made her better.

For them to arrive at their motel, Archie had driven them through Meridian proper. Meridian was a circus. Its Wastelands were falling apart like the ruins of an ancient city crumbling while someone fiddled a few miles north. The people, too, were zombies compared to the vibrant, gesticulating, loud, laughing crowd of Meridian's center, oblivious to its own illness.

The Wastelands was where the cancer ate Meridian's soul and spat it out.

Here, people clustered in alleys off the main streets to settle in for the night, cooking late dinners on propane stoves or eating wilted sandwiches handed out by social workers and volunteers on the edge of Cemetery Grove, because as bad as Cemetery Grove was, it was practically vivacious in comparison. The Good Samaritans who served there weren't fool enough to walk where Lis was now.

The last stop. Before death. Before oblivion. Before being forgotten, fading like old memories. It was so bad that people didn't bother hiding in the buildings — which were guarded by muscle-bound guards with flagrant automatics. And all because not so much as a single police car drove through the Wastelands, although sirens seemed to be constant — from a distance. Even the police had given up the Wastelands for lost, which put its inhabitants in greater danger from predators. Of all kinds.

Which was why Archie had settled them here. Cemetery Grove and its surrounding warehouses had some of the most intense paranormal activity, but also a contingent of hunters and an abundance of gargoyles and angels watching over it.

The Wastelands, despite the pocket density of its population after those who worked came home to their alleys at night, was unprotected. They depended on their clustered numbers to provide at least a superficial shield, but sleeping bags and tents might as well have been the covers of a child's bed, streetlights and battery lanterns their nightlights — not much use against the real monsters, who didn't need an invitation from people who didn't have a home to invite them into. And as bad as the people of the Wastelands had it, they made themselves even more vulnerable because they thought the worst monsters were only human.

Which was sometimes enough. Lis knew that as well as anyone who spent most of their life on the streets, while looking like she did — easy jailbait. Small and slight as she was, in the dark it was hard to tell she was a woman as full-grown as she was ever going to be. The same thing that made her a prime lure for demons beckoned to human predators, too.

Archie didn't know and wouldn't approve, but Lis was an equal opportunity monster hunter. Pestilence demons eliminated humans and demons alike if she dangled an arm, attached or not, in the gutter. Archie hadn't taught her to defend and disarm. He'd taught her how to kill things that were much bigger and stronger than her, and by the time a human being threatened her, with her limitations, she had only one recourse.

And she knew she was limited. If she hadn't known, and adjusted accordingly, she wouldn't have lasted this long.

Looking like a disaffected tween was apparently not an unusual sight winding between the sleeping bags, cardboard boxes, and tents. Lis tucked her hands in her hoodie pockets as she darted her gaze from one person to the next, not lingering long enough to seem threatening—on the contrary, probably appearing nervy and paranoid, high on something and enduring the crowd rather than retreating into any one of the buildings. Lots of people were let into those buildings, people without much money to spare, if any—hooked by the mouth to something that controlled their lives because it took them away.

She didn't have the luxury of oblivion. She had a place to lay her head and a job to do every night, which was more than a lot of people had to their name.

Lis was old enough now that she was starting to see hunters her own age just starting in their new profession, usually borne of grief and vengeance—a friend, a cousin, a brother, a wife, a child, taken by tooth or claw, leaving the witness behind in shock that eventually gave way to either childish fear or the kind of curiosity that could kill a man.

Sometimes she crossed paths with a hunter who thought she was new. Sometimes she crossed paths with a demon who thought the same. Both monsters and men tended to underestimate her.

At the intersection between the alley she'd entered and the one that cut a swath through a stretch of buildings, she found her first vampire, feeding on a woman in a sleeping bag. If Lis hadn't known what to look for, she might have assumed that the man and woman were having sex, which was the reason why no one was stopping them. When people slept in public, courtesy was sometimes the only privacy.

But Lis had seen enough vampires feeding to know when a neck kiss was way too deep, and although most vampires were possessive of the blood they bit from their victims, some usually welled just on the edges of their lips before they swallowed it down.

Lis didn't bother being discreet. In places like this, where the police either didn't bother or they bothered people to an early grave, Lis knew no one was likely to call them.

She grabbed the vampire by his hair and yanked him and the woman forward until she could get her knife against his neck. Then she dug the blade in as hard as she could. Stilettos were made for slashing and stabbing in close combat, not decapitation. The silver that coated the blade made more of an impact than the honed steel, hissing like holy water through the vampire's skin.

She could have tried to yank the vamp out of the woman's neck, but that would have been more risk to the victim, leaving her vulnerable to arterial spray if the vampire didn't work his saliva into the wound to remind the blood to clot.

As it was, the woman was still vulnerable, because the vampire had tapped the carotid with the full intention of drinking her fast. In the areas where Lis had patrolled in Houston, San Antonio, and Dallas, when a vampire fed on the fringes, they had no need to play at seduction like their more insidious cousins, the incubi and succubi, with whom Lis had fortunately experienced very little interaction. This kind of place wasn't for the game. It was a hunt to the death, pure and simple.

Which made everything pure and simple for her, too.

Once the vampire withdrew from the woman's neck, the victim burrowed into her sleeping bag, whimpering. The vampire crawled out with the control of a dancer and the angled limbs of a spider. Its eyes glinted silver in the golden light, and its fangs and claws were fully extended, eliminating any illusion that it was human. It hissed, not bothering with words for someone like her—with a knife in each hand and a shoulder holster holding her small revolver, not to mention the body armor and additional blades hidden all over her body in case the monster disarmed her of her first two. A vampire might try to persuade a civilian not to kill them. With a hunter, they knew better than to waste breath they didn't even need.

The vampire was a head and a half taller than Lis, and lean. It swiped at her with arms longer than hers.

Archie had taught her so many moves from a variety of self-defense disciplines. She could probably compete at the highest level with people more her size—like children—but the fact was that most of the monsters she faced were more formidable. A vampire had all the advantages over her, in power, in stamina, in reach, in natural weaponry, in thrall.

The best fight was the one that never happened, although she often chased after the ones who ran. The second-best fight was the one that was over quickly— even if she lost. Which she never had, although there had been a draw or two.

The best way to win was to not enter the fight on the monster's terms.

So she dropped to the ground in a crouch, then lunged forward while the vampire was still swiping air where her head used to be. Her first line of offense was cutting at the Achilles tendon—so close to the surface that it was easy to slice, and the vampire wore sneakers, so the tendon was exposed. A person—human or not—protected their head and heart better than anything else, as did the skeletal system. Most of the vulnerable visceral organs were within reach of sharp claws. But even if someone could touch their toes, that wasn't a position they tended to assume in a fight.

She cut with all her power and no hesitation, so accustomed to the motion that she barely thought about it anymore. Even for immortal monsters who healed quickly, it took *time* to heal. Time during which their entire leg buckled, useless. Screaming from unexpected pain, the vampire collapsed back onto the concrete. He'd already lost.

Even so, death throes could be violent.

He kicked at her with his good leg, connecting with the body armor on her side. It protected against bullets and took some of the force from the kick, but she couldn't remember the last time bruises weren't blooming somewhere under her pale skin. As long as they stayed superficial and she kept taking her iron supplements and vitamins, she always healed, if not as quickly.

Lis hooked her arm around the good leg, then brought her blade to the back of his knee, stabbing through his pants and into flesh before levering it to sever through more tendons.

Demons could often tolerate pain better than people, but unexpected pain surprised them into feeling it more. He rolled side to side, howling. And still no one got between them or yelled at her to get away, get off the man, stop attacking him.

That was another thing that was true in all the big cities she'd hunted in. The places where the vulnerable were, they didn't just ignore things that were none of their business. They also looked the other way when a hunter stepped in to stop a predator, because they knew better than all the blissfully ignorant in that city what fed upon those considered disposable. The dregs weren't usually pestilence's or conquest's preference, because of the thinness of the meat and blood, because of secondhand substances, because of the environmental pollutant particles people inhaled and swallowed, inadequately filtered by a system not made for the Industrial Revolution onward. But the unhoused, the addicted, the lost, and the desperate were all so very *easy* to hunt. Cheap fast food until they could procure something more substantial.

The people most at risk weren't always aware of the supernatural element, but they recognized predators. And they recognized she wasn't one. At least not to them.

She wasn't like a little dog, making a big noise to try to make people think she was bigger than she was. More like a stray cat—absolutely feral when someone got their hands on her without her permission. She would scratch, stab, bite, urinate, or vomit all over someone if it made them let her go. They were a bloody mess before they even registered how bad an idea it was to try to pick her up. She would and could destroy them rather than let them take or turn her. She hadn't lived to adulthood just to die—or worse.

She grabbed one of the wooden stakes strapped under her hoodie jacket—with a spare in her boot for good measure—and clambered up the vampire's writhing body.

Lis gave him no opportunity to plead or speak, to make her think she'd made a mistake and he was just a guy, pay no attention to the fangs protruding over his human-like teeth or the blood dripping down his face or the woman still moaning in the sleeping bag.

She wasn't here for a debate. She buried the stake in his fucking heart.

The stake's effect was immediate—as good as a bullet to the head.

After the vampire stilled, Lis shrugged off her pack and pulled out gloves, cutting knives, and pliers. Then she got to work.

When she was done with the body, she dragged it without interruption to the nearest gutter. Pestilence would already be attracted to a place like this. Like most hunters, she tolerated pestilence demons because they cleaned as much as they defiled. But the second they stepped over the line to the living, Lis wouldn't hesitate for a second.

Vampire hearts had no value on the mystical black market like the fangs she'd extracted from their special openings in the creature's gums. Archie would sell the teeth when they had enough of them to help fund their little mission, although she didn't think what she brought in funded all of it. She only knew that she wasn't paid but never wanted for basic food, shelter, or medical care.

Warriors don't need luxury, Archie had told her. *Luxury makes you soft. Softness makes you dead.* She didn't contradict him, but she secretly thought that his obsession with her health *was* a luxury. Those machines and home tests weren't cheap.

Despite the fact that they were worthless, Lis took the vampire hearts as insurance—even if vampires *could* eventually heal from a bullet or a stake to the heart, they couldn't regrow a heart or a brain—but also because she was only allowed to go wherever home happened to be once she had three hearts or the sun rose above the horizon, whichever came first.

Before abandoning the body to pestilence demons, she rifled through the pockets.

Vampires needed even less than she did in terms of food and shelter. The older ones tended to amass wealth through frugality, good investment, outright stealing, or thrall manipulation. That didn't mean vampires were universally rich. Where she tended to hunt, they were often as poor as the people they killed. It just didn't bother them as much.

But this vampire had a credit card—useless to her, since it was a paper trail—and a decent amount of cash in his wallet.

She pocketed sixty dollars. She'd give it to Archie along with the fangs and claws she'd removed. He handled the sales and the finances.

She gave the moaning woman twenty-five dollars and the change. For a few good meals, if she survived.

There were plenty of phones among the unhoused. If the woman lost consciousness or needed to go to the hospital, someone else could call. There was also a free clinic in Cemetery Grove that could probably suture her bite. But vampire saliva was an analgesic, antiseptic, and coagulant, when triggered after a bite— quite unlike the bats by the same name. Otherwise, vampires would cause a lot more accidental deaths in addition to the intentional ones, and staying secret from most of the world would be a lot harder.

There was something unsettlingly *tidy* about vampires, even though they were as brutal and messy as she was in their slaughter. Archie ascribed it to their demonic nature, attributes of the mystical means that animated their corpses. Their kills weren't always clean, but somehow their aftermath was, unless they *liked* making a mess. Lis thought killing should leave more of a mark in the world, even though she made every attempt to erase her own.

She tucked the last five dollars cash from the wallet into her functional bra, along with a gift card to Whataburger — although what a vampire needed with a Whataburger gift card, she couldn't say. She didn't even know if they *could* eat anything on the menu. Didn't matter. She took what she could get.

She'd been skimming off the top of her foraging since she was seventeen. If Archie knew, he said nothing. As long as she gave him most of it, he didn't seem to consider it a hill to die on. She just wanted to buy the occasional milkshake, breakfast sandwich, or secondhand book from the ratty paperback racks, something other than the texts Archie gave her to study — his version of education, in lieu of attending public school. He'd instructed her in basic math in the early years but gave her a book for everything else, encouraged reading widely and well when they visited a local library.

Otherwise, he'd taught her everything he knew about monsters so she could be prepared against whichever she met, and he'd taught her how a little girl could fight. It was all she'd ever really needed to know.

Lis washed her hands, her blades, and the stake with water and soap from her bag, then tucked the first heart and all her tools back in and stood, sliding the bag back over her shoulders.

After checking that her weapons were still in place and the vampire's kick hadn't damaged anything dire, she continued down the alley to find the next monster to slay.

* * * *

The sun was already coming up by the time Lis had the three hearts she needed, so she hadn't saved herself any time, but she usually kept going to sunrise anyway, no matter how many she killed. The three-heart rule was mostly for if she was injured, ill, or cramping and needed to cut work short to rest. If she was any of those three things and couldn't collect her three hearts, then she needed to find another place to rest that wasn't home.

Which was part of the reason she kept some money for herself. She always had a place in the alleys she protected, but she'd rather have a place at a bar or a twenty-four-hour restaurant, and she couldn't go in those places unless she bought something to justify staying.

Tonight she was not injured, ill, or cramping. Three vampires were all she'd managed to find. That was the nature of the hunt. Some nights she couldn't find a monster to save someone else's life, and other nights she couldn't swing a fist without hitting one. She averaged about three kills a night, but even one made that night a good night.

She knocked on the motel door three times.

There was a creak of old mattress springs. Then, muffled on the other side of the door, Archie murmured, "Password."

"Leviathan." Loud enough for him to recognize her voice as well as read her demeanor. There was a different password for each day of the week and a new distress word every month, in case she'd been taken captive and forced to lead them back home. Hadn't happened yet, but it only had to happen once to justify itself.

Archie opened the door, blasting her with cold air. He trained a gun straight at her center mass, still not inviting her in. Motels weren't under the same mystical strictures as domiciles, but the runes he'd painted on the inside made hybrid invitations mandatory.

He gave her a once-over, then settled his pistol back in its holster. He knew all the quick tricks to determine whether she'd turned, and she'd passed muster, which meant she could step into the motel without invitation. The last proof.

He locked the door behind her, then closed the blinds, the blackout curtains, and the decorative curtains.

"I called in some breakfast from the diner. It'll be ready for me to pick up in about thirty minutes." He pointed his chin in the direction of the bathroom.

Lis gave Archie the bag with salvaged vampire teeth and each of the hearts, neatly packaged in plastic, as well as eighty-three dollars, a gold necklace, and what looked like an engagement ring she'd foraged from all three vampires. The gold was real. Lis wasn't so sure about the rock. She'd squirreled away nine dollars in her bra, plus the gift card.

Brokers in the areas Archie tended to frequent were utter vultures, but in return for price gouging, the pawnbrokers and body brokers developed extreme short-term memory loss, forgetting names, faces, and cardinal directions if anyone happened to ask after the seller.

She removed her armor, her outer weapons, her clothes, then every last one of the weapons she'd strapped to herself underneath. She hid the money and gift card in her toiletry bag near the pads and tampons. Archie wasn't skittish around that sort of thing—he'd had to stop by a convenience store or pharmacy more than once to address a heavy or abrupt period—but it was still personal enough that he would never rummage through that part of her possessions, as a matter of courtesy. Not counting the card, she now had twenty-three dollars and a dresser of clothes to her name, which she wasn't even positive was her real name or just the one Archie had given her and reinforced until it was all that was left.

Lis Song. She was Korean and he was black, but no one ever looked at them funny, even when they went out during the day.

Maybe her thousand-yard stare appeared inherited.

She left the door open so the bathroom wouldn't become too much of a sauna, because she liked her showers as hot as she liked her bedrooms cold. She washed off all the sweat, blood, and grime, hissing at cuts she hadn't clocked, testing the tender places where she'd bruise, then letting all the tension from hunting unravel and flow down the drain with the dirt.

On the other side of the shower, after the scalding water had cooled to merely warm, she lotioned with the same product that Archie used, rubbing her muscles as well as someone could massage themselves. Then she pulled on a pair of shorts and an oversized T-shirt—not that most shirts needed to work that hard to drown her.

The cold air from the main room blasted her again, feeling as blissfully clean as she did. The unwinding of night into day was one of her favorite times, the closest thing she had to something to look forward to. To joy.

Her bed was the closest to the door. Archie had served in the first Iraq War and had been discharged without any lingering physical wounds, but an Achilles tear while hunting in Houston, then the back injury in Dallas, had ended his hunting career and led him instead to teach a protégé, paying his highly specific knowledge and wisdom forward. Archie could still fight, no question, and she knew to never doubt his shooting skills, but Lis was younger, more flexible, more dexterous, and she woke up faster than him. She could more handily fight anything that managed to cross the protected thresholds of the motel room.

She knelt next to her bed and clasped her hands on her quilt.

Archie pulled one of the chairs from the small circular table behind her and gathered her hair behind her shoulders.

She prayed out loud to God for resilience, endurance, and fortitude to continue in her mission for Him, sacrificing her life to save the most vulnerable. She prayed that He would grant His protection on all His children over the course of the day. Vampires would stay inside or underground, but almost all other demons could roam in sunlight, although they were as sensitive to it as she was.

Evil was an onslaught. She was just one warrior who always needed God to replenish her strength and ensure that her injuries were not insurmountable, that they would heal quickly, that she would be able to get up in the morning without creaking or groaning like Archie. That she would wake up at all. Or if she didn't, that He would take her somewhere she could finally rest, in return for being His good and faithful servant, eschewing all other things in service to the hunt against the devil's creatures, envious of what was God's.

Archie sometimes added in his own prayers when hers slowed. And while they prayed, Archie brushed her hair, the way he had when he'd first taken her in from the cold and the monsters, when he'd promised he would protect her better than her father had been able to but also teach her to protect herself better than anyone else in her life ever would.

After prayers, she clambered onto her bed with a biography of Harry Truman and switched the television on to C-SPAN for something in the background while Archie left to pick up breakfast.

Chapter Three

"I'd say you were drunk, but I'm the only one who's had anything to drink tonight." Rose leaned against Simon and laughed against his neck as he occupied himself with hers. Simon wasn't what she'd been drinking, though.

She'd brought Simon with her to the butcher and charcutier where she ordered her next container of blood to be delivered—by human courier—within a few days.

This butcher didn't follow Alliance standards. The shop was just closer to where she lived. If it became necessary, she had alternatives over the city—not to mention Sordid. In a pinch, she could drive somewhere else. There were plenty of butchers in Texas, and plenty of ranches not far outside Meridian.

Simon had wondered aloud how he hadn't known about this butcher, though he'd lived in Meridian most of his life, while she'd known them before she'd arrived. Rose had just smiled full-fanged at the man behind the counter, and the man had smiled full-fanged back.

Simon had just said, "Oh," and ordered a rib-eye that he'd proceeded to annihilate as soon as they'd found a decent alley where a man could eat a slab of raw meat and a woman could drink a pint of sow's blood without anyone making a fuss.

"God, you smell good with animal blood on your mouth," he groaned between catching her tough skin between his sharpened teeth.

"And with meat in yours." She buried her hands in his mane. She loved not having hair—it wasn't like she needed to worry about getting cold—but she also missed it and used his as a surrogate. He didn't mind at all as she raked claws over his scalp and used her grip to control his head, his mouth.

She took another swallow from her bottle but let some of it spill from the corner of her mouth over her chin to her neck, where he caught it with his tongue. His groan abruptly sharpened into a growl—like a distant chainsaw, but she felt it inside her. If her fangs hadn't already been out from drinking the pig blood, they would have extended from the abrupt rumble of his desire.

He licked the blood up to her chin, grabbing pinches of her skin on the way up, nearly tearing her flesh clean away from bone, which would have hurt like hell and been just as hot at the same time. If the human she'd been had known the things that would turn her on sixty years later, she would have been horrified. But time and experience had taught her how varied appetites could be, and being a vampire meant she could indulge in more than most. Simon taking a chunk out of her would hurt, yes, but it would quickly heal until no one would know it had even happened.

Of course, he never would do that to her, but the thought that he could, or that he might by accident from the ferocity of his hunger, led to her high, feral moan when he reached her mouth and licked deep in to follow the savory path of blood. She clung to his shoulders, arching to plaster her body flush against him, as though if she held him close enough, she would merge with his cravings. Meat in his mouth didn't have quite the same effect as blood in hers, but she could taste the life of *him*, in the rich blood flow pulsing through his tongue, and his rushing heartrate made him intensely fragrant, especially in an already warm night.

He caught her lower lip with his teeth, then released her just before wrenching his mouth away, panting and grinning. "Fuck, I want to eat you all up and leave nothing left. Let me taste you. *Please*."

They'd been going at it like this for months now, with nary a diminished return on the sex or enthusiasm. Part of it was him. Rose was so used to being surrounded by disillusioned oligarchs and plutocrats that a marauding werewolf inclined by nature to enjoy rather than endure the world was a novelty in and of itself. He went wild for new smells, new positions, for everything she wanted to try with him. He was game to make himself cower and crawl and bow and writhe if she told him to do it, and she only told him to because he could refuse at any time. But he didn't.

Sex wasn't something most werewolves lacked among their pack, but almost every time with Simon was like his first with her or anyone, except he had the stamina of both a wolf and an exceptionally virile forty-two-year-old man, even without the various shades of her thrall to motivate and extend him further.

He still ran with his pack, hunted with them, went out with them on the town to wolf-friendly places, from Waffle House to Sordid. Sometimes she joined them. But often, after running himself into a lather, he broke from the pack and showed up at her door or wherever she happened to be and either knocked on her door or ambushed her, his long naked body over hers, then at her disposal and whim. And her whim had yet to wane—as much a surprise to her as it sometimes seemed to him, since she'd been looking for a deliberate but casual fling that thus far hadn't guttered, despite how brightly it burned.

Maybe because he had the day as well as the night, and he could lounge in the light while she slept. Maybe because they did other things, too, besides whirl like a fur-flown dervish through her house or Meridian's many alleys. Maybe because he held no judgment of her for what she'd been even recently, although he'd been turned within a werewolf pack that had never hunted humans. Maybe because he never asked about what she'd been like but quietly listened when she did give him a glimpse into that life. She almost wished he had a *little* more judgment for her, but every swipe of his tongue over her clit seemed like forgiveness, absolution—all too fitting for their usual locale.

She pulled back, then guided his hand and its longer fingers, longer claws, to her shoulder. Using the claw of his middle finger, she dug a groove at the base of her neck. Blood—darker and thicker than human and werewolf alike—welled in the wound and slowly spilled out. Simon's hand shook as he gazed upon the black ink on the pale page of her skin. As though he wanted to maul her, rip her to pieces, bathe in the blood and flesh of her, lose himself inside.

"Have a taste," she said, soft and low.

"Oh, yes, please." His bestial voice dipped into a deep baritone that had her reaching for him even as he fell upon her, probing his tongue deep into the crevice she'd made him make in her.

Just another reason why choosing Simon had been one of the better decisions she'd made in the last five years. Werewolves were demon hybrids, even if they were the most human. Her blood couldn't change him into familiar or make him vulnerable to being turned. It did contain the most concentrated form of her thrall, which meant she allowed him to taste her blood sparingly. It was all too easy to become addicted to everything a vampire was — in some ways, even more insidious than sex demons. Sex demons only formed nests. Vampires forged shadow empires.

But Simon was devoted to every part of her that she offered — blood, clit, pussy, down to her feet — and she couldn't fault his enthusiasm, as infectious as the cloud of her thrall, which affected her, too. She raised her chin to give him more room as he grasped her by her shoulders and walked her back, back, back, without aim, just looking for something solid to shove her against.

He found brick wall instead of a dumpster, thank goodness, although neither of them would have let that distract them from Simon's hungry, wet moans into her wound, the scrape of his teeth to keep that wound open and bleeding, nor the way she tangled her fingers in his hair again and wrapped her legs around his waist so that her pussy pressed to his full erection, branding hot even though his pants.

He thrust against her through their clothes, holding her shoulders to protect her a little from the friction of brick. But the more insistent the cant of his hips, the plundering of his tongue, the gulping of her yielding blood, the more he dug his claws into her shoulders instead of protecting them. Rose squirmed deliciously as he tore through the fabric of her shirt. Then she moaned a little too high and loud for a public alley when the claws pricked through her skin, calling forth more blood and adding to the miasma of desire clouding them, binding them closer and closer.

Simon shuddered with restraint even while he dry-fucked her, until he couldn't hold back anymore and ripped not just her skin but her shirt, tearing it away from her entirely, then ripping again at her pants and underwear.

Now she was the one gasping and naked, knocking at the door of impending orgasm, while he was the one who slowed down long enough reach between them and undo the front of his pants.

Simon pressed his cock against her pussy, which swallowed him the way he swallowed her blood.

"You're a goddess," he moaned, still beset with the full wolf growl that made her strong body quiver as though she were small and weak. He grunted as she tightened her thighs on his sides, constricting his ribs.

She forced herself to relax and let her head fall back against the brick, allowing the sensations to flow over and inside her like a river released from a dam. She came before him, her breasts and abdomen slick with her own blood smeared from the violence of his carnal feed, her thighs slick from foreplay and orgasm — if the vicious things they did could be considered play and the light show in her head could be called a mere orgasm.

She laughed in the aftermath, stroking his hair and rocking with him to urge him in his indulgences. That's what she enjoyed so much about Simon — his utterly innocent hedonism. He was mature enough to appreciate the simple things, and even in darkness, he saw light. Within his viciousness, *he* was the one who found play, and she never had to worry that he would truly tear her asunder. He reveled in all that being a werewolf opened up to him, relished victimless violence, saw no contradiction in being a demon and being humane. He looked into Rose and saw the best of her that she wanted to become, without expecting her to extract her own fangs to do it.

When he slammed his hand into the wall as he jerked inside her with his own orgasm, brick dust crumbled over her head and shoulder.

She laughed again, holding him and relishing the little bursts of heat, like idle discards of his unquenchable inner furnace. Her heart felt as though it would beat any moment—at least faster than the deadly slow pulse that kept blood moving through her in semblance of life. Like breathing, it wasn't strictly necessary, but a body had its habits.

He lifted her away from the wall for the scrapes on her back and scalp to start the work of repairing themselves. Rose shifted her position over his erection, which wasn't flagging much, not with her blood still in his mouth. She wound her arms around his neck and kissed him hard, her fangs inciting him even more. With the help of her thrall, he wouldn't slow down for another two orgasms, and since he made a point to bring her with him for every one, that was just fine with her.

His eyes rolled back as she retreated from his mouth to kiss and caress her fangs down to his ever-tempting neck, even though that was somewhere she could never feed from him.

Rose jerked back with a scream as lightning seared through her lower back. She twisted off Simon, kicking wildly in reflex as another cut sent fire through her thigh, tearing through muscle and weakening the entire leg.

She collapsed to the ground, scraping her skin again, but she barely noticed, because it would heal in seconds. The cuts, which burned like sunlight deeper than just skin, would not. Tears stung little needles through her eyes. Vampires weren't supposed to cry, but when they did, they tended to cry bloody.

"Hey!" Simon's clothes were blood-soaked from what he'd smeared over Rose's front. His voice was still low, his growl ratcheting into something almost mechanical in anger and wariness. "What the fuck, girl?"

As soon as the pain shifted from its early scorching bursts, Rose registered the other person in the alley with them—what looked like a child dressed in black leggings, a black holey tank top, black hoodie, and straps over her torso and legs that looked like club gear, except they didn't have any tooling or enhancements. Not accessories—armor. Simon discerned her as female sooner than Rose did, but in Rose's defense, the knives in the girl's hands hurt her to look at them where the streetlights reflected off the blades. Which meant only one thing.

Silver—real silver—hurt any demon like a bitch, but it could kill a werewolf if it entered the bloodstream. Rose clambered to her feet and used every bit of her strength to shove Simon away.

Simon went flying against the opposite brick wall and crumpled to the ground, but Rose couldn't concern herself with whether she'd really hurt him. There was a world of difference between a hurt werewolf and a dead one, and she knew which one both of them preferred.

Rose put herself—naked, dripping, and wincing from the lingering effect of the silver—between Simon and the girl. But although she kept her fangs extended and grew her claws for good measure, she held her hands palms forward toward the tiny hunter. Rose couldn't make the mistake of assuming that because the girl had ambushed her or because she was as small as a lost child—under five foot by Rose's estimate—she was cowardly or weak. A cowardly or weak hunter would have run as soon as Rose's wounds weren't enough to incapacitate.

The girl planted herself and moved every limb like an immortal, with complete awareness and control. The face under the hood looked young—late teens, early twenties—but she held the small stilettos in her grip-gloved hands as though they were an extension of her.

"Hey," Rose said, as though soothing a scared stray, "we don't want trouble. It's okay. We're Alliance."

"I don't know what that means, and I don't care."

The girl clenched her jaw in resolve and ran straight at Rose. Rose curled her fingers to protect herself, but then the girl slid into the center of the alley as though stealing a base, and slashed at Rose's shins. The bones there were, by nature, protective, but knives scoring down to that bone still hurt like hell, especially with particulates of silver insinuating themselves inside. Like bullets, she'd work them out eventually, but not without issues along the way.

Rose's legs buckled, so she leaped forward to somersault over the hunter. She came back upright on her knees but flinched when she tried to stand.

Now the hunter was between her and Simon.

He'd managed to get to his hands and knees, joints popping, muscles writhing and knotting, eyes reflecting green as he bared considerably sharpened teeth at the hunter—who now registered him as something other than victim.

She held her knives out, one blade for each, her gaze darting between them. This time, when she clenched her teeth, it was out of fear. She backed up to bring both of them within her sight, but she wasn't retreating.

"Wait!" Rose held up a hand to Simon, although she didn't tell him to stop his transformation process. If a vampire didn't make the girl nervous, the beast might give her more pause, although a greater bulk also meant more places to cut. "You're either new or misguided, hunter, but either one will get you killed if you keep going after us. Fuck, that stings." Rose managed to stand, but she felt like she'd jumped off a four-story building onto her feet. "You're not allowed to hunt us."

"As vampire manipulations go, that's the most bullshit attempt I've ever heard," the girl spat.

"The Dietz-Mielle Alliance?" Rose searched for understanding but found none. "At least you're not breaking the agreement on purpose. The Alliance was formed when the vampires and werewolves of Meridian agreed not to hurt humans in return for hunters not hunting them."

"I never agreed to that." The hunter started toward Simon.

"Look at his earring!" Rose pointed at Simon's larger titanium cuff in his ear, now higher on his head and pointed. The cuff was more proportionately suited to him in his werewolf form. "I have my own. And our wrists bear the oath not to harm humans."

Simon's was no longer visible under the fur, so Rose showed where the Latin ink wrapped around hers.

The hunter stepped toward Simon, who was fully changed now, his clothes in tatters on the ground. He stayed low, ears back, looking between Rose and the hunter, caught between attacking in self-defense — and potentially being found guilty for breaking the Alliance anyway — and really not wanting to hurt the hunter. He'd never hurt a human in his life. Not like Rose.

The protection of the Alliance was eminently tenuous if a hunter decided they were fair game. Rose could take care of herself, although she didn't want to. But Simon...

"Stay away from him." Rose darted forward as fast as her supernatural speed would allow, then jumped to avoid the hunter's attack on her legs once more, although it still hurt to land. Jumping with her breasts free also wasn't pleasant, but the added firmness of vampire skin worked in her favor as well. "Can't you see he's not attacking?"

The hunter stayed in a crouch and swiped at Rose's legs.

Rose had to hand it to the girl. Hers was a strategy Rose had never seen, as effective as it was annoying, because Rose didn't have any weapon to combat it but the strength in her legs, and that had been sapped by the silver.

She'd only fought a few hunters in her time, and usually at the hunter's disadvantage rather than hers, because she wasn't a dark alley kind of predator. She preferred parties and civil invitations into other people's homes, then leaving people dazed and confused, with damp spots on their clothes between their legs and an inexplicable bloodstain on their bed or sofa. She hadn't usually gone out to kill, which was a good way to get caught. Victims slated for death were brought to the family home, onto vampire soil, where the law was less likely to even try to look — lest their own trail run cold.

That didn't mean she didn't know how to fight, because as civil as vampires pretended to be, fights with decades' worth of history often ended in ultimately harmless bloodshed. Even ancient grudges didn't lead to death so much as ruination, which was crueler. And sometimes fighting was foreplay.

Rose was quite good at fighting with that end in mind.

She fell to the ground, crouched on her weakened legs and braced on one arm. She prepared her claws and hissed at the hunter, who winced now that she had to contend with the deadlier parts down on her own level.

Rose deflected the first swipe of the silver blade, crying out from the burning wound across her forearm. She didn't have body armor like the hunter, but the problem with body armor was that Rose knew exactly what that armor could cover and what it couldn't.

She raked her nails over the hunter's hand. The gripping glove provided some resistance, but not enough, and the hunter grunted, yanking her hand back. Rose used the retreat to slash at the hunter's face, but not to do real damage, otherwise she could have angled the blow upward and punctured an eyeball.

The hunter cried out, briefly yielding the effectiveness of her weapons to cover her face with the cross of her arms.

Rose dug her nails under one of the armor straps and snapped it. The armor swung away from the girl's vulnerable guts.

Instead of disemboweling the hunter then and there, she grabbed the girl by her wrists, clenched hard enough to grind bone on bone, and kneed her in the now unprotected diaphragm—just to knock her breath out, not take it away entirely.

With the girl incapacitated, Rose squeezed her wrists even harder until the silver clattered onto the concrete. Then Rose slammed her into the wall in a much less fun way than she and Simon did to each other.

The girl gasped, gasped, gasped, eyes wide and animal-frightened from not getting enough air, mouth dark and wet and red. Her neck was exposed under the hoodie. Rose didn't even have to bite her. She could slash the girl's throat with one of her own blades and make it look like a mugging, protecting both herself and Simon from reprisal.

But Rose pinned the girl's wrists against the brick, because she didn't for a second think the hunter had only two silver knives on her person. Without use of her hands, though, she couldn't rearm herself. Then Rose pressed her knee against what would probably end up a bruised diaphragm and waited for the girl to get her breath back.

Rose read naked relief on the girl's face when she could finally gulp air, though she coughed and tried to double over out of Rose's hold. Rose didn't fall for that. The girl could catch her breath fine upright.

"Now, you listen to me, little miss, and you listen good. I'm well within my rights to kill you, since you came at me with a deadly weapon. I could even drain you dry, and no one would say anything against us. You're new in town. You're probably an excellent hunter. That's great. My friend and I, we're fine with you hunting the kind of creatures that hurt innocent people. That's called 'suffering the consequences of one's own actions'. It's the risk they take. But as part of the Alliance, we swore not to hurt anyone, and part of the reason we did that was so you people would leave us alone. We're not hurting anyone!"

"You're covered in blood, you monster!" the hunter snapped, struggling fruitlessly against Rose's grip. She tried to kick Rose's other leg out from under her, but Rose pressed her knee harder into the diaphragm. She'd taken the girl's air once. She could do it again and, at bare minimum, leave the girl unconscious in a Cemetery Grove alley for anyone to do anything with, while Rose and Simon made their escape.

"It's *my* blood, Buffy," Rose replied. She angled her neck so that what was left of her wound was visible. Unlike Simon or the hunter, she had no hair to get in the way. "See? The meat my friend was eating from that butcher paper over there? Steak. The blood I was drinking from that bottle next to it? Pig. Get it tested if you have to. We're not hurting anyone. And I don't want to hurt you anymore."

The hunter snapped her head forward to collide with Rose's nose. That didn't exactly trigger a font, but thick blood filled her nose and mouth to drip out like dark honey. And it stunned Rose enough that she let go of the hunter's wrists. Then the hunter slammed her fists in Rose's eye sockets, new bursts of wet heat. Again, not a gush, but a swell of nearly unbearable pressure. Rose stumbled back into the center of the alley, trying to regain her bearings as the hunter reached for another knife and a stake strapped to her back.

But Rose managed to keep her feet, and the cuts in her back and legs had healed to the point she could support herself better. When she held her hands up again, this time she made sure the hunter watched her retract both her claws and her fangs, even though that put her at greater risk.

"You're very good, but I already could have killed you at least twice, and I didn't. My friend and I are going to walk out of this alley, and we're going to do it with you either conscious or unconscious. Talk to other hunters. Ask around about the Alliance. Look for the cuff on the right ear. That should tell you we're safe for you and should be safe *from* you, too. We mark ourselves as what we are, which potentially puts a target on us among less scrupulous hunters, but we do it for a little peace. Please don't make me kill you just because you didn't know any better or didn't care."

The hunter kept her knife and stake in hand, poised for an attack, but neither she nor Rose came after each other.

Rose waved for Simon to leave the alley, even though he was quadrupedal and would be walking under Cemetery Grove streetlights — hard to explain even in Meridian.

The hunter pointed her weapons at Simon but still didn't reach for the gun at her shoulder, which would doubtlessly serve silver-plated bullets.

"Thank you," Rose said, as politely as she could under the circumstances. "Now me. I'd planned to wear my friend's shirt home, but that just went flying out the window, didn't it?"

The hunter didn't laugh, didn't so much as grin, and only then seemed to realize that Rose wore nothing but her own blood — or rather, she reacted to the fact that the vampire she'd been fighting was naked. Rose couldn't read the response beyond a sort of mild confusion. Not fear or anger. Not arousal. Just the barest bemusement that she brushed away, leaving her pretty little face inscrutable once more.

Most hunters were all business all the time, but it was odd seeing the look of a sixty-year-old hunter on someone so young. Rose had only ever seen martyrial resolve like that in vampires straining against the burden of time that moved on without them.

Rose backed away slowly, still with all her more physical weapons sheathed and her thrall throttled back, even though it responded to fear the same as it did to feeding, as a defense mechanism.

"See? Interaction between vampire and hunter doesn't have to end in a bloodbath. Talk around. If I'm as full of shit as you think, someone will tell you you've been scammed, and you can seek me out in vengeance for the embarrassment. Although I'd say I was more humiliated by this than you."

She reached the streetlight, which sent the hunter into comparative shadow, but she remained in position.

Simon closed a hand over Rose's arm. Rose jumped and looked behind her, which could have been fatal. When she realized her mistake, she swiftly looked back at the hunter, who hadn't moved.

"We can't go home like this. I'm going to turn again," Simon said. "And you're going to ride me. We need to travel by rooftop. Ready?"

Rose nodded.

As soon as the body against hers was covered with fur, Rose grabbed hold of the mane at his nape and pulled herself up just as he loped into a run. When Rose glanced back again, the hunter hadn't left the alley. No one with legs that short, no matter how fast she sprinted, would be able to compete with werewolf stride.

Rose released all the tension she'd hoarded through the fight into a blustery sigh through Simon's fur and held on with her claws in his tough hide and fists tangled in his fur as he shifted into bipedal wolf form to climb up the nearest fire escape. Then he fell forward again on all fours to run over the Meridian rooftops among the angels and gargoyles who surveyed, silent and still.

* * * *

Lis had let demons go before when they were beyond her ability to fight—knowing her limitations ensured that she was lethal under the right circumstances and alive under all others—but a vampire and a werewolf, even fighting together, shouldn't have been outside her ability.

Fighting werewolves directly was generally ill-advised. The best method for dealing with them was knowing where they would be, then taking them out from a distance with silver-plated bullets or shotgun shells filled with silver pellets. But in theory, this one should have been a cinch to eliminate, because he hadn't tried to fight her head-on. He'd stayed on the alley's edges rather than risking his hide against her silver. Which was smart. What the two monsters had done had mostly been smart.

Except for the part where the vampire hadn't killed her.

The vampire had been right when she'd said she'd had ample opportunity to kill Lis. It wouldn't have been the first time Lis had walked the line between life and death. She'd been fed from multiple times, had been to the hospital twice for exsanguination. If it weren't for Archie using some of the blood he regularly drew from her to keep a supply in his private fridge for emergencies, she would have been in the hospital at least five more times. She could handle the pain of a bite—and the ways that the bite weren't pain, overwhelming though they could be.

Lis was used to demons trying to lie or manipulate their way out of a fight or insinuate themselves close enough to hurt her. But despite the bullshit the vampire had spewed about some fabled Alliance between demons and hunters, the vampire had fundamentally outsmarted Lis on the field of battle, and she could have killed Lis in a matter of moments, or she could have made it last, and Lis wouldn't have been able to stop her.

But the vampire had put herself in danger just to allow Lis to live.

Lis didn't believe in life debts. She didn't owe the vampire shit for *not* feeding on her. That was just common courtesy — which should have been far from the vampire's vocabulary once outside the niceties of society.

Vampires could pass for humans after dark, walk among them, even convince humans they weren't a threat, and Lis was sure there were vampire hunters who looked good in heels and knew what each utensil on a full place setting was for. But on the streets, Lis encountered demons in their far more natural state, because in the shadows and among the unseen, no one had to pretend anymore.

She'd found this vampire in the most animalistic state she'd ever encountered one, given that in all her years, she'd never come across one without clothes. She was sure they engaged in sexual seduction within the kind of social situations Lis didn't frequent, but there was never any need for that kind of duplicity on the streets, where they were always just straight feeding. Both victim and predator may have been enjoying it, but she was far more likely to walk in on naked humans than naked demons on her patrol.

Lis had assumed that the vampire had been preying upon the man, latched onto him like the leech she was, but despite the state of them, the man had turned out to be just as corrupted as the woman, and the vampire had been the one bleeding, the werewolf feeding upon her, to mutual satisfaction.

Which meant demon feeding upon demon, which was not within Lis' purview. They hadn't been any danger to anyone.

Except all demons were dangerous. Just because they hadn't been killing anyone right then didn't mean they wouldn't feed together upon someone now that she'd let them go. That death would be on her for not taking them out when she had the chance.

And why *hadn't* she killed them when she'd had the chance?

Because the vampire gave me the chance.

It didn't make any *sense*. Monsters preyed and hunters saved. That was the way the world worked. In the world she was used to, the vampire would have had her, and she'd be dead — or close to it.

There was no reason why the vampire and werewolf should have left her alive. In fact, by not killing her, they left the door open for her to make hunting them her new project. She knew what they looked like, and she knew their feeding grounds — even if they hadn't been feeding on people at that particular moment. They'd even given her the tools to hunt others like them. If what the vampire had said was true, the silver-colored cartilage cuffs could help her discern demon from human in a crowd.

Lis stood in the alley, still as a gargoyle herself, for longer than she thought was normal, even for someone like her, who didn't live in the normal world. It reminded her of a line in a children's book she used to love, that she stood there puzzling until her puzzler was sore.

When she moved again, her abdomen ached, and her face and hands stung. The scratches were shallow. They might scar, but they'd be lost among the rest. She'd had worse from overenthusiastic stray dogs. The diaphragm bruising concerned her more, but she could breathe okay for now. Archie would examine it later.

She retrieved the blades that the vampire had forced her to drop and sheathed them in their wrist straps. She had to remove the body armor around her trunk. The vampire had rendered it useless for now. Archie might decide its integrity had been entirely compromised. It wasn't the end of the world. Before Archie had determined she wasn't going to grow anymore, she'd patrolled in double-layered cardboard and duct tape — surprisingly effective, not to mention cheap.

With the vampire and werewolf gone, she made herself a target by staying in one place too long. She couldn't let the strangeness of her encounter with the couple throw her off, or else the vampire might as well have killed her. Perhaps that had been her plan, but as evil plans went, it was unreliable.

Lis set her confusion aside to come back to later, once she'd finished patrolling.

Chapter Four

After gathering her three hearts — two vampire and one rogue pestilence demon — Lis found the only twenty-four-hour coffee joint in Cemetery Grove. It smelled like espresso, of course, and cinnamon and vanilla. She immediately recognized two vampires sitting together, a vampire sitting alone, and four hunters scattered through the facility. It was four o'clock in the morning. Even Meridian tended to call it a night around this point — an hour when nothing felt real and the world seemed deserted. Only monsters and hunters were awake after the devil's hour.

She ordered a chai latte and a breakfast croissant sandwich. In typical coffee-shop fashion, it nearly cleared out the extra cash she'd collected from her last three kills. What change was left she put into the tip jar, because it was too cumbersome to keep.

While she waited, she observed the vampires and hunters.

Not just in Meridian but in all the other cities and towns she'd hunted in, there were always a few establishments where neither side brought the fight. There had to be neutral territory, for everyone's sanity, especially during this early morning darkness, like holding one's breath. Counterintuitive, how cooperative these late-night or twenty-four-hour places could be, and Lis had just accepted it all this time without assuming that if demons could control themselves in one place, they could control themselves over a broader territory as well.

The vampire couple drinking hot mocha lattes at their table didn't have tattoos or the earrings that the vampire woman had referenced. The solo vampire drinking an iced caramel macchiato wore a jacket that concealed his wrist, but he bore the same silver cuff as the vampire woman from the alley.

Lis ate her breakfast sandwich so fast she could barely enjoy it, always so unbearably hungry after hunting. Her chai latte in hand, she prepared herself, then slipped into the booth bench across from one of the hunters.

She knew from her own experience that hunters were amenable to neither interruption nor social interaction. They weren't amenable to much of anything, especially during their quiet times. Hunting was a solitary sport. She was lucky to have Archie—and to not mind his company—but most hunters she'd met over the years had been loners like her, prickly as honey locusts. They certainly didn't want to talk to a punk kid, any more than she wanted to talk to crusty old men. And they were overwhelmingly men, although she was finally starting to catch up in age with younger hunters, who tended to start in their twenties — the decade when shit was most likely to hit the fan, due to a combination of independence and cluelessness.

She looked young and new to every hunter she had to interact with, which was mostly from walking into them by accident when they weren't looking down wherever they were going. When it came to hunters jealous over location, Lis always retreated. No reason for her to leave her blood behind at a scene when someone else was willing to instead.

Sometimes she'd watch them, see what other hunters' moves were, compare their methods to what Archie taught her. Most hunters engaging in hand-to-hand combat took too goddamn long — not only wasting time but taking years off their life in a cockfight show no one else was going to see. She didn't underneath their need to prance and preen in a boxer's position like there was respect, money, and a girl on the line.

But that was in the field. Hunters out of the field usually just wanted to eat, drink, and unwind in peace and safety before heading home. She knew better than to interrupt, in no small part because she didn't really know how to talk to anyone who wasn't Archie, and the only reason she knew how to talk to Archie was because they'd been talking — or comfortably not talking — for fifteen years.

"I just need to ask a few questions, then I'll get out of your hair."

"What's your damage, kid?"

She hadn't tried to correct people when they called her 'kid' for about three years now. The only time her age was really relevant was when she wanted a beer.

"I'm new to Meridian."

"Don't sound like a question."

"Heard about some Alliance," she said. "How can that possibly be real?"

The hunter set down his grilled sandwich, raising his eyes from his meal to meet hers. His entire demeanor changed—thankfully not for the worse. If anything, his grizzled antagonism softened. Like he was too tired to fight another day.

"Sure it's real. It's real like this place is real." He nodded his head at the entire coffee shop. "These places are more useful to hunters than they are to demons. Even demon bars are more useful to hunters than the kind that accept mixed company. Because we're the ones with the advantage. Don't you forget that."

Just another hunter assuming she hadn't been doing this long enough to accumulate the most common of wisdom for an uncommon profession. She didn't bother contradicting him, though. He wasn't wrong about the rest of it.

"When the Alliance happened," the hunter continued, "most of us thought the hybrids were going to play us for fools—wear the accessories of contrition, then sin anyway and pretend they were saints so no one would hunt them while they hunted."

Lis nodded.

"Turns out there are vampires and werewolves and even a few purer demons who just don't want to deal with the hassle of hunters. By and large, reports of werewolf and vampire attacks went down, particularly werewolves. When they want to be part of city life, their social instincts are strong enough that they're willing to forego human meat entirely for the opportunity to run their territories. Just stay out of the parks at night and you rarely cross their paths."

"And the vampires?" Lis asked.

The hunter inclined his head toward the solo vampire with his macchiato at the bar. "You see the cuff, you leave them alone. That's what we agreed to. True, not everyone agreed, but if one of us kills an Alliance demon, they all gang up on that hunter. It's pretty much a suicide mission. Not worth it."

"But they're evil. Even if they agree to only maim and not murder or drink vegan blood or something, they're evil. But we just let them live — whatever life the dead can lead?"

Shadows returned to the hunter's eyes as he raised his sandwich again for a big bite. "We let evil people live all the time just because they're human. Under the Alliance, we let not-so-evil evil live, as long as they don't hurt humans."

"Why not just eradicate them?"

"There's no eradicating evil, kid. You should know that early," he said with his mouth full. "And there's plenty of evil to eradicate without going after lighter shades of gray just because their teeth happen to get sharp. It's good for us, too, you know. Saves time and valuable energy. You see a titanium cuff or one of those oath spells around their wrist, you know to move on to some demon who's an actual threat."

She'd already guessed that the cuffs weren't actually silver, given that the werewolf was alive. There was self-denial and then there was self-mortification, and although the vampire and werewolf claimed self-denial in one respect, neither vampires nor werewolves were inclined to curb their appetites, much less punish themselves for them.

And for the first time since the alley—now that survival instincts had subsided—she could really consider what she'd walked in on.

She heated under her hoodie with a wave of arousal so strong she didn't know what to do with it. Never had. Manipulated desire was something she was used to, but that was because she recognized the telltale signs it came from outside of herself. If it wasn't hers these days, she could easily ignore it. But when it came from her... It swept not just through her body but her mind. If she weren't sitting, it would threaten to knock her on her ass.

She didn't like it at all, hadn't since puberty hit and, with it, these dizzying tornadoes of physical *feeling*—like vertigo, except the world stayed on its axis, while she was the one tilting.

Then the feeling was gone, as quickly as it arrived. Although it seemed like everyone in the coffee shop should know, not even the hunter across from her blinked. She pushed back her hood to let the air conditioning cool her face.

"We coexist in these liminal places, tolerate the witch, and we don't waste time hunting werewolves for their pelts when there are demon wings we can sell and plenty of vampires who refuse to give up ill-gotten human blood." The hunter sipped his coffee—unadorned black. "That answer your question, new kid?"

"I'm new to Meridian, not the hunt. But yes." She climbed out of the booth, looked back at the cuffed vampire, then took her chai latte along with her to go.

* * * *

Simon got himself and Rose back to her place so they could wash off and Rose could change. Simon was still restless and upset, not from anger so much as fear from how close they'd come to a hunter picking them off. He kissed Rose's cheek before leaving to run through the parks with his pack until sunrise.

Rose changed into house clothes, although she fully intended to go out, so the clothes she chose covered her body — leggings, black long sleeves with a hood attached, and a long black coat, in case she cut it too close with the morning sun.

She returned to the alley where she and Simon had been interrupted. Then she opened her sense of smell until she could practically peek into the past. The hunter's scent lingered, and since Rose had drawn blood that would take a while to completely close under a scab, it was easy enough to follow her trail through crowded alleys that had mostly gone quiet in sleep, although there was almost always some activity among insomniacs and other nocturnal creatures.

Rose was more put together than most of the people walking around at that time of night, but there might have been something in the surety of her stride and complete absence of anxiety that kept bad actors from approaching her or even attempting to pickpocket — which would have been fruitless. She kept her keys and money in a compartment in her boot, not her pockets, but she was also sensitive enough to feel even the slickest of sticky fingers — and the best pickpockets didn't live in this part of town.

Rose's home was on the western edge of Cemetery Grove. She lived there because she'd wanted that particular property and a little quiet, not because she couldn't afford to live closer to Meridian's more vibrant center. She'd never had any reason to go south into the Wastelands. No one she knew did. Like everyone else, she didn't enjoy the reminder that people lived like this. Rose was actually a little relieved the hunter's blood-scent trail wove all through the area, because that meant it was at least marginally protected. This hunter would never receive accolades for her service, nor would she be able to sell valuable parts like some of the more industrious and ambitious hunters who used incubus or succubus wings to pay their rent.

Which begged the question for Rose how her hunter could afford the lean pickings. Mission-oriented hunters tended to be the rangers of their kind and could sleep wherever they laid their head — and wake up at the slightest alarm — but she didn't like to think of that little girl risking her life all night, then risking it again every time she closed her eyes. Did she have family? Was she sneaking out at night, then climbing into her bedroom window in the morning? Did she go to UT Meridian?

Or was she protecting home by patrolling these alleys?

Being human was sometimes such a thankless existence. When Rose had turned into a vampire, she'd immediately been drawn into the family home — more like a gutted and reconfigured luxury hotel. She'd had access to family funds as well as her own streams of income, plus beautiful clothes, beautiful people, and drains in every communal room.

Turned werewolves tended to enter a more nomadic and houseless existence, but that wasn't universal. There were often handfuls of wolves who wanted their day-to-day life more average despite their night-to-night activities, and they often housed other wolves who preferred a den to open air. Those wolves didn't need roofs, which made living outside less distressing.

Despite the little girl nearly killing her, Rose still lingered unhappily on the image of her huddled cold in nothing but a raggedy blanket or sleeping bag, enduring like the martyr so many hunters became. Although she was young, she'd moved with the confidence of years, suggesting she'd started entirely too early, when a girl was supposed to be skipping classes, running laps, figuring out what they wanted to be when they grew up, and falling in love with all the wrong people but making all the right friends.

Instead, she'd been doing this, patrolling among the helpless because she wasn't helpless, going up against beings who could crush her like a bug if she didn't get her silver bite in first.

Rose followed the scent back out of the Wastelands — *thank God* — and into Cemetery Grove, to the coffee shop a few blocks from Melody's bar, demon-friendly but not demon-exclusive. Neutral ground. So the hunter understood the concept of places where she couldn't hunt the clientele. Perhaps it wouldn't be such a big leap to citizens she couldn't harm within the city limits. Hunters tended not to be the most ideologically flexible, but this hunter was young. Young enough that her moral compass might not have been petrified in place just off north, with no room for nuance or choice.

Rose had known that not all hunters would respect the Alliance, but she'd become complacent after months of silently interacting with those who did. She'd lived too long to assume there was anywhere she'd be safe, whether she was human or vampire. She should have known better. And now she would.

She wasn't even sure why she was following the young hunter, except that thinking about her made Rose sad and protective. She knew a little something about ideological inflexibility and changing her mind anyway.

Like regarding the young hunter with concern rather than merciless pity.

When the hunter exited the coffee shop holding a hot drink in a paper cup, Rose climbed a fire escape. She wasn't as fast at running over rooftops as Simon, but she had the strength to jump when she needed to, and she landed without too much noise.

Rose stayed far enough behind, dipping in and out of view, that the hunter didn't appear to notice her, but Rose could sense impending sun, like the slightest haze of smoke in a newly burning building. Indirect sunlight would only be unpleasant, but if she got caught out too far from home, she'd have to find somewhere to break in until sunset, and that would just be no fun. Half of why she loved her home was because all her things were there. Sure, she slept most of the day, but she'd be so bored the rest of the time.

The hunter didn't seem to be in a hurry, however, and although she cast a paranoid eye in every direction, toward every movement or voice, she lacked the intensity of a predator seeking prey.

Like most hunters—and Rose—her shift was reaching its end.

Rose followed her out of Cemetery Grove back into the Wastelands, then to its western edge, where what might generously be called civilization started back up again, with neon signs and lights on behind plate glass and people at counters finishing out their third shifts as well.

The rest of the Wastelands was utterly without tenants, commercial or private. All the denizens were technically squatting, and any electrical power happened to be on by accident or suspicious circumstance. There were no convenience stores, no restaurants, no apartments, no businesses whatsoever. It was a ghost town filled with living people who might as well have been dead to the rest of Meridian. The vendors who served the Wastelands seemed to know where the line was between no man's land and the land of the acknowledged living. It wasn't even subtle. On one side of the street, buildings were dark, boarded up, broken into, stripped clean of every last inch of value and left a vacant, worthless shell. On the side the hunter walked to, there were active storefronts — worn and faded as trash in a desert, but with unmistakable signs of life.

The hunter kept going, even while Rose adjusted her hood to make sure she was covered and tightened her long coat around her, ready to pull it over her head if needed.

The hunter veered into the parking lot of a motel that looked like it had once been painted cream and red but now just flaked and blistered in varying shades of sun-bleached brown. Rose climbed down the fire escape of the last Wastelands building, then ran silently across the street as the hunter ascended the stairs to the second floor, where she knocked three times on one of the doors.

Rose strained to hear what the girl said and caught the tail end, although she wasn't sure she heard correctly.

" — Tim Roth."

The door opened on a black man who had seen his share of rough years, grooves dug deep in his face, although the rest of the skin seemed too smooth to call it aged. He had some freckles, but not many, and his close-cropped hair was salt and pepper. To the casual observer, he looked like he could have sold vacuum cleaners or encyclopedias door to door in another time. He spoke too softly for Rose to hear, but she recognized the deadly glint of a gun. Rose ducked under the walkway beneath the room, worried that the girl had knocked on the wrong door, but there was no gunshot. The girl's light footsteps entered the room and the door closed behind her, followed by a series of locks — the motel's lock and deadbolt, but also another one that had been added for good measure.

Rose went up the stairs and stopped outside the room, where she slid down to sit under the window, pressing her ear to the wall. The wooden embellishment on the walkway railing mostly shielded her as dawn broke, and she was close enough to home that she might be able to cover herself with her coat and dart from shade to shade. She just wanted to make sure the girl was all right with the man, wanted to understand what had brought a hunter into the night so young. Wanted to know who would do such a thing to her.

There was the click of a plastic box opening, then the rustle of what could only be a first aid kit. For a long time there was no other sound, no speech, only small, soft, tinny rock music from the room's clock radio.

"Ever heard of something in Meridian called the Alliance?" Without the tension of a fight, the hunter's voice was loose but flat, to match the blank mask of her face.

"A devil's peace treaty," the man replied, with the certainty of a fire-and-brimstone preacher, although he was as softspoken as the hunter. "Who's been filling your head?"

"Another hunter."

"Well, you're not this other hunter, Lis. Meridian is a mystical whirlpool of evil, worse than anything I've exposed you to before. It will try to suck you in, too, in the name of exception, nuance, relativity, ease. But you're a hunter of monsters. It doesn't matter what those monsters pretend to be. They are what they are, and you cannot give them one inch, not one solitary inch, or else it's your soul they'll be taking next. You have a job, a mission, a moral compass, and an obligation. Don't let Meridian make a fool of you like it does the others. Now go take your shower. I'm making sausage and eggs with the hot sauce that you like. I'll dress these properly when you're done."

An idealist, then, as rigid and absolute in his assessment of demons as many hunters, even those who adhered to the Alliance agreement. Which was dangerous in and of itself, but Rose didn't think he was a direct danger to the hunter—Liz or Lis, hard to tell through the wall, but she thought the end sounded harsher than a Z.

Then all Rose could hear was water from the shower and a limping walk.

Direct sunrays had crossed the horizon. Rose felt like she stood too close to a firepit. She adjusted her hood over her head and the rest of the coat around her. Then she ran. She was less than ten minutes away from her home on foot, and there was still plenty of shade in the early morning. She made it home without even a sunburn.

Chapter Five

Now that Rose knew where the young hunter patrolled, and since there were few others she needed to worry about in the area—even most mission-oriented hunters had given up the Wastelands for damned—she searched for her among the alleys as soon as the sun was below the horizon.

She stuck to rooftops. People tended not to look up, especially since Cabrera's famed artistic influence didn't extend this far south.

Rose found the girl after less than thirty minutes. She patrolled with her hands in her pockets, shoulders hunched, hood up as though she was the one who had to hide herself from the sun, like some disaffected teenager who would blow up at the first person who tried to talk to her or put a hand on her shoulder. Given her nervy glances and the state of her clean but sew-scarred clothes, she looked like she belonged. Rose would never have guessed the girl was a hunter, much less good enough that she'd managed to survive for however long she'd been fighting, despite her obvious disadvantages.

Lis encountered her first vampire of the night in a mostly deserted alley. Guards farther down squinted into the dark to figure out where the sounds they heard came from, but they didn't bother to investigate. If it wasn't a risk to the business they protected — and from whiffs of burning plastic and human vomit, said business probably had something to do with the injudicious distribution of meth and heroin — it was none of their business.

The girl killed the vampire in three minutes.

Rose considered herself lucky, although she could already tell that part of the reason why Lis was so good in places like this was that the vampires here were the kind who had no support, who'd been turned on a whim or a dare or for a laugh, or even by accident, if the victim bit back while the vampire was feeding. Vampires without family to teach and mold them were scrappy and, during their feed, absolutely animal. They took what they wanted how they wanted it, each feed as desperate as the first, their hunger seemingly insatiable if they didn't know where the next meal would come from. No finesse, very little connection with the manipulative side of their thrall, and not particularly sophisticated in terms of strategy, because they could usually overpower their human prey, then control them with the natural thrall of the bite.

Vampires with animal instincts were dangerous, no doubt, like confronting a mountain lion or rabid dog. But a vampire with finesse, who knew how to use all their tools, was even more dangerous.

Lis was handy with her tools, and like the vampires she fought, she was vicious as a feral cat, but she had the finesse that the vampire lacked. She had training. She moved to an eight count like a dancer or gymnast and was efficient with every move—none of the frills or shows of strength other hunters wasted their energy on. Get low, then get them lower, short bursts of force on targeted areas, incapacitation at weak points, then a quick kill.

The only reason why Rose was still alive might have been because she'd thought to jump when the hunter went low. And perhaps because, although she'd marveled at how capable the girl was despite her size, Rose hadn't underestimated her based on that, nor on her age or the fact she was a woman, because Rose had lived for so long among other women as immortal as she was, often turned young, and often stronger than they appeared.

As she followed Lis through other alleys and watched her handily kill and field-dress three other vampires, it didn't escape Rose's notice that the vampires the girl encountered were men. Vampire families tended to keep turned women like jewels, to display status and conquest and put them to work on behalf of the family. Outside families, women were turned to become companions when the tomcats got too lonely, and they might even hunt as a couple for a time, before a family saw an opportunity and stole the woman away to a more comfortable life.

That abundance of women had never led to an overabundance, however, since the women working in service to a family were also more vulnerable to hunters—who were, once again, mostly men and took powerful, manipulative women more personally.

As far as the heads of families were concerned, the uneven gender population evened itself into something more sustainable over enough time. And vampires, of course, had plenty of time.

"What do you think you're doing?"

Rose jumped, covering her mouth to keep a squeal of shock from alerting Lis to look up. She wasn't usually so easy to sneak up on, but she'd been watching Lis cutting out her fourth vampire's heart, and how often did something sneak up on people on rooftops?

Simon leaned over the roof's edge, then winced in distaste. He guided Rose away and lowered his voice further, into a rumble that tried to be threatening but was undercut by the worry in his expression. "Are you trying to torture yourself? She didn't succeed. She didn't kill us."

"I'm not worried she's going to kill us. Now that we know her, we can be more careful. I'm worried *she's* going to get herself killed."

"She's a hunter. She knows what she's getting into."

"How old do you think that girl is?" Rose really wanted to know, because she couldn't trust her own assessment.

"If I hadn't gotten a good look at her, I'd think she was *young* young. But freezing in the middle of an alley and afraid for the life of you and your mate, you get a damn good look at a hunter — down to the pores. I'd say early twenties. Nocturnal life helps her avoid sun damage, but environmental pollutants and telltale signs of too much stress are dead giveaways."

"She's got this down to a science, and her handler seems like a father figure with a moral absolutism streak. Simon, I think this girl was cultivated as a hunter way too young. She's fighting a war she should have only just started — if at all. And it was by someone else's design. She doesn't have to be doing this. She doesn't even know what she's missing. This is all she's known. *This*." Rose leaned over the side of the roof again and pointed down at the systematic way the girl removed the vampire's fangs. Rose winced in sympathetic pain.

Simon put his hands on her upper arms and rubbed at the tension there before resting his chin in the curve between neck and shoulder that seemed made for that move. "Still don't see what that has to do with you."

"I don't think you can understand. Not directly."

"Is it a woman thing or a vampire thing?"

"Both. Don't get me wrong. I had a typical youth before I was turned, but... I know what it's like to be plucked out of my life and into a pool of blood. I know what it's like to be praised and encouraged and supported only for what I can do for them in return. It's bad enough that hunters are created by tragedy or greed. Do we really need them reared from the cradle?"

He guided her away again, toward the other side of the roof so they could talk less sotto voce. "It's not nice, I'll give you that. But hunters are made for all kinds of reasons. So are warriors. She's old enough *now* to make her own decisions, and she's decided to keep going with it. Think you might be overidentifying a bit, with that soft, changed heart of yours?" He pressed his palm against her chest.

Rose sighed. "Maybe."

"Or maybe, with your newfound independence, you're partial to picking up strays," he added with a grin.

"Also maybe." She closed her eyes and rested her head against Simon's chest, where his heartbeat was much more prominent than hers.

Just because the girl was old enough to make her own decisions didn't mean she felt secure enough to make them. There were more ways than vampire thralls to manipulate. She and her handler were a cult of two. Girls like her obeyed because of a combination of moral imperative, affectionate control when obedient, and disproportionate punishment when disobedient. Independence wasn't as easy as hitting an age of majority and moving out.

If the girl had been hunting for as long as Rose thought she had — or, even more horrifying, longer — she wouldn't be able to imagine what else she could be, without the tools to be anything else. Like, say, a formal education, ties to anyone outside of her handler, or more than a controlled allowance. She clearly had enough to go to a coffee shop, but not enough to replace rather than crudely mend her clothes after substantial damage.

Rose had lived sixty years with her family coven, but she couldn't die of natural causes, and at least her prison bars had been elaborate wrought iron. Hunter lives were harsh, brutal, and usually short. She didn't have sixty years to build up courage to escape.

But Simon was right. Unless the hunter decided to hunt them, she wasn't their problem. Rose couldn't help someone who determined a monster by what they were and not what they did. Trying would just get Rose killed for her trouble. The hunter would have to figure out shades of gray on her own. No one could force her to see them, least of all a vampire.

Simon shifted to his wolf form before running across the cluster of buildings to the far end of the block. He looked back to see if she was coming.

Rose returned to the edge of the roof to silently wish the hunter well.

A group of vampires was just as silently closing in on Lis, who was busy making sure the last vampire heart was secure in its plastic bag. She didn't hear or see them approach, as though made of the shadows themselves.

A small family could have heard about Lis' impact in the Wastelands, but they could also have just been a vampire pride who'd zoned in on a girl separated from the herd. Although werewolves hunted in packs, vampires didn't usually hunt in groups greater than three — not least because they tended to be possessive over a body's blood. But small families hunting together wasn't unheard of.

There were seven vampires, five men and two women, each of them lean and hungry, silver glinting in their eyes like forgotten ferry coins as they crossed into indirect streetlight.

Rose beckoned frantically at Simon.

"What is it?" To Simon's credit, he could have sounded annoyed or frustrated that Rose was this invested, but he didn't. He mirrored her concern and urgency with his own.

"They're going to kill her."

* * * *

A sole scraping against the rough asphalt alerted Lis to the clandestine approach of several beings. Supernatural, by her blind assessment. People in the Wastelands generally weren't that quiet when they walked, even while sneaking.

She left her bag on the ground and carefully palmed her knives, pretending she hadn't heard anything. Still kneeling, she rocked onto her toes and waited for the subtle footsteps to get closer.

Then she pushed herself standing and spun around, her knives glinting bright in contrast to her dark sleeves.

Her throat dropped into her stomach. Her stomach dropped even further as she darted her gaze from one shadow to the next. In hand-to-hand combat, she'd never fought more than three demons at a time. Nests and families were supposed to be taken out with precision targeting from a safe distance.

She knew she couldn't take on seven vampires, and the seven vampires didn't care that she couldn't take them on, given that her inability to take them on had probably factored into their plan.

She had one chance.

Lis dipped down to snag her bag and ran the other direction down the alley, heading for the light. Light itself wouldn't protect her, but being in full view of other people could — although if this group of vampires knew the first thing about the Wastelands, they'd know they could bring her down in the middle of the intersection, drain her dry, and leave her there, and no one would do a single solitary thing until pestilence demons crawled out of their sewers and dragged her dead body down like urban alligators.

She considered her gun. She didn't do well in a firefight. She was better with guns when she was in complete control of the situation. If she shot at them, the silver would sting like hell, and maybe she'd hit the heart, though she was more accurate with headshots. However, in a sprint, there was no guarantee of accuracy. Even if she got two or three of them that way — which was generous — that still left five or six of them left to avenge the dead.

Running was good for one purpose only — to make herself more trouble than she was worth. It worked best with human monsters, who usually didn't do that much cardio and couldn't sustain the chase.

Vampires had more stamina than her, and all of them could run faster.

The first one snagged his claws into her shoulder before she reached the alley's mouth and swung her into the wall with a shrieking laugh. The others joined in, like hyenas. She knew it was coming as soon as her hoodie pulled against her momentum, so she managed to put her hands up to keep from smashing her face or losing her air. The gripping gloves saved her from some scrapes, but her knife handles bruised her palms.

Lis whipped around again, blades first.

"Little girl thinks she knows what she's doing," said the vampire who'd stopped her. He sneered down at her, fangs visible. "Playing hunter in the bad part of town. It was only a matter of time before something swallowed you up."

"Just glad it could be us," said another vampire, a thin man with a big mouth and gaunt cheekbones. His fangs seemed too big for him, and he slavered rudely.

Lis couldn't stop to think. As soon as the first vampire started for her, she dropped, bracing her fists on the ground as she slammed her boot into his knee, locking it back. The second vampire reached her, smile turning upside-down and inside-out as he parted his mouth to expose what seemed like more teeth than there should be. He struck at her shoulder, but she was farther down than he could easily reach, and she punched his nose and upper lip, stunning him and unsettling his balance from his bent-over position.

Then she slashed at the grasping hands of the first vampire. He jerked back, hissing.

But she was only making them mad and inciting the other five, who closed in.

The vampires stayed on their two feet rather than meeting her on her playing field, so she lunged for the first vampire. His Achilles tendons were protected by boots of his own, but she latched to his leg — an extra burden in more than weight, because every time one of the other vampires tried to attack her, he was at risk, too.

Once attached, she stabbed behind his knee. When his leg buckled, she acted as a kind of splint that kept him up, even while he clawed at her head, snapping her rubber band. Her hair spilled in every direction, including her face, but she was used to fighting in the dark.

She hugged the first vampire's leg harder as two others slashed at her shoulders and back. Her armor deflected some of their claws, but one got her in the neck through her hoodie. Her blood had been drawn in multiple places now, and although she couldn't smell it, they certainly could. It made them more eager to get to her.

Lis buried her left blade into the vampire's upper thigh. Hardly fatal, but as she dug, pulled, then withdrew it again, the vampire screamed like a thousand bats at the clear night sky. Then she stabbed the groin at her eye level. The flesh there was much more yielding. She felt more than heard a rupture.

Nothing, not even Lis, would keep him upright anymore. When he collapsed, Lis released him, rolling again to the side and pointing her knives — one now quite bloody — at the others. She kept her back to the wall, which at least limited the directions from which the other vampires could attack her and protected the hardest part of her to defend.

But that still left the other hundred-eighty degrees of her accessible.

Lis crouched again to slam into the second vampire's knees and go after his exposed Achilles tendons, but the two women mimicked her, catching on.

She stabbed at the second vampire's abdomen, cut, twisted, yanked back, then spun herself toward the women who came after her with their fangs extended and claws like blender blades heading straight for her face. The incapacitation of the first two vampires wouldn't last forever, not even for long, so she'd have to do this multiple times before she could hope to get a chance at their hearts.

She wasn't going to make it.

Lis had fought clever vampires before and lived to regret it. Fighting four at once had convinced her that she absolutely could not attack nests alone. She'd barely made it out of that one. She'd been lucky.

Luck could only get her so far.

She swiped at the two women, but she had two hands to their four. They tore at her jacket and the gauntlets underneath, caught her cheek, crossing the wound made by the vampire in the other alley. She hadn't needed stitches then, the scratches too shallow and thin to require anything other than covering them overnight with some Aquaphor and bandages where they hadn't already closed. She might need stitches for the ones left by these women—if she made it long enough to need anything but a priest.

Is this it?

It wasn't so much that her life flashed before her eyes. The various scenes of her life overlapped into one image, because in her clear memory, her life had been hunting or preparing for the hunt. Skulking and stalking through the darkness. Fighting monsters of all shapes, sizes, sex, and species. Sleep, train, hunt, study, sleep, rinse and repeat, ad nauseum.

There was comfort in routine. Any break in that routine had either been when she and Archie had moved cities to pursue new quarry, investigate some old trinket, hide from more organized evil, or find some ancient reference to demons in a rare books section— anything to make her more effective in the eradication of evil.

Her life had been one thing and one thing only, and she was honored by it. She carried the burden because she could carry it, because she knew what the rest of the world didn't know or didn't want to know. This was her sacrifice, even if no one else knew she made it.

But with all her life narrowing to one moment—the one she was presently in indistinguishable from the first—she became all the more aware of what had been excluded. The rest of the world. People who raised their faces to the sun and closed their eyes because they weren't afraid of what would get them when they did. Who people were and what they did when they simply weren't afraid, when they were ignorant of evil and its impact on their world. They had the lights, signs, and streets, and she had the alleys, as much forgotten and disposable as the humans she protected, no matter where she lived.

No one but Archie would even think to look for her, but that wouldn't be until morning when she didn't come home, and then he wouldn't find her. As a hunter himself, he would understand that this was the risk, the price, plain and clear in the contract they'd signed when they'd strapped on their first stake and sworn allegiance to God in holy-water-bathed silver.

The good thing, though, about knowing she was going to die was that she didn't have anything left to lose, and it didn't matter how injured she got. As long as she took some bloodsuckers with her.

Lis swiped again at the women, aiming for their faces rather than their forearms, which put her face within their reach as well. She barreled into one of the women, toppling her onto the concrete, since the vampire wasn't as used to balancing in a crouch. But this put Lis face to face and body to body with the vampire and left her back completely exposed, which both women took immediately advantage of. The vampire beneath her grabbed her by her loose hair and jerked her head to the side to expose her neck, which she couldn't protect with any kind of body armor without compromising maneuverability. The vampire behind her shredded the back of the hoodie and tried to find a weak spot in her armor while also tearing back her hood to get a good biting spot at her nape.

This is it.

The vampire woman laughing behind her shrieked before she was torn from Lis' back, ripping most of Lis' hoodie into something significantly more ventilated.

Lis managed to get her blade into the chest of the vampire beneath her. With a cry, she fell on top of the handle to push it in to the hilt, then angled it up to cut through the heart.

The woman beneath her went slack.

Lis shoved herself up again, aiming her blades at the chaos in the alley, then froze. Because other than the first two vampires still recovering on the ground and the vampire she'd just killed, all the other vampires were occupied.

At first, she thought some hunters who'd decided to give the Wastelands a spin had swooped in to rescue one of their own. But even though the woman had been naked the last time Lis had seen her, it was impossible to mistake her face and the distinctive silhouette of her shorn head.

And although the man had been clothed the last time she'd seen him — until he'd been too furry to remain clothed — at that moment, he was naked and in bipedal werewolf form. They never showed certain anatomical realities in the movies. Werewolves were apparently only partially sheathed while in their bipedal state. She'd never had the chance in all her hunts to see a werewolf so clearly and up close, since they usually stayed on more rural outskirts of suburbs. She'd only ever seen werewolves either in their full wolf form — something actually closer to a cross between a wolf and a bear — or in their human form, the cave in which they hid their evil. The bipedal form was just a state for them to phase through. She'd never seen one linger in it, and she was briefly fascinated.

None of the demons she'd ever encountered before were as big as a bipedal werewolf, who towered somewhere around nine or ten feet — although, for her, other beings above a certain height were all just 'very tall and will not notice you when it puts its feet down'.

Lis watched, stunned, as the werewolf pulled the second vampire woman's head right off her shoulders — another effective way to kill them that was out of Lis' reach without an axe, and hatchets were heavier than she liked her weapons.

The woman from the alley hissed at two vampire men, who hissed back at her like a pit of vipers fighting over the same mates. When one of the men tried to go after Lis again, the woman clawed the vampire's mouth from corner to ear, giving him a sloppy, lopsided grin.

"Go! Run, if you value your lives. Just go!" the woman tried to convince them, but the vampires still alive frothed with hatred that left them unable to so much as form words.

The man with the cut mouth tried for Lis again while the other confronted the woman.

No longer stunned, Lis dropped again to stab the man in both thighs and yank down as far as she could through the vampire's tougher body. The man stumbled forward. Lis swung her leg to catch him across the shins so that he face-planted onto the alley. Then she crawled forward to jam her silver into the base of the skull. Silver to the brain. Good as the heart.

She took the opportunity to go after the vampires she'd wounded, who were well enough to wriggle but not yet to stand. She stabbed each of them in the heart, then clambered back to her feet, prepared for any other creature to come at her. Her pulse was a staticky rush in her ears, and she was as unable to speak as the vampires had been. She felt like a cavewoman, ready to kill friend or foe who tried to touch her.

So it was a good thing the vampire woman and her werewolf didn't try. They kept a respectable distance fifteen feet away, the werewolf still in bipedal form, although he hunched over with his hands on the ground, strangely simian behavior.

The vampire held up her hands again. "They're dead. You're okay. We saw them jump you, and I couldn't just leave you like that. You're okay, Lis, I promise."

Lis jerked her right blade toward the vampire. "How do you know my name?"

"I was worried about you last night. I followed you to make sure you'd be taken care of."

Lis laughed. It wasn't something she was used to doing, and she was pretty sure her mouth twisted in the wrong direction, but adrenaline and absurdity were a hell of a cocktail. "I tried to kill you. You almost killed me. I might try to kill you now. You were *worried*?"

The vampire woman slowly lowered her hands again, her whole posture relaxing. The werewolf didn't relax, but the fury in his eyes when he'd decapitated the vampire had dissipated.

"We told you we're not going to hurt you. Defend ourselves, yes, but we won't hurt you."

Lis strode forward. The werewolf twitched, curling his lip in threat, but the woman touched his arm and didn't otherwise move when Lis brought her blades within six inches of the woman's chest. All she needed was a good jab, and the woman would join with the rest of her kind.

The woman didn't flinch. She met Lis' gaze with a warmth Lis didn't recognize, didn't know what to do with. But it wasn't cruel, and it didn't *feel* like a lie. Some demons were subtler with their manipulation than others, but Lis didn't sense so much as a grain of thrall emanating from her.

In fitted high-waisted jeans, a soft, heather gray T-shirt tucked in, and slouchy boots with decorative studs wrapped around, the vampire appeared unsettlingly human, far more normal than Lis in her slashed and torn clothes. Anyone looking in on them now would assume Lis was the dangerous one.

Lis knew what Archie would say. That the devil was fooling her with masks and costumes, tricking her with kindness, engaging in a long con to tempt and destroy her, body and soul. That it was all part of the game and the way a creature like her enjoyed the hunt—by convincing her victims that she was harmless.

Except Lis knew she wasn't harmless. But even if Lis were fast enough to kill the vampire, she'd still have to contend with a werewolf who could relieve her shoulders of her head in a heartbeat. Perhaps that was what gave the woman confidence to stand against her.

But Lis didn't think so. Contrary to everything she'd ever been taught, she lowered her blades.

"That's a nastier cut than mine there." The woman raised her hands again to point at Lis' face, this time without claws.

Lis let her, even though she wasn't sure why.

"And your clothes are in shambles," the vampire continued. "I shudder to think of the damage I can't see. Do you have field first aid for this kind of thing?"

Lis nodded to her backpack, which had been wrenched away during the fight.

"Puppy, could you?"

As the werewolf edged around Lis, he shrank into his human self. This time, he was the one who was naked. Lis had seen naked men before, but it wasn't something she was *used* to seeing, especially from a man without any sense of urgency to cover himself— because although they looked human, they were animals, and animals didn't have the same shame as people, who'd eaten of the apple. Out of her own sense of shame, she deliberately didn't look — as much as was possible when she needed to keep her attention on him while he walked behind her.

Equally cagey with her, he crouched by her backpack. Opening it exposed four bagged hearts and a prescription bottle of vampire teeth. He grimaced in disgust.

"Charming."

But he nudged the hearts aside to find the flexible black canvas kit, which he tossed at Lis. Catching it meant adding an obstacle to using her knives, but neither werewolf nor vampire took advantage of the opening.

Lis pulled out one of the bigger adhesive bandages from the kit, then clapped it over her cheek, wincing against the sting that had awakened as soon as adrenaline wore off.

"I meant a field suture kit," the vampire said.

"It's fine. Arch — I can sew it up myself once I have a mirror."

"In the meantime, you're inviting every vampire between here and St. Theresa's to midnight tea," the vampire said. "I have a place where you can be safe 'til sunrise."

Chapter Six

"Are you sure about this?" Simon asked as quietly as he could without whispering. "You're leading a homicidal serial killer straight to your home?"

"I just told her I know where she lives. Besides, knowing where I live doesn't make it easy to get into," Rose replied. "Look at her."

"I see her," Simon said. "But just because she looks like she needs chicken soup and a stuffed animal doesn't mean she's safe."

Rose tucked her arm around Simon's, as though they were on nothing more than a romantic late-night walk through the worst part of town while Simon could still get picked up for indecent exposure. "I take a homicidal serial killer home every day. I think another will be just fine."

"I'm not —" he started to protest. "Oh, you. Well, I'm not comfortable with her at my back."

Lis had agreed to sheathe the knives, but after she'd insisted on taking each vampire's heart and teeth, that didn't reassure much. And she couldn't fit all the hearts in her backpack, so she walked behind them with four vampire hearts in sealed plastic bags like late-night groceries. That occupied her hands, but Rose was still just as aware as Simon that the girl had more than enough weapons within reach as soon as she dropped those bags.

"You don't have to stay," Rose said. "This was my decision. And it's my home. You didn't sign up for this, for fighting, bloodshed, harboring a hunter. I'd understand, Simon."

He looked over at Lis, his eyebrows drawn together but the set of his mouth inscrutable. Finally, he shook his head. "I'm not leaving you alone with her."

Rose rested her cheek on Simon's arm and smiled. "She's just staring at your ass."

Simon punched her shoulder. Although he remained tense as stone, he couldn't hold back an almost shy grin. "I didn't know I'd be baring it to anyone but you."

They turned onto Rose's street and crossed an intersection to get to the building.

"You can't be serious," Lis muttered. "You live in a church?"

"Whether there were any abandoned churches in the area was the first thing I asked my realtor." Rose ran up the steps to the double doors, then crouched to retrieve her key pouch from her shoe. "This one suffered a fire in the sacristy—which isn't as ironic as it sounds. Just an error by an acolyte with the candlelighter. They were already overbudget and underinsured, so they let the bank take the church two years ago. Given the location, they've had some trouble unloading it, but it suits my needs perfectly."

She unlocked both the main lock and the added dead bolts. The hunter and her handler weren't the only ones protective of their space.

"How can you stand living on consecrated ground? How do you not burst into flames just by stepping over the threshold?" Lis asked.

"I think the consecration was decommissioned by abandonment," Rose said, only half joking. "Demons can enter churches, you know. It's the occasional religious icon they don't like, and I had the chancel renovated, so the built-in cross was removed. But I can behold a cross without hissing madly. I'm not Bela Lugosi."

"You still react to conviction," Lis said.

"I'm not going to deny I've got a little demon in me, and it has rules, just like everything else in this world. I *am* going to say that most people, not just vampires, react negatively to a certain level of conviction. Please, come in."

"I don't need your invitation."

"No, but it's polite to wait for it." Rose gestured for Simon and Lis to enter before her. Then she shut the heavy doors behind them.

Simon went for the first lamp while Rose did up the door locks, the chain locks, the combination padlock, and the large gate latch. The door wasn't impenetrable to, say, construction machinery, but it would take a lockpick way too long to get through to justify the trouble.

"I know the security measures look intimidating," Rose explained, "but they're to keep people out, not in. The combination lock is set to all zeros."

Simon kept lighting lamps, putting distance between himself and Lis, then ducked into the wing that led to the Sunday school rooms. There was even a basement level that used to be for fellowship. Now it housed Rose's books and acted as a sort of display museum of the life she'd left behind. It was protected by more locks, and she was the only one who knew where she'd hidden the keys.

"Make yourself at home," Rose said, gesturing to the church interior. "I'm going to get some of my own first aid supplies. Meet me in the sacristy. All the smoke and fire damage is gone now, and it seemed like a good place for my fridge. It's not like I need a giant kitchen, is it?"

Lis didn't move from the front of the sanctuary.

Built-in carpet led to the chancel, where the altar should have been. The track of the carpet looked original to the building. The dark red carpet itself looked new. The rest of the sanctuary had been gutted — only a few refinished pews under the stained-glass windows acknowledged its history — and reconfigured instead as large living room lounges and a study, with couches and chairs arranged in multiple discrete sections. Some pieces appeared to have been chosen for comfort, others purely for aesthetic. A large desk and free-standing bookcases demarcated the study near the chancel, and a large-screen television established a casual living area in the more comfortable seating arrangement across from it.

Lights switched on outside the church, backlighting the arched windows depicting the Passion of the Christ and the rose window above the chancel, which showed prominent Old and New Testament scenes in its slices. If there had been an installation with a cross below the rose window, it was gone, replaced by some kind of wrought-iron sculpture behind a large king-size bed, unmade but plumped with pillows and blankets like a nest. On one side of the bed was a wardrobe, dresser, and shoe rack. On the other was a mounted television screen that could flip out for easier viewing from the bed.

A portion of the building had been opened up to the right of the chancel, exposing a wood and iron staircase that led to what Lis assumed was the steeple. Church bells, real or recorded, were supposed to call to churchgoers and cast away evil spirits. Perhaps gutting the steeple bell tower had done the opposite.

Above, attached to the vaulted ceilings, medieval-inspired chandeliers with flickering imitation candlelight provided added illumination and atmosphere.

It should have been blasphemous, replacing a church with luxury living, replacing an altar with a bed, but although the design indicated taste and indulgence, the entire home was surprisingly comfortable, even modern, despite vintage and antique touches. It didn't feel formal. Nor did it feel mocking of the body it had invaded. On the contrary, Rose had made no effort to cover sacred images, not even curtains to keep the sun from coming through during the day, and had she kept the cross on the chancel wall above her bed, that would have seemed far more blasphemous than it did without.

Lis did notice that the only place in the room where sunlight wouldn't threaten her through the windows was the chancel, clouded in soothing shadow.

Vampires didn't necessarily need it, but a strong air conditioner ensured that the sanctuary was comfortable, dry rather than the strange humidity endemic to every motel room Lis had ever slept in, no matter how much air conditioning they pumped in. The floors on either side of the carpet in the central aisle were porcelain tile and would be cool to walk on barefoot. The walls had been plastered smooth, the beams from which the chandeliers hung stained dark. From the cream-bricked outside, it was clear that this was one of the older churches in Meridian, but from the inside, it looked and smelled like new, with the lingering odor of fresh paint, plaster, and grout.

Lis didn't know what to do with any of it. It wasn't the dungeon she'd imagined, in either the 'basement of a medieval castle' or the more modern SM sense. Lis could practically smell money along with the paint, but it didn't *feel* ostentatious, the kind of luxury too garish or too ornate to be livable. And there were entirely too many windows, depicting things that should have been abhorrent to a vampire. Yet she'd made it not just a den or a dungeon but a home, somewhere that invited Lis to remove her boots and rest.

The most pernicious and insidious of spider webs.

Simon returned to the sanctuary in a black long-sleeve shirt and dark green sweatpants. His wariness hadn't changed. The cautious regard was mutual.

"I think your host would appreciate if you would remove your gun and any additional ammunition and place them there." Simon pointed to the side table near her in the narthex. "I'd also request that you remove your knives, but I get the feeling that's a harder ask, and it would be a bit hypocritical, since we keep our weapons close, too." He flexed his hands but kept his claws in. "It's instant death I object to more."

Lis set her bags of vampire hearts down by the side table. She also shrugged off her backpack and removed her hoodie. There'd be no creeping around in the shadows in this place, and certainly not with most of it shredded. That left her still in body armor, plus the blades strapped to her arms and hidden under her clothes.

She removed the holster with her gun, the box of ammunition from an inner pocket of her hoodie, and the stake strapped to her back. She didn't empty the ammunition from her gun. If she needed to, she wanted to be able to run to the table and shoot immediately.

But Simon didn't look like a wolf about to attack. He looked like a wolf who wanted to run. In her experience, most monsters outside the Wastelands and rougher areas of Cemetery Grove tended to prefer running away to fighting, because the odds were better that they'd survive escape more than a fight.

It didn't mean Simon was harmless, despite the cuff, despite the tattoo, no matter how mild he seemed as he rounded the sanctuary to the most comfortable sectional across from the study.

Her usual assumption about demons more willing to run was 'coward'. But given that he'd entered the fray and killed on her behalf won him at least the consideration of leaving the gun and blessed silver-dipped bullets behind. The fact she could throw one of her blades at him and achieve the same end was not lost on her, and perhaps not on him, either.

Lis left the sanctuary and entered the sacristy to the left of the bedroom chancel. The room was much smaller than she expected — a cramped galley kitchen with a microwave, a small oven, a rolling island for prep space, and what looked like the single extravagance of a large refrigerator, which was where the vampire stood, studying her selection of blood that took up half the fridge, although Lis was surprised to see food in there as well.

"Do you want anything to eat?" the vampire said. "The blood's mine, of course, but the rest is edible for you. I don't just stock my fridge with fakes for the look of it. A glass of water? Milk? Beer? Wine? A slice of cake?"

"Do you keep them for you or your wolf?" Lis wasn't sure she should eat anything from a vampire's fridge. On the other hand, vampires weren't fairies or goblins. There wasn't any established lore on not eating what a vampire fed you, just on generally not accepting food from strangers.

"I have a sweet tooth. The milk and meat is mostly Simon's, if he wants them. Really, it's *all* available to you. I just know your stomach won't respond well to uncooked blood. How about cake and ice cream after we address your wounds?"

"You're not going to convince me to trust you with dessert."

"After the night you've had, tell me you don't crave comfort food." The vampire opened the bottom freezer. "You know, I have Simon's pizza leftovers in here somewhere…"

"Please just direct me to your sewing kit." Lis wouldn't have even added the 'please', except the vampire kept turning her back on Lis, which was either very stupid or very brave, and she honestly wasn't sure which. Either way, the vampire was making a show of trusting her a lot more than Lis was willing to trust her in return.

The vampire closed the freezer, then grabbed a Dr Pepper and a glass bottle labeled 'cow's blood'.

"Who sells animal blood?" Lis wanted to add a certain unveiled disgust to the question but remembered that the motel room she shared with Archie had a whole mini-fridge devoted to what Archie drew from her.

"People who sell animal meat. There are plenty of recipes that require cooked animal blood, and it's used in some fertilizers and at certain research facilities — not to mention ritual use. And of course, there are those who drink it. The businesses don't care, as long as they make a profit."

"And no one questions it?"

"Has anyone ever asked you questions about what you do in your motel room with your handler? Of course no one asks questions. Some might speculate, but it's none of their business and they don't want it to become their business."

"He's not my handler." Although now that Lis said it out loud, she wasn't sure how true that was.

"I assumed he wasn't your father, but maybe that was misguided."

"Not my father, either." Lis stopped herself from fully explaining what he was — teacher, mentor, father figure, caregiver, researcher, supervisor, a bookshelf of roles that ultimately came down to making sure she could be a better hunter than anyone would ever give her credit for at first glance, so she wouldn't have to think about anything but making it through the next night, and the next.

The vampire didn't push for clarification. She passed the Dr Pepper across the island and gestured for Lis to join her near the field aid kit.

"What use do you have for sutures and bandages?" Lis asked, but she sat on the barstool next to her.

"Some vampires put themselves in the path of more injuries, and some of those injuries do take longer to heal — like amputation," the vampire said, picking her tools between sips of blood. "However, mine isn't for me."

"Then who —"

"I'm only recently part of the Alliance," the vampire said. "Let's leave it at that. Do you need painkillers?"

Lis shook her head. Archie sometimes gave her oxy when he needed to suture, but if it was somewhere she could reach with her good hand, she didn't bother with meds unless she had trouble sleeping after an injury.

The vampire was quick and sure with the cleaning and stitching of the deeper wound across Lis' cheek. She checked all other cuts made by the vampires' claws, but most of them required only cleaning and covering, if they hadn't already closed.

"I know from listening that your name is Lis," the vampire said, "with an S sound instead of a Z. Is it short for anything?"

"Elisabet. I only go by Lis." No point in concealing the information. The vampire already knew her name, and her family was safe from retribution, given that Lis wasn't even sure that was the name on her original birth certificate.

"I'm Rose. My friend is Simon. I'll get some cake and ice cream together, if you want to go ahead out to the living room again. I also have a regular sewing kit, so do you want me to do some repairs on your jacket?"

Lis shook her head. But she swept the trash off the island into a bin and accepted the Dr Pepper to take with her into the sanctuary — presenting her back and anticipating. But no attack came.

And Lis didn't understand, unless Rose intended to cajole her into becoming one of those mindless drone donors who gave their blood willingly. But the vampire wasn't *doing* anything to her. No plucking at her heartstrings, or other areas of her body. Just inviting her into a cool, comfortable home, stitching her up, and offering her cake — which she *could* spike with anything to knock Lis out or kill her. Some vampires drank from the drugged because it was a high for them, too — but also a risk. What use was it to poison perfectly good human blood?

And why waste the money on animal blood? Why bother sourcing that animal blood when there was an abundance of human blood, what a vampire was made for and far more invigorating to consume?

That was ultimately Lis' bewilderment — Why would a vampire bother doing things the hard way when it was *so easy* for them to do it the easy way?

The werewolf had turned the television on to some music channel with the image of water rolling over the screen. He glanced up at her entrance but deliberately forced himself into a posture of relaxation. If Lis could be in the same position and still jump up at a moment's notice, a werewolf would be even more capable.

She joined him, sitting on the chaise across from his sectional. She'd never had an occasion to join someone in their parlor before, and she found that sitting on a chaise made for average people made her look absurd, with her short legs awkwardly swinging from the edge of the cushion. Simon's lips twitched, as if he were trying very hard not to smile.

Lis frowned and scooted forward until her feet touched the ground, then gathered throw pillows behind her so she could lean back, although it was still awkward. The motels she'd lived in never had anything other than hard chairs. She'd usually lounge on the beds. She didn't want to lounge here.

Rose came out from the kitchen with slices of chocolate cake and a scoop of ice cream in soup bowls. For some reason, using a bowl instead of a plate seemed the most endearing detail, because the cake looked like good quality but the presentation was unpretentious — the way Lis and Archie ate together, without care for manners or messiness as long as everything performed its desired function.

Rose set the platter on the coffee table between the two couches, then settled back on the couch with Simon, on Simon, to present him with his serving while holding her own.

Lis took the last bowl and cautiously started to eat.

The hunter she'd spoken to had said the Alliance was a real thing, not something the vampire had made up to try to slither out of battle. And Archie hadn't denied its existence, just said it didn't matter. If she wanted to confirm that the Alliance was a real thing, that there were creatures in this town willing to not hurt humans, she had to put that to the test.

With chocolate cake and ice cream in a vampire's renovated church.

The last time Lis had been to church had been when she'd given confession after killing a man, a human man — in self-defense, of course. Archie didn't know about that. Otherwise, her spiritual education was handled through books Archie gave her and which they discussed together. She didn't usually immerse herself in the experience of spirituality, but she found herself oddly drawn to the rainbow of colors from the windows.

"They can't be good for you in the daytime," Lis finally said, half her cake eaten.

"The way the church is oriented, the light never reaches the bedroom," Rose replied. "I had the agent do an assessment based on different times of year. She apparently had to bring in an astronomy professor from UTM, which is dedication, but it guarantees I don't sizzle in my sleep. If I'm awake, I can usually duck around more direct beams or cover myself with a coat or a blanket, but even if I step into them, the colors filter the light into something less fatal. It's hard to kill vampires with sunlight when it isn't sustained. I haven't had an accident yet."

"Why would a vampire put herself in the position where she might get burned at all?"

"You mean, why don't I find myself a nice basement hovel?" Rose asked. "Or shut myself into a maintenance closet? Or maybe I should check into a motel and put up black-out shades? In my family home, most of our daytime was spent in interior rooms or with black-out shades, too. You're right, though. It doesn't make any sense to take the risk. When *you* finish your night and see the sunrise, there's probably a sense of peace, because the vampires have to go to ground while you can walk in the light. It probably gives you some satisfaction to be able to turn your face to the morning, to warmth, to life. I miss it. It took a long time, but I miss it, and the family doesn't allow dangerous renovations like this. So when I left them, I chose a new home with lots of light, as well as safe places within it. I can't turn my face to the sun, but this makes me feel almost as good."

Lis had never once in her life thought that a vampire might not always enjoy being a vampire the way she sometimes didn't always enjoy being human, especially after a bad night—the kind where other demons didn't jump in and help her out of a situation.

Which was another thing she'd never dreamed that other demons would do—and the only reason she was still here, eating cake and ice cream, which didn't seem to be doing anything to her but making her stomach happier now that panic had withdrawn and hunger had taken its place on her priority list.

She'd never had dessert before dinner before.

"I'm guessing you have all the curtains closed in your motel room to sleep during the day," Rose said. "Do you do anything other than hunt and sleep?"

"I study. I read. We watch TV too." And other things, like train and research and test, but that felt like proprietary information.

They finished their dessert. Without a bowl in her hands, Rose wrapped her arm around Simon's neck and leaned her head against his. His long hair was golden against the tarnished pewter of their clothing.

"Why do you do it?" Lis finally said.

"Do what?"

"Eat cake, ice cream, animal blood, raw animal meat. Both of you are made to eat human flesh and blood, of which there's an abundance in the city. Why would you deny yourselves? *How* do you deny yourselves?"

"That's an interesting question, considering you deny yourself all the time." Simon said. "Don't you? You're a human being, a social creature, usually of the daytime. But the way Rose tells it and based on what we've seen, you've made hunting your whole personality. You sleep, eat, breathe, live bloody like us, run under cover of night like us. Unlike us, though, you've devoted your life to shortening it. You've denied yourself a *life*. So that others may live, right, martyr?"

Words which could have been so cruel, laced with either anger or dispassion, instead took on a warmer tone. Almost like sympathy.

"You know you don't have to live like that, don't you?" he continued. "You could walk away anytime. Move from Meridian, live in the light. You might never encounter another monster again. Instead, you choose to forego earthly pleasures in favor of spiritual battle. Right? This is a mission for you. Well, Rose and I don't sacrifice as much. We still have some fun in our lives. But my pack had an agreement with hunters long before the Alliance made us mark ourselves, because my people were here before the city rose from the earth, when this was a nothing town, and we keep the state land safer by patrolling where hunters can't go. Only a handful from our number have slipped and eaten the wrong kind of meat. They were dealt with, either by hunters or the pack. And Rose made the decision to stop. How long have you been hunting, girl?"

Lis held her legs as though she'd punch or kick something if she didn't. Tension drew her shoulders inward. She didn't like it, this self-conscious feeling of being judged and found wanting, even though Simon kept his interrogation gentle. "Fifteen years. Almost sixteen."

"Jesus," Rose breathed.

"So being a hunter twenty-four-seven is pretty normal for you," Simon said. "Most of your living memory is fighting demons. Just like I was brought into a pack that didn't eat human meat. Which means it was probably harder for Rose to make that decision than it was for you or me. Because she tasted pleasure and had to relinquish it."

"Well, not completely," Rose interjected. "There are still ethical ways to drink human blood. From a bar that serves donations, for instance. Donations to the bar, not stolen from blood drives — just clarifying. If I wanted, I could always get a donor, but that has its own ethical issues. Still, animal blood with the occasional sip of human isn't going to kill me, and although it's not as good, animal blood certainly isn't unpleasant. After all, humans are animals. And there are so many pleasures other than human blood in this world."

Lis tightened her grip on her legs. "Have you had enough of it to know?"

"I've been what I am longer than fifteen years," Rose said quietly. "What do you think?"

"I think, 'How could you just turn around after being human and drink people to death?'"

This time, a chill threaded through Rose's reply. "I'll let some things slide because you've probably never asked the vampires you've killed why they do what they do. You don't understand what it's like to fundamentally change. To die without decaying. To become something new — a different species. To feel like yourself but in a funhouse mirror. After all the vampires you've killed, maybe you think you understand their hunger. But you don't, and you don't understand bloodlust. It's so much stronger in the beginning. And like you said, we're built for human blood, not cow, not pig. It calls to us."

"Then why fight it? Why fight your nature?"

Rose tilted her head slightly, her dark eyes deeper than human, as though they captured light in a different way, absorbed it far back in the hole of the pupil. "Because no matter how good it tastes, it's not worth the price. Even when you make them like it, you know that at some level—perhaps the cellular, starved of oxygen—they're screaming. And I never liked that. I was only able to cover it up and ignore it for so long because, like you said, it's what I'm made for. But just because you're made for something doesn't mean you have to do it. If I could consume nothing except human blood, maybe I'd compromise with a donor. But I *can* consume other things. So, once I couldn't look away from my cruelty anymore, from the devastation I caused, the lives I stole from the world, I couldn't justify the bloodshed. I couldn't pretend what I did was a mercy."

Lis stood, unable to endure the tension anymore. Simon and Rose flinched, but when Lis didn't lunge or retrieve a blade, they settled back on their sofa.

"A mercy?" Lis finally asked.

"Most predators don't kill so kindly that prey welcomes death, sighs instead of screams," Rose replied. "It's as seductive for them as it is for us."

"Is that what you're doing to me?"

"Do you feel seduced?" Rose asked. "Is it the chocolate cake? Was that too much? Does your handler not allow dessert?"

"Of course I can have dessert," Lis snapped. "But you eliminate the competition, invite me into your home—"

"You're welcome. And you didn't have to come."

"What do you *want* from me?" Lis couldn't remember the last time she'd raised her voice. Possibly sometime in her mid-teens, when she and Archie had hit a rough patch. And even then, they'd tended to shout-whisper because motel walls were so thin.

"We just didn't want you to die like that." Rose stroked through Simon's hair but didn't look away from Lis. "I invited you because I'm occasionally hospitable, and here's where I keep the needles. There's no malevolent plot. I have all the blood I need without risking my life to take yours. And if I were seducing you, you wouldn't have to ask. Surely, in all these years fighting demons since you were *way* too young, you've felt a vampire's thrall."

Lis didn't move, which was as much a 'yes' as nodding.

"You're free to leave at any time," Simon said. "You're not a prisoner here. I'm not saying you have to trust us implicitly after knowing us for a consecutive hour, but we did save your life and we did lead you to where she sleeps. She's taking a leap of faith. Don't screw it up."

Rose continued petting his hair, finally looking away from Lis to smile down at him. "Puppy, she's had a rough night, and she's in the belly of the beast. She's right to be suspicious."

"Well, her suspicions could lead to us being dead, so I'm right to be suspicious, too."

But Simon leaned into her strokes, and Rose leaned against his head. For a moment, there was just the two of them, as lovely and cozy as the rest of the sanctuary.

Rose pressed her lips to Simon's hair, then his forehead, before looking back up at Lis. "You see? Our lives aren't just about meat or blood. Abstaining from one pleasure doesn't mean we have no others to enjoy. Can you say the same, killer?"

Again, there was warmth in her enmity that kept it from being accusatory. Because Lis *was* a killer. But they were killers, too. They'd killed vampires right beside her.

Rose raised Simon's chin with an extended claw and kissed his mouth, which had thinned with tension but softened quickly in response. When they parted lips, Lis glimpsed tongue pressing to tongue, and Simon's low moan shivered with a growl.

As in the alley the previous night, arousal shot in two directions within her, like fire set to accelerant — up to her mind and down to her lower abdomen, where it spread like fingers. Lis' toes curled in her boots and she made fists, her breath hitching as she fought to tamp down such an overwhelming rush, worse than wine or harder liquor.

Lis pulled out both knives attached to her forearms. "Stop."

Rose's lips lingered against Simon's before she reluctantly looked up, glancing from the blades to Lis' face. When Simon opened his eyes, the irises and pupils both seemed larger than normal.

"I'm not doing anything to you, Elisabet. Let me show you." Rose stroked her palm down Simon's shirt, then to the front of his pants. He inhaled suddenly and sharply — not quite a gasp. Like a sigh in reverse. "I'm going to use my thrall on the puppy here. You'll get the residual effects. Some of it I can control. Some of it I can't. I'll show you what I can control, and you'll step back until you can't feel it anymore. Then I'll pull it back. Even what I can't control shouldn't reach you once you're outside my sphere of influence."

Lis stepped back slowly. She couldn't tear her gaze away. Rose kept her palm over Simon's pants. It was an awkward angle, a little bit behind where she sat on his lap, but that didn't seem to deter her or bother Simon as she gently moved her fingers against the heaviness she held, pressing her palm against his cock in a soft, steady rhythm. Not quite gripping, not quite stroking, but suggesting.

"So he's your puppy? Your slave? He's under your thrall?"

"It's just a term of endearment. He's not my donor, my servant, or my slave. I *could* make him those things. I've enthralled the living into service before. But when I use my thrall on him, I use it because it feels good, for both of us. More often than not, I don't even use my full power. It's best used sparingly, and we do just fine without it. But when I turn it on like this..."

Simon combed his fingers through his hair and threw his head back on the couch, arching into her touch, groaning, growing right before Lis' gaze, because his erection pressed against loose pants that did nothing to hold him down.

And Lis felt it, too, that external influence, like walking by someone wearing too much perfume and suddenly finding oneself with a head full of scent so strong that it smelled artificial. It affected her body as though the desire were her own, but it felt...thick somehow, like it took up too much space.

Lis struggled to breathe, her heart racing. Every cell in her body seemed to orient toward the couch, where Rose stroked over Simon's cock now with firmer, more intentional strokes, though she watched Lis from under hooded eyelids. And when Simon could open his, while his hips jerked to meet Rose's hands, he watched Lis, too, with a strange mixture of curiosity and commiseration — without the misery.

Lis stumbled behind the chaise, even as she licked lips that seemed fuller and as folds just as full responded more sensitively to the shift of her leggings. She felt open, spread, wet on the inside and dripping to the outside. She wanted to fall, tumble back into that bed across from her, into the soft cloud of duvet and pillows. No amount of customization could make the same of a motel bed. She wanted a hand on her like Rose's on Simon, and when she wasn't paying enough attention, hers crept to her inner thigh.

But she shook her head, her hair swirling over her shoulders and cheeks, and kept stumbling away, even though the sight of the vampire tenderly jerking her werewolf off was impossible to look away from.

Simon's heavy breathing became harsher. He brought his hand around to Rose's thigh and curled his fingers, brushing against her in a tease, before smoothing up her abdomen to her breast, which he cupped familiarly and with great relish. Her nipples tightened enough to see them through her bra. Lis knew it had nothing to do with the air conditioning.

When Lis had backed halfway into the seating area behind the casual one, the intrusive arousal faded, leaving behind tingling in places she simply wasn't used to being this aware of. When out of motel rooms, she was hunting and more concerned with not getting killed. When in motel rooms, Archie was right there.

It wasn't like she'd never done anything about it before, though. When Archie was deep asleep enough to snore. When she was in the shower. When she was in a dark room alone during her patrol. And sometimes, when she was trying to sleep, her thoughts would turn mortifyingly pornographic. More often than not, she would just fill her mind with the mission or with things so boring that she'd fall asleep before she was tempted to try anything. But sometimes…sometimes…

Sometimes, when she was patrolling and more mentally than physically weary with the chase, she crossed paths with someone who met her eyes and seemed to want the same thing at the same time. In the earlier days, it had just been make-out sessions. But once the boys had started pressing, and once they'd starting being men, Lis had allowed things to go further, her body whispering to her that she wanted it.

The whole process, once it had started, had been sticky, messy, and she sometimes had endured the whole thing on cold, hard concrete, and occasionally it had been painful or just…there. Like *she* had just been there. A hand on her mouth and another on her breast, a body heavy over hers, grunting loud and harsh in her ear. This sense of being poked, probed, invaded, not knowing what to say or how to stop, better to just let them get it over with, squeeze until they came. Until it felt like they took something from her without offering anything in return and left her alone, either rolling over on their back to pass out or leaving her entirely, her function finished. She didn't even know what she was supposed to ask for or demand.

She could bring a pestilence demon down in three minutes but didn't know what to do with a man she wasn't supposed to kill.

And a few times, she *had* killed them, sometimes before, sometimes after, because there *was* a difference between taking what she allowed but didn't enjoy and taking her to feed on her resistance or pain or fear.

Killing, as Rose had so aptly pointed out, was what she did. It was who she was. And she was good at it.

She wasn't good at this. She didn't understand it and found it hard to believe that people weren't just faking their way through the idea of mutually good sex, that there wasn't just taker and taken.

But she wasn't used to the woman being the taker, and she wasn't used to the taken being the one enjoying it so much, the way her body in its throes of frustratingly physical arousal was telling her she *could* enjoy it. Was it the thrall that did it? Was that why people fell prey to monsters? Because their thrall made it feel as good as their body lied to them that it should feel?

Lis took a few more steps back, even when she was sure she couldn't feel Rose's thrall anymore, until she was maybe fifteen feet away.

"Can you still feel it?" Rose asked, with her own breathlessness, even though she didn't need air like a werewolf or a human.

Lis shook her head.

"Okay. I'm pulling it in. There should be no residual thrall left, and now you should be able to tell the difference between what's thrall and what's real." Rose leaned her head back to bury her face in Simon's hair, kissing his neck with her enthusiastic mouth wet in the shadow.

On a downstroke, she pushed the sweatpants off his cock and grasped him like she wanted him harder than her self-control. Even from a distance, Lis discerned the slide of Rose's fangs from their sheaths. They nudged against his skin as she licked and sucked at him, calling his blood to the surface without breaking through.

"God...oh fuck..." Simon grasped the back of the couch and pushed his cock into her hand, pushed his neck against her mouth, and when he looked to Lis, his eyelashes fluttered beautifully.

Lis' knees went weak, as though from another punch of Rose's power, but it wasn't from Rose, wasn't from outside her. It was as though something wild crawled and clawed through her, *begging*, even though she *knew* what it begged for wouldn't be as good as it seemed to think.

"Right now, he's breathing me in." Rose's voice lowered to a purr as though to match Simon's steady growl. "It comes from my skin like a scent, and werewolves are more sensitive to it. He feels it from my teeth, too. Don't you, puppy? Self-denial doesn't have to be for everything, everywhere, all the time, forever and ever, Lis. There will always be another monster, another demon, another day, another night. You can't kill all the monsters in the world or even just in Meridian by sheer force of will. You've got to have some way to let off steam, or else the pressure is going to cook you alive, and we might not be there next time. When was the last time you did anything just for yourself? When was the last time you let yourself feel good?"

Rose stopped stroking Simon to lick her palm, which left his cock long and flushed and thickened, curved against his shirt with head gleaming. There was something so terribly, rudely visceral about the sight of a cock uncovered and untouched, blood-filled with desire. Lis' mouth watered despite previous experience of cocks shoved down her throat to make her gag.

"I don't... I can't..." Lis shook her head again. She grasped the back of the couch in front of her, the third of three couches between her and the couple, as though it were the edge of a cliff. She bit her tongue to keep from telling them things they didn't need to know, no matter how personal they were willing to be with her. It was a trick, a trap.

Rose brought her slickened hand back to Simon's erection, wringing it with relish. She encouraged his hand over her breast and licked a line from his chin to the angled end of his jaw.

"Can you feel anything?" Rose asked, this time with a higher plaintive quality before licking her fangs. She seemed to enjoy that more than teeth alone could explain.

Lis couldn't answer. She knew Rose meant her thrall, but Lis *did* feel something, and it didn't come from Rose. She didn't want to give Rose the satisfaction of saying it aloud.

But Simon's nostrils flared, and he still stared at Lis, even as he offered himself over completely to Rose. Sometimes his eyes rolled back, but he always returned his gaze to her, not just panting now but inhaling deep swallows of air and everything hovering within it.

"I'm going to bite him now," Rose said. "A different kind of thrall. You shouldn't feel it, but he should come, and so should I."

Simon brought his hand from Rose's breast up to her mouth. "I'd say I would never have agreed to be with you if I'd known you were like this, but I think we both know that's a lie. Fuck, I'm ready."

Rose sank her teeth into his wrist with a wet slide that startled a whimper from Lis — even though no new wave of vampire power hit her, just an explosion of her own sensory disorientation. A strangled, almost sobbing cry wrenched from Simon's throat, who watched Lis watching him as his cock twitched and spent over his shirt and Rose's hand.

Blood pooled in Rose's mouth, outlining her lips, but she sucked fast and hard enough to keep it from spilling over like Simon's cock. Her head fell back, but Simon held his arm against her in a way that made Lis think of hands over her mouth or fingers over her tongue, keeping her stifled.

Rose was neither quiet nor stifled. She rocked on his lap and moaned with each swallow until Simon kissed her cheek and her neck. Then she slowed her gulps, licking at the skin more than drinking, her fangs gradually receding, until the wound no longer gushed or seeped.

Then she leaned back and kissed him. This time he was the one consuming her, conjured by the blood in her mouth until she was whimpering and he hardened again.

Rose guided his mouth from hers with one last swipe of their tongues between them. Then she stood to grab some towels and water from her bedroom to help them both clean off. Simon was the most relaxed Lis had seen him since they'd met—perhaps because she hadn't tried to kill them while they were at their most vulnerable.

"So you see," Rose said, handing Simon a dampened washcloth, "if I were seducing you with my thrall, hunter, you would know."

Chapter Seven

Which wasn't to say that Rose wasn't seducing Lis the more old-fashioned way, but after decades of the vampire way, shameless flirtation and exhibitionism seemed positively innocent.

Perhaps such innocence was relative, because Lis threatening to break the back of her couch in two and her stone-blank face showed how overwhelmed she was, but the blood-flush in her cheeks, lips, and other parts of her body Rose could smell suggested that the feelings she struggled against weren't entirely bad. Rose also knew that sometimes too-good feelings could be a struggle, too, for certain kinds of people, particularly those prone to self-denial in other respects. She'd tortured a few priests and nuns that way in the past.

But she wasn't trying to torture Lis. She'd just wanted to prove that if Lis experienced these feelings, they were her own, and that they weren't bad just because they were good. That she could loosen up and enjoy herself for once, especially after nearly dying. Nearly dying should have been the wake-up call to live a little—and might have been the only reason why she'd come to Rose's home and allowed herself to be a witness to the ways Rose and Simon enjoyed life, despite one of them being dead.

If the supposed enemy could do it, why couldn't the white hats? It had never made any sense to Rose, the weight of misery that hunters seemed to carry with them all the time. Grief, she understood. Oh, she understood that plenty. But it was like hunters *wanted* to get hurt, wanted the beatings and the early death and the nights alone, unattached, untethered. As though they wanted to fade away, violent red slashes obscuring that they were ever there. Wanted to get lost in a file somewhere until no one remembered their name or cared what sewers their bones calcified in.

And with Lis twenty-two years old, killing since she was a child, it was just so fucking *sad*.

"Lis, are you all right over there?" Rose cleaned her hand and her shirt, then dabbed at her mouth to make sure that, between her and Simon, all the blood had been swallowed. She stepped closer to the hunter, but Lis raised a blade again. Well, one was an improvement on two.

"Hey, it's okay. You can stay here longer if you'd like, and I can warm up that pizza. I'm also pretty sure I can figure out spaghetti if you give me a few minutes."

Lis backed down the central aisle. "I'm leaving."

Rose followed, but at a distance. "I don't know what I can do to prove you're safe here when you're convinced that the slightest bit of comfort or pleasure is a trick."

"You're evil. Anything you try to convince me of is all just part of the hunt. I don't know what the endgame is, but I do know there's an endgame."

"This." Rose gestured to the church, the bed, the chairs, Simon. "This is my endgame. I've had grander luxury, control, power, adoration, and I took my payment for my time. But as it turned out, this was all I really ever wanted. I'm satisfied with my werewolf's blood. I don't need yours. You don't have to do anything you don't want to and, more importantly, I only wanted to show you that you *can* do some things that you want to. You had to grow up faster than most, but even by the numbers, you're a grown woman, Lis. So please, I beg of you, don't let this be the last chocolate cake you ever have."

Lis' back hit the locked double doors next to her bags and discarded hoodie. When Lis stopped, so did Rose, so Lis could see that she *would* stop.

"I eat chocolate," Lis said.

"Often?"

"Enough."

"And what about the other things that you clearly crave?" Rose asked softly. "You think I can't smell where blood flows, hunter?"

"I don't…" Lis grabbed her bags of hearts, shrugged her backpack onto her shoulder, and draped her hoodie over her arm to hide the content of the bags. Then she started on the multiple locks. "It's not good. When it happens, it's not good. It's uncomfortable and wet and sweaty and heavy, and when it doesn't hurt, it's… I don't feel. I don't feel… I still… I still try, but it's not enough that I try, and sometimes they don't ask."

"Oh, Lis. No. That's not sex." If Rose's heart weren't a cold, barely beating lump, it might have broken right there, a pang as strong as arousal through her chest, but like fingernails on a chalkboard instead of down her back. "When were you ever with someone who cared if it was good for you, too?"

Lis undid the last lock and jerked the door open into darkness that seemed all the darker against the soft, warm light of the sanctuary. "I need my hearts counted. I need to go."

"Want anything for the road?"

Lis ran into the night. Rose sighed as she shut the door and redid all the locks.

If she'd grossly miscalculated, there was a possibility that, before the night was over or as soon as the sun was up, Lis and her handler might show up and try to break in. It wouldn't be easy to get in through the double doors, and there were similar measures on the door to the former sacristy and to the Sunday school wing. She'd also boarded up many of the Sunday school windows, but they were easy enough to cut through with an axe or chainsaw. Presuming they valued her death more than the destruction of sacred images, they could break in through the stained glass, or they could get a ladder and climb the roof to the bell tower steeple. They could just wait for Simon or Rose to open her door.

She'd known the risks, but she'd hoped Lis' visit would go better.

"Well, that's just the most pitiful individual I've ever met," Simon said, sprawled on one of her nicer sofas. "Too bad she can kill me in a matter of minutes."

Rose flexed her fingers, showing off her claws. "I can kill you in a matter of minutes."

"But that's not what's on your mind."

She grinned and crawled over him as he slid to the side in an even more awkward arrangement. She tucked her hands under his shirt to push it up over his chest until he took the collar to pull it off himself. Then he untucked hers from her jeans. They scrambled to remove everything while remaining tangled together, and if claws tore skin and teeth left bruises or puncture marks, at least their clothes managed to make it through the removal intact. That wasn't always a given.

"I felt you watching her," Rose murmured against his mouth, her fangs partially extended to tease him as well as herself.

"So were you. You wanted her watching." He massaged her sides, then around to her back, digging into her muscles. Even though they were supposed to be tight, it still felt good.

"She doesn't know what it's like for someone else's touch to bring her pleasure, Simon. Given how uncomfortable she was just *feeling*, she barely knows how to give it to herself. Her body only knows how to be a weapon. All she's known of sex is to be used." Rose straddled him. "I want so much better for her. But I want you to use me."

He grabbed her by the back of the neck like a kitten and whipped her around. They seemed to be flying for a moment, but they were really just falling — her onto her back on the rug, and him onto his other hand and his knees.

He shifted his grip from the back of her neck to the front, squeezing — an obviously empty threat. Then he slid his hand up to rub her lips roughly against her teeth. When her fangs pricked her gums, she moaned, reached for him, but he shook his head. She touched his chest anyway, so he grabbed her by the neck again and forced her around onto her stomach beneath him, hiking up her hips.

Long and dense and hot and hard, Simon leaned in over her. Even as he forced his fingers into her mouth, over her tongue, brushing against her fangs in the process, he whispered her ear, "You sure?"

She nodded, then wailed as he shoved into her, taking her like an animal until she howled with him and both of them had blood in their mouths.

Servant to noble, if there was one thing a vampire knew how to clean, it was blood.

* * * *

Lis walked home in a daze, which was not a good idea at all, although some part of her remained aware of her surroundings.

Nevertheless, she tripped on the stairs up to the motel room, then knocked on the door with her bags still in hand, so they swung and smushed against the door like revolting pendulums.

Archie put her through the usual rigmarole, which she could sleepwalk through by this point. It wasn't until she entered the motel room that the powerful air-conditioning woke her up.

Archie took the sealed plastic bags from her. "Looks like you had a productive evening. Good. I actually need to keep a few of them today."

He stored some in one of the fridges, then took an orange juice box out of the one they used for their food.

Lis fell into the other hard chair and started removing the armor on her right arm to expose the crook of her elbow. "Do we have to do this today?"

"Bad night?" He fetched vials, syringes, needles, table, everything he needed to take her blood.

"Nearly died."

"You nearly die every night."

"This time was really close. I wouldn't have come home if someone else hadn't saved me."

"You owe other hunters nothing. It's their job as much as yours. Or was it those cops I hear about that don't know half of what they're doing?"

"Alliance." She glanced up to search Archie's reaction.

He clenched his jaw, chin prominent and defined, with scars sketching lines among the natural texture of aging skin and stubble. "So we're doing this again."

"This isn't a debate. It's fact. Alliance rescued me tonight. I was a second away from a small family of vampires draining me dry."

Archie jabbed the butterfly needle into her arm. He had to move it around a few times to find a vein. "We're *not* talking about this."

"And yet my lips are moving and sound is coming out. You don't get to ignore me right now, because I don't have the luxury of ignoring—"

As soon as her blood started filling the first vial, Archie slapped her across the mouth. He didn't hit her hard, but it had been a long time since he'd hit her at all, not counting during training.

"I'd hoped we were past you mouthing off to me with such blatant disrespect."

"I was this close to not coming home, but *you're* alive," she said through gritted teeth. "You're alive, and you stay in here all day and all night, while I go out there and risk my life because you can't do it anymore—"

He hit her again, a little harder this time. "You know better. I do what I can. I do things you can't. We each play our part. For instance, I thought I made it abundantly clear that monsters will say anything. They'll spew hate at you to make you afraid. They'll drown you in kisses to make you think you're loved. The world is much simpler than they try to make of it. You're a protector. Any creature who is a threat must be eliminated. It's not just about whether they're an immediate threat to *you*. I didn't raise you to be this selfish."

He replaced the first vial with the second. The room was so quiet that the sound of her blood pouring inside the vial was audible even over the rumbling air-conditioning.

As soon as he finished with the fourth vial, he opened the orange juice for her and slid it across the small table. He put three of the vials in his various machines and one in the fridge after scribbling the date. Then he did his count of the vampire hearts, sitting shrunken and purple in their own thick, nearly black blood. He put two of them in the fridge. The others he tossed into the trash, which he prepped to take out.

"I'm sorry you had a bad night," he finally said, grimacing as he sat. "I know how terrifying they can be. And I can't tell you how glad I am you're still alive. But even if you reap the benefit of a monster's nefarious plan, that doesn't make the plan any less nefarious. It's not whether or not they want to kill you, just whether they want to kill you now or later. Putting a little more effort into later is worth it when the fly flits right into their web. You've been doing this for sixteen years, Lis. You ever met a demon who didn't want to corrupt you?"

Lis didn't say anything while she drank the juice, although she craved something more substantial and savory after cake and ice cream.

What she wanted to say was that, when she went into alleys in the bad parts of town looking for dangerous demons, she was going to find dangerous demons. Lis and Archie never hunted beyond the bad parts, because the less bad parts were where things got messy, weren't they? That's where the demons were more integrated into people's lives. Archie could call these cities Sodom or Ninevah for opening themselves up to corruption, but that seemed like wearing a pair of sunglasses that cast everything in a damning shade of red.

Most of the humans who interacted directly with her wanted to corrupt her too, because that was the part of the city she was in and the only people who approached her when she made herself so unapproachable were people who didn't care whether she wanted them there or not.

But she knew for a fact that not all people were like that, or else what was she doing every night, saving them? She walked among people just doing their best to get through the day or night. Those were the people she was saving. It was reductive to assume that the better parts of town were better solely through deals with devils or that most of them weren't doing the exact same thing as the worse parts of town—the best they could.

Whenever she crossed paths with other hunters, she acknowledged them, and they acknowledged her. They weren't chatty. But it didn't escape her notice that the only hunter with whom she engaged in regular interaction kept her isolated. Archie took care of everything so she didn't have to, monitored her to protect her, trained her to survive. Lis didn't question that. But although hunting was a solitary profession, it was perhaps not a coincidence that they only ever hunted where others rarely did. To fill in the gaps, yes, but it also made him the only influence on her life—emotionally, financially, ideologically.

She didn't have money. She couldn't trust that her name was real. She had no formal education, which meant no test scores or GPA or diploma, although Archie had made sure she'd had a well-rounded informal education. She didn't have anyone else to turn to. Her world was Archie and the monsters she killed, with very little exception.

As long as she wanted to keep being a hunter, that was mostly fine. Through training and testing by fire, he'd made her into an exceptional hunter. And she'd by and large accepted most of what he'd taught her about demons as fact, because he'd proven himself through their research, experimentation, and experience to be correct.

But now she wasn't so sure.

Which put everything else into question, from the Alliance to each and every demon she'd ever killed. Well, maybe not all of them. Neither Rose nor Simon were arguing that every vampire or werewolf or full-blooded demon was good, or even neutral. But they made a decent preliminary case for some, while Archie wanted to hear none of it.

Archie framed her face with his hands, staring down at her from his standing position. Then he tucked his arms around her and held her against his coat. She closed her eyes and accepted the rare show of affection. He tried to make it all about business, a commander to his soldier, and he often said he wasn't her father. But they both knew, without speaking, that although that was true biologically, it wasn't on every other level.

"I'm glad you're alive," he repeated. "And if you're having doubts, I promise you won't always be so confused. Things will become so much clearer. Just give it time. You need something to eat. Something that will fill that cold, sinking pit of fear. Philly cheesesteak pizza? I have some errands to run, so you can call to have it delivered. Did you find anything off the original owners of the hearts?"

Lis pulled out a hundred forty-four dollars in cash, two wedding rings with diamonds, and two just gold. She also handed over two watches, some necklaces, and earrings. These she was less sure of in terms of whether they were valuable or just shiny.

She'd given away thirty dollars and seventy-six cents. She'd kept sixty dollars and a Freddy's gift card. Now that she knew vampires could enjoy food other than blood, the gift cards she'd taken from so many back pockets made more sense.

Archie gathered the jewelry into a velvet bag he used to bring items to pawn shops or places to sell gold and silver, then put most of the money in his wallet. He left some of the cash and a pizza delivery menu on the table. It was one of the only ones that served their area, but the pizza was decent as long as she put red pepper flakes on it.

Then he grabbed his duffel, which held what he'd pawn that morning as well as some of his own hunter's tools. After a backward glance to make sure she was mostly okay, he left.

She did up all the locks, then went to take her shower. She'd get delivery afterward. Philly cheesesteak pizza, breadsticks, and a nineties action movie sounded like just the thing before sleep.

Chapter Eight

Archie stepped out into a world awakening.

Lis' vision was more sensitive in light, but his night vision suffered these days, so doing things during the day would naturally fall to him, even if he'd wanted Lis to get out more. But it was hard enough keeping her in this life without encouraging her to see what kind of world lay beyond it.

That was one of the dangers of raising a hunter rather than letting her come to it on her own by unnatural circumstances, like the rest of his colleagues. You could create the perfect killing machine, but show her a pretty dress or a nice house and she might start wanting something more. She'd had the same inspiration for her life as many hunters, but the memory of her father—as well as the rest of her family—was fuzzy, dreamlike. The mission was simply her life. It wasn't in her gut, not even when she came so close to dying, because she'd grown up knowing her work might come to that.

The longer he spent with her, watching her grow and become an eminently capable hunter, the idea that such a strong young woman's life would likely be cut short hurt his heart more and more. The best she could hope for was dire injury forcing her to retire, like him. He'd managed to stay in the hunting world by finding her, but he had to confess even to himself that he hadn't left her many options beyond what he'd shaped her into.

That tonight had been such a close call — *Eight vampires at once. God, what was she thinking?* — and that she seemed to have been targeted by a pair of demons who must be laughing at how they made her doubt him... Archie wanted the world for Lis. If that meant making her job, and that of every other hunter, clearer, then he would move heaven to hell for her. Or hell to earth.

His first stop was the diner, where he ate toast and took some coffee to go.

Then he drove north. He was pretty sure that when Lis pawned things for herself, she only used the nearest brokers and accepted the worse fleecing in return for something she could actually use, since hunters avoided wearing jewelry without some sort of mystical protective properties. Archie went to where the pawnbrokers were only slightly fairer but jewelry stores bought the wedding rings without question.

After tucking the cash away, he headed for Meridian's historical downtown district.

The jingling bells rang at magic shop Book & Candle.

There were stores like this in every city he'd lived in — someplace that looked like a tourist trap but offered real magical components. There were crystals, incense, and jewelry that probably paid the bills, along with dubiously published paperbacks about the craft. But there were also bookshelves of previously owned hardbacks, some in locked cabinets because they were old enough to have some value. And in the weapons display case gleamed an arsenal of knives, some decorative, others for self-defense, but all of them sharp and most with silver work on the blade.

When he couldn't hoard magical books for himself through purchase or theft — to protect the world from those not convicted enough to trust with their secrets — he usually made copies or took pictures of relevant pages found in scrutinized rare book and private collections. But there was supposed to be a book here in the magic shop that had been referenced in other works. The only other copy he knew of was in a private collection unavailable for public viewing, even by appointment, nor were there scans of its contents — so dark and dangerous the text was rumored to be.

Given that so many of the books he confiscated into his own possession were intended for service to evil, unraveling them for use against evil often meant working backward or looking for analogous beneficial materials. The only thing miracles and dark magic had in common was blood. The book in Meridian's magic shop, *Ars Cruor*, dealt specifically in dark blood magic.

As though God had known what he needed and how soon he needed it, and had arranged just in time for him to find the last piece in the puzzle.

Thank you, Father, he prayed silently as he stood before the locked glass cabinet. *I won't be able to keep her much longer if she doesn't believe, if doubt creeps into her faith in me, in You. Thank You for this gift, this miracle, and for all that will be done with it in Your name.*

He was reluctant to leave it behind, as though someone would know how much he wanted it, break through the glass, and run out of the door with it in the time it took Archie to flag down an employee. But he forced himself to keep going and gather ingredients for his most recent experimental phase. This was his second visit to Book & Candle. He'd tried to get his ingredients at another shop in the area, but it didn't compare to the selection and quality here, which meant he had to swallow every moral and ethic to approach the vampire who worked the counter without killing her.

The vampire seemed to know by looking at him that he didn't want or need her to smile and give the good sales rep routine while he arranged containers of roots and powders from his shopping bag onto the table. She twitched when he retrieved the jars of vampire and pestilence demon teeth Lis had collected over the last three weeks.

"I'm going to need an exchange," he said, also not bothering with being polite, but also not raising his voice. She was afraid. That was enough, for now. "And I want that *Ars Cruor* from the book cabinet."

The vampire backed away from the counter. "I don't have the key for it. I need to get Violet. Is that okay?"

"Yes."

The vampire backed into the hall behind the counter and knocked on the door to the storage room. "Vi, I've got someone wanting to sell to exchange, and he needs something from the protected bookshelf."

After a few seconds, Violet came out, wearing her typical modern witch costume.

She'd already chosen her side by pretending to be neutral. Archie wouldn't have a problem burning her in her own hearth if he thought both sides of Meridian wouldn't rise up and gut him on her front step as a warning. Most hunters in Meridian were almost completely dependent on her for the mystical side of their jobs as well as acting as a body broker, since her prices were the best in town.

This was one of myriad ways Archie kept Lis pure. She never had to sell a piece of her soul to do her job. He bore that burden for her.

Violet covered the tops of the two teeth jars with her hands. "Do you have a count, or do I need to do it by hand?"

"Sixty-two fang pairs, a hundred thirty-eight individuals of pestilence."

The fact Violet accepted vampire teeth didn't appear to bother her own vampire, or at least she didn't let it show.

"Nine hundred for the lot. I assume you want the jars back."

Archie nodded.

She took the jars to the storage room, then returned with them empty. "The *Ars Cruor*?"

He nodded again.

"That shelf ain't cheap. The book's even less so. I couldn't take less than fifteen thousand."

"Cash or check?"

"Cash. Can't risk the check bouncing," she replied.

"What do you take me for, witch?"

"I don't take you for anything. It's store policy. I can put a hold on it for a week if you need to gather the funds, or there's an ATM in the square."

Archie clenched his jaw. He hadn't anticipated the book would be that expensive, but given what he'd read about the information it contained, he was more surprised the witch was selling it at all. And that she'd priced it within a careful hunter's means.

He reached into his duffel and pulled out a padded manilla folder. Inside were five bricks of hundred-dollar bills from when he'd closed out his account in Dallas. He'd redeposited the majority of it in a Meridian credit union, but since most of his transactions were in cash...

Of all the things to be afraid of in Meridian, a mugger wasn't one of them. These days, he had to be more careful with demons, but humans without combat training — even a twitchy bastard with a gun and an itchy trigger finger — were no match for him.

He put down one brick, then slit open another and split it in half. "Will that do?"

Without so much as a blink, Violet swept the money over to the vampire. "Please count that to confirm and ring the rest up. Come with me, sir."

He followed her to the bookshelf, where she took out her keyring of many keys and opened the glass cabinet while muttering under her breath. Archie didn't think she was speaking English, nor any other language he knew.

"Given the ingredients you chose and the *Ars Cruor*, I take it you're interested in blood binding?" the witch asked.

"It's none of your business what I use it for."

Violet pulled the book from the shelf, then resealed the glass. Archie suspected that if he tried to infiltrate it with Mjölnir itself, the pane still wouldn't break.

She carried the book with her to the counter. "Hannah, please go to the storage room and put the money for the book in the cash box." She handed Hannah her keyring.

Hannah slid four hundred dollars back to him. "You were over." Then she did as Violet told her.

"It looks like you owe a hundred twelve for the ingredients, before taxes. Should I just take it out of this?" Violet gestured to the cash.

Archie nodded.

She boxed the ingredients, arranged them in a paper bag with a handle, then carefully arranged the book in there as well.

As Archie raised a hand to take the bag, Violet grabbed his wrist and slammed it to the counter.

He reached for his gun.

"Freeze." Violet kept her spell soft and even, presumably so she wouldn't alarm the vampire in the other room.

Archie couldn't move. All he could control in his entire body was his eyes.

"I've read the *Ars Cruor*. I know what you're doing. You're looking to unblur some lines. While my position won't permit me to deny the sale, I feel compelled to offer this warning—These spells don't just work on inhuman monsters. You're not the one who gets to decide who's a sheep or a goat. Then the llamas don't know where to go, and it's a whole barnyard mix-up that's not nearly as funny as it sounds."

"*Let go of me, you bitch.*" He didn't know if she could hear his thoughts or not, but she released his wrist and pushed the bag toward him.

"Magic is good for a lot of things," she said. "But it excels at practical use with clear, uncomplicated outcomes. I'm not saying it *can't* unravel the mysteries of the universe and tidy up the messiness of being people. What I'm saying is that it doesn't tend to be good for that. If anything, magic tends to make these things even more inscrutable. If you must proceed, sir, please do so with caution."

Archie grabbed the bag and left the establishment without engaging with the witch any further.

That was what he feared was Lis' problem — letting the enemy make whether they were her enemy into a debate. Once she engaged, she already acknowledged the possibility that evil was good, which opened the door for the unraveling of every other tenet. You didn't argue with evil. When you couldn't kill evil, you got away from it as soon as you could so the black sludge of their influence didn't slime you so badly that you couldn't wash it away.

If Lis was losing sight of what was evil and what wasn't, he had to move quickly. His experiments thus far with vampire hearts hadn't yielded much fruit. He could bind the heart to the vampire it had belonged to, which wasn't much use because that vampire was dead. But if he could bind a vampire heart to *every* vampire, that had a lot of potential for a hunter who couldn't fight the good fight like he used to — which was why he now used aerosols, grenades, guns, and spells.

Like the witch had said, magic *was* good as a weapon, with clear parameters and outcomes.

And if he could affect all vampires with one spell, his contribution to the hunters' crusade would reach even farther than when he had fought. If he didn't have the power to erase monsters from the face of the earth with his finger, like killing a mosquito on his arm, then maybe he could make it clearer to Lis who the monsters were.

When things were less human, they were a lot easier to identify. And a lot easier to kill.

* * * *

He hid his duffel in a secret locked compartment in his car, then headed further east, toward the industrial parks, less bright and shiny than the Meridian business district but no less industrious. Whole sections stood almost empty or abandoned after businesses past went belly-up. To an innocent observer, it would seem almost by design.

To a more attuned observer, they would *know* the empty buildings were by design — as a tax write-off and as convenient spaces for the wilder creatures of Meridian to inhabit, like hornets' nests.

The buildings spread over several miles in each direction, interspersed with vendors close to the street and at intersections, like building blocks left by a particularly orderly child, in blandly functional design intended to look clean and modern and feeling instead like an afterthought in comparison to the more intentional artistic design elsewhere in the city.

Some Meridian hunters used the district as their hunting ground. Others knew better than to hunt here. There was almost unprecedented access to nests, families, covens, hives, but that meant that an attack on one demon could easily become an attack on twenty.

Archie drove through the park, clocking the demons who weren't bound by sun restrictions. The sex demons were easy — well-dressed, but not in business or business casual clothing, and all of them gorgeous even from a distance. They were on the edge of full-blooded, despite enough human traits, habits, behaviors, and sometimes whole lives that some hunters considered them hybrid. Their human faces were veils. Archie had seen a sex demon's true face before.

Truer hybrids had more difficulty hiding. It was why a full moon forced the change upon a werewolf and why vampires couldn't walk in direct sunlight.

Archie wasn't looking for demons, although he'd love to drop a grenade in the middle of most of these buildings. He also had more than enough vampire hearts and blood to work with through Lis' quota. What he was missing for his experiments were werewolves.

He could instruct Lis to search for werewolves on her next hunt, but although he put her at risk every night, he wasn't actually sending her out there to die. From the Wastelands, the closest access to urban werewolves were the city parks where Alliance packs ran. The problem was that the space afforded them in the parks meant that they ran together. Lis' fighting tricks against bipedal opponents would lose all their potency against the quadrupedal, especially in groups.

Which meant the task was on him to enter deeper into the rotten heart of Meridian, where its evil denizens didn't just manage to endure but thrived, because this town had been built for them as much as for human business.

That was the thing about Meridian that just wasn't as true in other big cities. Meridian had been *made* for monsters, demons, hybrids, witches, cultists, and acolytes, and as a result, for angels, gargoyles, and hunters. There were as many places of worship as there were large businesses, as many people preying as praying.

Evil was drawn to humanity, so the denser the human population, the denser the population of demons. That was just math. But Meridian called the demons home and made for them a space to roost. They barely had to fight to find a place within its strata. And as a result, compromises were made for everyone to get by, to survive, to keep families safe and housed and fed in exchange for relatively small sacrifice.

Other cities didn't have protections for its demons as inane as the Alliance. They didn't pretend demons had every right to be there as humans. And Lis was wavering. After sixteen years of the mission, she was looking for ways to cut corners, like every other Meridian hunter. They'd lost the plot as much as the rest of this godforsaken city. Archie refused to let Meridian change her, too.

He drove deeper into the city, out of the industrial park and into the warehouse district, which performed a similar function, but the buildings here were older and made of brick rather than concrete. There were plenty of abandoned buildings here, too, but also more architectural detail and variety, they were packed more densely together, and there were more places to hide.

Which made it perfect for urban werewolves who wanted nothing to do with the Alliance. They resented all efforts to police them, resented that hybrids had to make themselves known but hunters who held to the Alliance or not didn't have to prove a thing. They knew better what they really were, not domesticated wolves but feral marauders.

Most of the unmarked packs still didn't kill a lot of people. Their viciousness didn't lend itself to low profile, and living in a city among humans rather than in the greater safety of rural areas meant it was better for them to defer attention. However, they had a reputation among hunters as viciously brutal thieves, though they tended to leave their victims alive—for better or worse. Whenever that victim described themselves being attacked by a band of monsters, their accounts were dismissed as the ravings of the understandably traumatized. Just because they didn't kill many humans didn't mean they weren't still wild dogs that needed to be put down.

Archie pulled into an open lot among a number of other dated cars. It looked like it had once been paid parking, until someone had yanked the machine out. If Archie were a werewolf, he would use such a place as a net for unsuspecting tourists who didn't know that this part of town could be as bad as the Wastelands.

He, however, was not an unsuspecting tourist. He slung his weapons bag over his shoulder, checked that the guns in his shoulder holsters were still where they should be and all had their silver-coated ammunition, checked in the bag for his shotgun with the silver ball bearings inside. More ammunition was hooked to his belt under his trench coat. Like Lis, he kept silver knives strapped to his forearms—as a last rather than a first resort for him. He had yet to use them since his own patrolling days.

Then he exited his car, unconcerned about the valuable book left behind. The lock on the secret compartment was custom-made with silver coating and strong enough that most supernatural beings couldn't break it. The compartment kept the car's mileage higher than it could have been, but it was worth the security in places like this. The packs around here could use his money more than his meat. Meat was plentiful, money less so for the half wild.

He set out into the urban forest of red brick and rusty iron, one hand on the shotgun in his open bag, grenades and smoke bombs laced with colloidal silver within reach as well.

Sun up, most hunters had gone to bed, as had most demons who didn't work a day job. Werewolves were nocturnal by necessity but tended to be crepuscular when they didn't give a shit about where or when they were supposed to hunt, and there was so much more to do in the city during the day, which meant unmarked werewolves tended to get up with the sun.

Archie looked the part of a hunter, perhaps, except for his limp and the timing, but he could also seem like easy prey. No one took his bait, however. Other than flashes of movement in the windows of buildings he passed, this part of the warehouse district could have been a ghost town.

He swerved into an alley and climbed a fire escape, wincing at the strain on his leg. He settled on the second-floor landing after making sure that the window was intact, then tucked himself into a corner, arranging the shotgun across his lap.

Half the hunting game for someone like him was waiting. The fire escape was a blind, his quarry a lot more dangerous than a deer.

He waited almost forty minutes and, in that time, only saw a group of what looked like construction workers taking a break.

As soon as they were out of sight, though, a pair of boots slammed on the fire escape railing behind him. Archie whipped his shotgun around, only for a thick clawed hand to grab the bore and wrench it from Archie's grip.

The man smiled bigger than his face seemed able to hold, his interlocking teeth pressing against human lips, forcing them open. He was shirtless, but his pants and boots suggested that he intended to keep bipedal form. That still left him a lot of room to overpower Archie.

"What do you think you're doing here, loitering on my doorstep? This isn't your home, Pops. Here, you're breakfast. Or if we want to be really bougie, brunch."

The man's face distorted as his jaw jutted out. His legs strained against denim that had been loose before.

Archie didn't bother with banter. The demons who talked too much were the real ones to worry about. To the trained, it was a threat, that something so dangerous could also afford to be casual.

Archie pulled out his pocket pistol and shot the monster in the belly. The beast laughed, maybe because he assumed Archie was new to the game and using untreated bullets. Then, when the beast staggered, comical confusion on his partially turned face, Archie shot him in the head.

Heart untouched, except for the silver rushing through the creature's veins.

He didn't fall so much as collapse.

Archie didn't worry that police would show up. People would assume the gunshot was just a car backfiring or they'd simply mind their business. If he glimpsed a black-and-white, he would climb into one of the abandoned warehouses until they went away. He knew how to make himself unseen, unnoticed, half the battle of being a good hunter. Looking like a child was Lis'. Looking like a harmless gimp was his.

Archie worked quickly, extracting the teeth and claws for resale, then removing the heart and storing it in one of his plastic bags. Once finished with the body, he used leverage tricks to flip it back over the fire-escape railing. It landed in the alley with a crunch to the head that made even Archie wince.

Then he retrieved his shotgun and waited for the blood scent to call the wolf's brethren. For his experiments, one heart wasn't enough. He'd need at least three.

Chapter Nine

When Rose opened the door to polite knocking, she knew there could be a rocket launcher on the other side, but she opened it anyway.

Lis was on the doorstep, sans rocket launcher. She also didn't brandish any knives, although the position of her hands at her side suggested she could grab them in a half-second. She wore a different hoodie from last time, dark gray instead of black.

By now, the shallow slashes from Rose's nails had already almost closed, they'd been so thin and clean. The other cuts across her cheek featured more prominent scabs, shiny from remnants of petroleum jelly that she probably used in conjunction with bandages while she slept.

The sun had just crossed the lowest rooflines, although some indirect light compelled Rose to step back into the shadow. She searched for any other movement, but unless the people walking on the sidewalk were undercover hunters working with Lis, there was no additional danger. Rose doubted Lis easily worked with anyone. Most hunters hunted alone.

"Lis. I thought that if you were coming back, you already would have."

"Are you afraid of me?" Lis' dark eyes were shrouded by the hood, but Rose could see her well enough.

"I knew I was taking a risk."

"Why'd you take it?"

The girl spoke so flatly, but Rose didn't think it was because she felt nothing. Fifteen, sixteen years of hunting, she'd killed most everyone she interacted with. She might have had a normal childhood before she'd been pulled into the underworld, but the kinds of things a little girl would witness while learning how to be a hunter would have undone all that, and television might not have made up the difference. It wasn't as though she needed expressions and inflection while stabbing a vampire to death.

"Would it insult you if I said that you remind me a bit of me?" Rose asked. "It's not a narcissism thing. I just like you, and I wanted to show I trusted you so you might trust me."

"What will happen if I decide to trust you? You sit on my lap next?"

"Vampires are dense, so I'm heavier than I look. I wouldn't sit on you like that."

"I mean, would you seduce me, add me to the harem of people under your thumb while you pretend to be kind?"

"Not unless you ask nicely." The sun had finally set enough that the indirect light was only a soft burn on Rose's skin as she walked out onto the steps and closed the door behind her. "I just thought you could use more than one person to trust. But I can't make you trust me. I can't even make you want to trust me."

"Why do you want me to trust you?"

"Because I spent over fifty years doing what I was supposed to do. Most of the time, I even enjoyed it. But whether you're dead or alive, Elisabet, there's more to life than the one thing you were made for. I don't want you to take as long as me to figure that out. However, if there's one thing age and wisdom teach you, it's that you can so rarely teach age and wisdom." Rose shrugged. "All you can do is put it out there and let those without age and wisdom take what they need. I'm not going to stalk you or hunt you, and I'll thank you to grant me the same courtesy, but I can't force you to do that, either."

Lis was one of the most inscrutable people Rose had ever met. Her face was still a lovely thing to look at while it was inscrutable, although some people might have considered the set of her mouth to border on bitchy.

"If I wanted to kill you, I'd do it now," Lis said.

"You would try."

"I'm going on patrol. Would you come with me?" She quickly followed up, "I'm not afraid to go back out. I don't need your help. I'm inviting you. You and Simon. If you want to join me."

"Why?"

"Maybe I want to try trusting you."

Lis didn't have to set a trap. She could fall to a crouch right here and murder Rose on the steps of her own church home. Rose wanted Lis to take a chance on her. Suspicion flowed both ways. Trust had to, as well.

"Simon isn't here. He'll catch up with me after his pack has a good run. I'm a homebody, and he gets restless. Is what I'm wearing okay?" A dove gray crop top and black leggings, just something to wear around the house.

Lis nodded.

"I'm not going to kill vampires with you."

"You killed vampires *for* me."

"Yes, but that was because they were *going* to kill you. Most vampires you can handle yourself. And I'm not going to attack vampires for doing what they're meant to be doing, even if that means killing humans."

"After what you did for me, and with what you chose by joining the Alliance, why not?"

"I can see how that's bad from your perspective, and there's no reason why prey shouldn't fight back and protect their own. But just because a predator *can* eat other things doesn't mean he's meant to. *I* don't want to do it anymore. That's a choice I make. I'm not going to make it for others. It's not sporting."

"I don't understand the distinction."

"You don't have to. It's a line *I'm* drawing. I'm not going to kill vampires for killing humans any more than I'm going to kill you for killing vampires. However, if you find yourself the target of another family, I'll step in. Because that's not sporting of them, either. Can you accept that?"

Lis needed a moment to think. Then she nodded.

"Let me get shoes on."

* * * *

It wasn't the strangest outing Rose had ever been on, but it was on the top twenty list — patrolling for vampires on the streets of the worst neighborhood in the city while in a hunter's company.

She had gone on walks aplenty, because even though it was rough, Cemetery Grove was beautiful. Then, just ten or fifteen minutes in the car, she could be in the vital center of Meridian.

The Wastelands was the antithesis of all the versions of Meridian she frequented. It was bleak and frankly the kind of tragic she didn't like to look in the face. Poverty was something she'd never had to deal with. She'd contended with homicidal intention, Machiavellian strategy, and vampire politics, and she'd left everything she'd ever known to come here to Meridian, but she'd left with her share of what she'd earned on commission and investments. She'd bought and had a church renovated to her specifications. She would never go hungry. She had everything she would need for three lifetimes, and by then, savings and investments would have enough for three lifetimes more.

These people didn't have enough for a week. Rose contributed to Cemetery Grove food banks and the free clinic, but this made her want to do more, and she wasn't sure what that was supposed to look like. Part of the reason vampires amassed wealth for three lifetimes was because they could very well last that long, and being immortal meant that people started to question the fact you didn't age after about fifteen years, so vampires couldn't maintain steady jobs the same way humans could. Even if they moved every fifteen years, they often had to change their identity, too, because they couldn't be eighty years old on all their paperwork when they looked twenty-five. In an increasingly digital age, with better and better anti-counterfeit measures, government bureaucracy had become more difficult to navigate for immortals. As a result, they'd developed their own extralegal infrastructure to accommodate mortal requirements, which required connections. Most vampires lived in comfort, but their worlds could sometimes seem so small. They built those worlds in the largest hangars, hotels, and warehouses to give themselves an illusion of space, yet even though vampires were apex predators at night, it was a daywalker's world.

So she didn't feel guilty about being rich. She wasn't sure how to help so many people who weren't, or if she was even supposed to, beyond what she already did.

Lis had no such reason to feel guilty. She had somewhere to live, but it wasn't a home. In that sense, she was one of them, transient, with her shelter shut to her all night while she made other transients like her safer. One of the most effective deterrents for monsters was four walls and a roof. These people didn't have that, but they did have one badass hunter — even though she looked like she'd be a hundred pounds in the pouring rain.

Size mattered in a fight, but she knew how to use what she had, and Rose had to give Lis and her handler credit for that. He hadn't taught her as though she were a five-foot-seven MMA fighter. He'd taught her to fight as a child, and when she hadn't grown *up*, those methods still served her so well that she'd survived into adulthood against most odds. And if she managed to meet her requirement of killing at least three demons a night, that was over a thousand demons a year. Felled by one little girl. Rose nearly reeled at the thought.

People who didn't acknowledge Lis with more than a glance or two noticed Rose more readily. She probably should have dressed in something more innocuous than even her house clothes. But it was too late to go back home now, and beyond wardrobe, Lis made no additional effort to stay under the radar.

Down one of the alleys, Lis found a pestilence demon dragging a man, drunk to the gills, into its gutter. She used her boot to block the demon from biting her. Then, when she couldn't get a good angle on the creature's neck or any of its other vulnerable parts, she simply cut off the hand holding the man's sleeping bag.

The demon slunk back into its gutter. Lis used the slipperiness of the sleeping bag to drag the man back down the alley to where the population was denser and he could be watched over by the others.

"If you don't bring home a heart, it doesn't count, does it?" Rose said.

Lis shook her head.

"And you can stop at three?"

"I can. I usually go 'til dawn, regardless of quota."

"Fuck."

"It's my job," Lis said. "I don't stop 'til my shift's over, unless I'm sick. But some days are also just harder than others. It helps that I have permission to take some time off if I reach my minimum."

"You don't even get weekends and holidays off, do you?"

"Halloween. Christmas Eve. Christmas. Merry Christmas."

"Halloween?" Rose thought she knew why, but she was curious.

"Even in places like this, too many people walk around looking like monsters. I might stab something I shouldn't. Arch— My mentor gives me candy, and we get to watch the horror movies I like."

"What horror movies do you like?"

"Seventies and eighties slashers, mostly. The classics."

Rose still thought of Universal and Hammer monster movies as classics and seventies and eighties movies as new and modern. All a matter of perspective—and birth date. "Why do you like them?"

"They're violent. Visceral. The effects are sick. But they're just effects. If you've ever seen the real thing, you can tell. I like that it *feels* real but doesn't *look* real."

It was the most frivolous thing Lis had ever said to her. Rose thought that was promising.

Further on, Lis killed a vampire feeding on a twelve-year-old boy. The boy went running off, so the vampire couldn't have taken much. Lis then settled onto her knees to cut out the vampire's heart with the same clinical precision as before, as rote as the wandering, the finding, the killing.

Killing was so much a part of her life that she probably didn't even register it as killing anymore. She didn't get off, and she wasn't cruel. She confronted something deadly with her own deadly force, and she did it in such a way that it was as quick and painless as possible for all involved. Locate, incapacitate, kill. As mechanical as a factory job.

It was both sad and impressive at the same time— which was *also* sad and impressive at the same time.

Rose wondered if Lis knew that she was a prolific killer even by hunter standards. Most hunters were lucky to find and kill one demon a night. Part of the reason for that was because they hunted areas where demons were more likely to hide within a human population, either in their domiciles or within crowds. The other reason was that Lis was killing low-value targets. If hunters wanted to make a living, they might kill a vampire if they crossed its path, but sex demons and rogue werewolves sold for far higher—anything with wings or pelt. The demons she did kill would be of greater value if she had the tools to harvest more, but her handler had taught her to simply kill, retrieve the bare minimum, then move on.

Eventually, the alleys Lis patrolled were much less populated, like the one in which she'd been jumped by the vampire family. Didn't mean there weren't people in the buildings. Rose smelled drugs. She smelled sex. She smelled drugs and sex together. She smelled men and women in various degrees of high. She smelled power trips and ego boosts and just enough blood to make her edgy.

Lis slowed her stride to walk with Rose at her side instead of at her back. The fact didn't escape Rose, however, that Lis had spent the last few hours with a vampire at her back without constantly checking whether the vampire was going to kill her.

"You said you changed how you lived your life and left the world you knew because of what you were created to do. What were you created for?" Lis asked.

"Within families, turning is initially almost always about companionship," Rose replied. "That can backfire in a very *Bride of Frankenstein* fashion, but when it's done right—effectively, I mean—the companion you choose was already companionable before turning them into a vampire. And once you're turned, they get you hooked. On the blood, the thrall, the sex, the whole drug of other people's lives. On pretty jewels and party dresses. The nightlife. One great big party. None of these things are bad in and of themselves — unless you're the human in the equation, of course. But then the time comes when the head of the family pulls you aside and says no one rides for free. Then they teach you to take all the things they got you hooked on and hook those things into someone else."

Rose transported back to those early years in service — the embarrassment, the resentment, the shame. Yet she'd served her family for decades in the way she'd been chosen for, all while her sire had praised her and lavished her with love when she returned once more to the fold, not empty-handed.

"Like so many other women in service to the family, my task was to go out into the world and seduce wealthy men or women — usually men, because they were more generous in their wills. Sometimes we were simply mistresses, the most torrid of affairs, but more often than you might think, we became spouses. Mistresses and escorts would receive gifts and financial compensation for their time, while spouses were invariably written into the will. Oh, it was so unfortunate we never produced heirs to inherit our husband's estate, and we sometimes had to convince them through thrall that we'd been on that wonderful trip to the Maldives and spent the morning sunning on the sand. But devotion was its own spell. They didn't complain about all the places we couldn't go during the day when they didn't want to leave our bed all night."

"You were prostitutes." No judgment, just a statement.

"Of a kind."

"Black widows."

"We rarely killed our husbands. We didn't have to," Rose said. "A human trophy wife might feel the weight of age, the pressure of time, the sense of the power of youth and their lives as they know it retreating out of reach. A vampire doesn't have to worry about those things. We can give our partners years of our life without relinquishing a single ounce of the youthful beauty we were selected for."

Lis stopped walking and turned around, crossing her arms. "So you what? Just lived with them until they died?"

"Sure. If we were mistresses, we let them put us up in fine apartments. If they gave us jewelry, we had the jewels replaced with paste. If they gave us an allowance, some of that went toward expenses, but we sent the rest home to our family. We treated the windows and bought good curtains, and when they visited the apartment, we filled their heads over and over again, sometimes feeding on them, but sometimes just calling in takeout and having the kind of time they would usually need pharmaceutical help to have. They left the little blue pills at home when they came to us.

"And when we were finally wives, we didn't let the spark die. We were devoted. We took care of our spouses and were taken care of. We leaned on servants, often hired through the family so that they'd deftly work around our limitations. We told the men we were sensitive to light, and that's why we had to wait for evening parties out on the deck and wear wide-brimmed hats until the sun dipped below the fence. Any inconvenience was more than made up for in the dark. The family had similar policies regarding gifts and allowances for wives as for mistresses, but they were much more flexible with the timing, because what we waited for was inevitable."

"You said you rarely killed your husbands."

"We didn't exsanguinate them to kill them. God, that really would be suspicious," Rose replied. "After years of wedded bliss, we wouldn't be so gauche as to invite an investigation. If the natural process took so long that our power waned from their physical or mental deterioration, the family provided potassium or digitalis, and an eighty-five-year-old man died peacefully in his sleep. We didn't even leave a puncture mark if we licked the wound afterward.

"Don't mistake me, Lis, the family basically sold us to these men for millions, for our shares of estates and antiques and heirloom jewelry, but our task wasn't to bleed them dry. It was to be loving, doting partners and give them the time of their lives because we could afford the time to do it. I was good at it. I remained mistress to men I wasn't terribly fond of, to women who at the time and in their position couldn't afford the social cost of being with me more publicly. But when I married men, I learned to love my time with them, sometimes even love them. I was a good wife. A vampire can learn to love almost any bed. We're subject to our own thrall when we use it on someone else, so it's mutually beneficial. I didn't resent them, and I mourned their passing. But after yet another funeral, yet another hearing contesting the will, yet another name and background I had to learn, brushing my long blonde hair and avoiding mirrors so no one would notice I wasn't in them, then going to the family home and assessing my commission while my sire kissed my neck and told me for the seventeenth time what a good girl I was…"

Rose smoothed her hands over her scalp, with its short, soft, pliable hair. "I realized they were doing the same thing to me that they were having me do to these humans. Mutually beneficial and not entirely unpleasant, but still all about the end transaction, while they got to sit in their obsidian tower like dragons and count their gold, their work done in making us. Most of their women — and sometimes men, to be clear — catch wise to the way they're used. As long as they've given good decades to the family, it doesn't resist too hard when they leave with their share."

"So you bled your men and women dry, but just financially, so that makes it okay," Lis said.

"I tricked them into mind-blowing sex and the occasional surreptitious feed. I didn't trick them into giving me gifts or buying me condos or marrying me — any more than anyone does, I suppose," Rose said. "I came by these things as honestly as any pretty young thing. If I stole anything, it was by siphoning inheritance, given that I would never have children, nor die and pass my part of the estate on. Generations worth of wealth died with me. Instead, I signed titles over and transferred funds to the family home. Regardless of how much or little I liked my spouses' families, I felt worse about that than what I gave my partners. Which is why I was so damn good, I guess. I was earnest, and there was so much to love about my life if I just ignored how it was all part of the family's design. I might have even ended up doing it on my own if I'd been left to my own devices. Now I don't have to."

"Who do I have to kill?" Simon jumped down from the gutter he'd climbed down as though it were a ladder. Rose supposed a few more holes in the flimsy metal wouldn't hurt. "You two look really intense. Do I have to stand between you, or should I stand back?"

This time he wasn't naked, which meant he'd stopped by Rose's home first, where she'd left a note and he kept clothes for just this purpose. He couldn't always carry keys to her place, but he was uniquely able to retrieve the spares where she'd hidden them in a building near the church. He wore a loose tank top and sweatpants again—clothes in which he could partially grow into his bipedal werewolf form if he had to.

"I was just explaining my history as mistress and trophy wife," Rose said. "And she's giving me a 'the rich really are different' look. She's not wrong."

"You little gold-digger."

Simon hugged her around her waist from behind and pressed a kiss to her head, followed by another stroke of his cheek. Rose smiled at how much he liked her shorn.

"Werewolf packs also tend to share wealth," Simon said, "although 'wealth' is a generous term. We don't need much. We live a long time, but we're not immortal, we don't require housing or protection from the sun, and we have all the food we could need in the wild. And if I feel the urge to roll in the lap of luxury, well, Rose and I found each other, didn't we? One person in my pack has a steady white-collar job, and we think she's weird, but we love her. Someone in another pack brings in cash flow by writing naughty romance novels. She's pretty popular these days. The rest of us do temporary construction work, because we're strong but don't enjoy binding ourselves to a schedule for too long. The wolf doesn't always understand the concept of work, and the last thing you want to do is beast out at a bad boss."

Lis watched them with that wonderfully bitchy set to her mouth, but Rose didn't think the intensity in her eyes or around her brows was anger. Perhaps she was reconsidering her own financial situation. Nothing wrong with mending clothes until they'd frayed or fell apart too much for repair. Nothing wrong with motels or being kept. Rose had noticed during Lis' foraging, though, that she'd put some of the cash in her bra and given some of it away, but stored the bulk of the rest in her bag with the body parts. The fact that Lis' bra wasn't a place her handler would search answered at least one question Rose had been keeping to herself.

"I just do the same thing most nights," Lis finally said. "My mentor ensures that hunting is all I need to concern myself with."

"And you get three nights off a year," Rose said.

"I can finish my quota in a few hours, sometimes less. Then I might do other things."

"Like chocolate cake and ice cream?"

"Bars. Grocery stores. Searching abandoned buildings. Reading. Studying. There's not a lot to do after sundown."

Rose laughed. "There is if you go downtown, hon. Ever taken a ride there?"

"What's for me there? I don't...dance, don't drink much, don't talk. Everything I do, everything I need, is here."

"There's more to Meridian nightlife than drinking, dancing, and drugs, and the only one of those they don't have down here is the dancing. They have rooftop movies, ghost walks, evening church services. UTM offers night classes for GEDs, ESL, and some associate's degrees. There are a lot of concept restaurants that close late, too. Simon and I met at an Alliance speakeasy, which is one of the few places I can consume ethically sourced human blood. There's so much life happening in this world. If you don't have to stay here all the time, why do you?"

"Everywhere I go has a place like here. It's what I know. It's where I belong." Lis gestured to the tense brick and concrete sentinels around them, with eyes peering out from dark panes. "I'm not exactly like the people who live in the alleys or sleep in these buildings, but I'm more like them than I'm like you. What can Meridian's nightlife offer someone like me? A world that's too loud, too bright, that knows how to smile, that forgets what lurks in the darkness they're dancing in. And what can I offer it? A knife to the gut."

"Life shouldn't be over at twenty-three," Simon said. "And, as Rose proves, you're never too old to change. I understand encountering an ever-present darkness and wanting to shine a light. However, if you don't give yourself a chance to live, eventually you're going to wonder what the point of living is. The more you seek out the darkness, soon there won't be a light left to shine."

Simon kissed Rose's head again, then tentatively rounded her to approach Lis, who twitched when he reached out to brush his knuckles against her beautiful broad cheekbone. "I've seen it happen before. Not every werewolf or vampire adjusts to being turned. The hunger is difficult to endure for someone who doesn't find a way to live with it, not just in spite of it. You don't hunger like us, hunter, but even though you're strong and healthy, don't think a vampire or werewolf can't tell you're still starving. There are other ways to die."

"What should I do? Lounge on a cushion with a hookah pipe while someone feeds me grapes?" Lis asked.

Rose and Simon laughed. Rose hadn't known that Lis could joke, even if she was frowning a little more.

"Maybe in your free time?" Rose said. "Why the hell not?"

Lis still looked at them like they were the ones who were slightly mad, then turned around to continue her patrol.

Rose and Simon walked arm in arm, giving her some space while she ruminated on what they'd told her and how that must have clashed terribly with her dystopian view of the world, because she was always in the most desperate and forgotten parts of it.

"Interesting night out," Simon murmured.

"She asked," Rose replied. "I was stunned enough she came back without a semi-automatic pointed at my forehead."

"Still think she can be saved from herself?" Simon asked.

"I'm trying to save her *for* herself. She's the only one who can get herself out of the situation *he's* holding her back in. *She's* fine."

"*She's* a set of Cutco knives."

"Don't pretend that doesn't do it for you, puppy."

"I'm not saying I don't like Cutco knives. I'm saying my mama taught me not to play with them."

The vampire and the werewolf were probably talking about her, which was a new experience in Lis' life. She wasn't sure she liked being talked about — or not being able to hear it — but it was…nice she'd spent enough time with anyone that they had anything to talk about at all.

Her life should have been none of their business, except she'd made it their business by trying to kill them, then by inviting them to join her in hers. And she wasn't even sure why she'd done that, except when she thought about the church home, she remembered the beautiful, deep, jewel-tone stained glass and the echoes of Simon's cries through the vaulted ceilings, and she remembered the novel sensation of *company* — not just living parallel but perpendicular to another being who acknowledged her existence beyond a death rattle or the briefest gratitude.

She turned into a side alley. Its mouth on the other end opened onto the main street. Between where they were and the exit, three men sat on concrete steps leading to a plain gray door. As she approached alone, distanced from Rose and Simon, two men stood. All three grinned the way other mammals grinned, to show their teeth. Their happiness was not hers.

One of the two who stood, a big white man with small facial features, approached her, while the others grabbed waistbands next to the guns they carried.

"What's a little girl like you doing wandering so far from home? Looking for a little something? We might got what you're looking for. But I don't know if a little girl like you should be getting anywhere near that stuff. Or if you know what the price is."

Lis would usually just ignore men like this, but the big guy had put himself in the middle of the alley, blocking her way. Two other men were coming up from the street, but they were customers. They'd have other things on their mind.

Bouncers sometimes used, too, but it would be the kind that made them more confident and mean. His beady eyes gleamed without substance or depth as he stared her over and held the stiff jut of his jeans. If there was an erection there too, she couldn't see it.

"I'm passing through." That Lis had to say anything at all meant things were already wrong.

She could reach for her own gun, but they'd recognize the movement. She reached for her knives instead, but she didn't like that there were three guns, three dudes hyped on powder and testosterone, and close walls with the risk of ricochet.

"Well, there's a toll for every road around here, and the only way through is that door. I'll show you the way."

Lis backed up, but the man grabbed her shoulder to pull her back in.

She pulled out her blades.

The man thought a little girl with knives was hilarious, and he reached for the gray gunmetal in his waistband in response. A bore to the temple was good incentive for what men like him wanted from girls like her. The other two were getting their guns ready, too, and weren't afraid of her blades at all.

In less than two seconds, she grabbed the big man's hand and slashed his wrist.

The wrist-slashing kept him from using his dominant hand to hold the gun, although he'd squeezed the trigger when she grabbed him. The bullet hit the wall and bounced off somewhere before the gun fell to the ground.

Once her knife was buried in his groin, bursting something in the process, he doubled over. She grabbed him by the neck and whipped him around, letting his weight push her against the wall, because the brick would mostly protect her back. She used the man's great big head to block hers. They could shoot their dude, and the bullets might do considerable damage to her even through him, but although the other men's guns were trained on her now, they didn't seem willing to shoot their friend.

"I have no business here," she said to the other two with guns. "Like I said, I'm passing through."

"Jesus fucking Christ, shoot her!" the big man screamed. "Bitch stabbed my junk! Kill her!"

Lis dragged the man along the wall with her, continuing to use him as a human shield while he spilled blood from his wrist and the front of his pants went dark. As long as he could hold himself up, she would be able to keep using him like this. If he lost control of himself, she would have to make an antelope run for the street and hope the other two thought she wasn't worth the effort to chase.

"Let him go!" shouted one of the other men, a white boy with tattoos on his face and hands. He twisted his gun in that annoying way people had to try to seem intimidating and shot at her, but she ducked completely behind the big man, who howled as the bullet grazed his shoulder.

Lis glanced behind her at the opening to the street. It seemed so far away, and her human shield was already getting heavy, between his blood loss and her throttling.

"Fucking bitch whore!" he sobbed at her, not sure which part of himself to put pressure on, the one that might save his life or the one that might save his dick.

"You take me to the nicest places, Lis."

The two men still with guns in their hands pointed them at Rose as she approached with a smile that seemed all the more bright and beautiful framed by her shorn head. Simon had fallen back, but he strode behind her with the same nonchalance.

"You can drop the poor man, hunter." Rose smoothed her hand over the glimpse of skin between the top of her leggings and the start of her crop top, in case the other two men needed help knowing where to look. She wasn't wearing a bra underneath, and every step clearly short-circuited even their adrenaline-shocked systems. "This is all just a big misunderstanding. Who's in charge here?"

The black man with the braids stepped in front of the younger tattooed boy. He lowered his gun and switched his aggression from violence to sexual intimidation as he gazed down at Rose, his smirk set in badly trimmed facial hair. "Looking to score? Best in Meridian right through that door. Give you a discount on my dick if you're nicer than your whore friend and she sucks off my boy over here. And she'll do that for free, on account of my other boy's hospital bills."

"Well... Aren't you the big bad guy?" Rose purred without blinking. "Does threatening a little girl make you hard? Do you want somewhere warm to come?"

"Fuck yeah." He stepped closer to her, daring her to retreat or fall to her knees to pay the piper.

Lis dropped the big man as he slipped into semi-consciousness, but she held herself against the wall with a gasp as Rose's thrall poured with the focused intensity of a sunbeam on the man in front of her. The fact that the desire Lis felt in response was so strong at incidental radiant thrall frightened her more than a little. She whimpered as she pressed herself back against the wall, an ache inside her opening, begging to be stroked and spread and stretched — everything sex had never been but her body seemed determined to tell her she wanted, needed.

But she didn't have to imagine what it was doing to the man, because he jerked forward into a comical bow, mouth open wide as he shouted, growled, and grunted at the same time, coming hard in his jeans before he could even get a finger on Rose. And when he tried to grab at her, he came again, and again, until there was nothing left to cream himself with and he was just spasming like he'd grabbed at an electrical wire instead.

When Rose let go of him, he fell to the alley like she'd cut his man strings. Then she turned to the younger guy. "Would you like to come?"

Afraid or not, he nodded, wide-eyed. Then he fell back on the stairs, sliding down with a dull thump of his scrawny tailbone against the concrete, as he held his crotch and rolled his eyes back.

Ecstasy was a hell of a drug, but Lis stumbled away toward the alley's mouth while the men were incapacitated, away from the influence of the thrall humming through her like a beehive, telling her to do things she shouldn't, demanding things of her that were painful and violent and felt like bleeding and sometimes she even did.

"Lis, it's okay," Rose called after her. "It's over."

Lis ran past the sickening flicker of bad streetlight before finally pausing, panting, clenching her eyes shut as she tried to bring herself down from such useless biological desire. She distracted herself with the step-by-step process of breaking through rib bones to get to a heart, the dry prattle of a newscaster, taking out roach motels and fly paper to the nearest dumpster. Until she could control her breathing. Until she could control herself.

But that was a joke, wasn't it, when someone like Rose could just decide she'd make someone come, and they did. Lis wasn't in control here. She was the one who'd invited Rose to join her in the first place, and why? Because Lis thought she was interesting? Poised? Wise? Because Lis wanted to be with her or because Lis wanted to *be* her? All of the above?

Simon turned the corner first. "Lis, what are you running from? She wasn't targeting you."

"But I still *feel* it!" Lis grabbed at the sides of her hoodie as though trying to tear her hair out.

"There's nothing wrong with what you're feeling," he insisted as Rose joined them but still kept some distance, troubled. "It's just desire. You must feel it all the time. I mean, you have an outlet of violence, but you don't seem to like it *that* much. Surely you must—"

"What I feel doesn't matter."

"Is that you talking?" Rose asked quietly. "Or your mentor? It's okay to want sex. It's okay to pursue it for your own pleasure. It's okay to make your pleasure a priority. My God, if all you've ever felt of sex was like—" She gestured back at the alley. "No wonder you don't enjoy feeling it. Because then there *isn't* an outlet, is there? You have this thing that you crave, that you hunger and hunt for, and it's so disappointing when you get it. But, Elisabet, what if it doesn't have to be? What if you just haven't known where to look for it?"

"Because I didn't look for monsters who make it their bread and butter?" Lis shot back. She was angry that there were tears in her eyes and mucus catching the back of her throat like a fishhook. She didn't cry much and didn't like it when she did. It felt like eating needles and expelling the tips out of her lacrimal glands.

Rose bent down and lifted Lis' chin, not letting her hide the ugly, blotchy contortions of her face, the greater pronouncement of her frown, the wrinkling of her brow. "Are we monsters?"

The answer should have been obvious, automatic. Vampire plus werewolf equals monsters.

Yet she couldn't say it.

Rose wiped Lis' tears away with her thumb. "Those three won't remember you anymore. I also gave that big guy's wrist a lick to help close the cut, if you care — and I'm not saying you should. But I think we've had enough of this place for a night."

"I need three hearts before I can go back home."

"Come home with *us*. The only heart you need for that is yours, safely inside your chest. Let us show you what it's supposed to be like. No thrall, at least what I can control. You'll know what you're capable of, what you deserve. Come home with us."

Chapter Ten

With just one vampire heart in her bag and a drag in her step, Lis followed Rose and Simon back to the church, where they repeated their ritual of bringing it back to life with light.

It was one thing to bow out for a night when she was sick or cramping, but when she bowed out before quota when nothing was physically wrong, guilt sloshed inside her like tar. Because she wasn't out there, someone was going to die bloody, and it would be her fault.

But that was true when she stopped after three hearts, too, wasn't it? That was true when she stopped at ten. It was true when she stopped at sunrise. While she showered and slept and ate, people died at the hands of monsters, human and demon. While she walked around looking for trouble, trouble had already found someone somewhere else. If she let herself feel guilty about all the people she could have saved, there wouldn't be enough priests in the world to absolve her of her sins.

She did what she could. Just because she wasn't in the right place at the right time shouldn't make her responsible — not when she gave everything. Almost her whole life. And eventually, soon, she'd give her death. She already knew she wouldn't be able to escape it for much longer. Training was getting harder in new ways. Sleep wasn't working as well. The foam cover on the beds wasn't enough to make them comfortable. And the walls of the motel rooms were closing in.

Her world was hard and small and too dark even for her light-sensitive eyes.

Lis didn't scrimp on food, but Rose and Simon were right that there were holes in her that remained hollow, no matter what she ate. And lately, they seemed to be spreading. She saved humans every night, but she didn't feel right. Didn't feel human. As though she'd had to become a monster to fight monsters.

And what did that say about Archie? Despite all his diatribes about monsters, he was the one who'd decided to mold her into something so similar to a monster that it was indistinguishable at certain angles, and he'd made that decision before she'd even had her first period.

She understood why, even when she resented him for it. Childhood was a time to explore, but also to shape and control, then reinforce and polish in adolescence, to let the hot metal cool and harden. Much harder to cut carbon after pressure had made it a diamond — took another diamond to manage it. Teach a child to become a hunter, they'll be ready by the time they're an adult, if they make it that far.

But although she accepted her responsibility, she understood more and more every year how much he'd kept from her. And as she watched Rose and Simon resurrect the sanctuary, she resented that the monsters seemed more human than she did, and the vampire more alive.

Rose spoke quietly to Simon, then headed for the kitchen. Lis shrugged off her bag and removed her hoodie and body armor while Rose ran a blender. Simon joined Lis at the front of the sanctuary, but he didn't force her to talk, just leaned against the wall on the other side of the entrance from where she leaned, as though they were bookends.

She felt naked without her body armor, and she tried not to fidget with the blades on her arms, because Simon seemed to get restless when she did, as though afraid she would fling one or both at him at any second.

Rose came back out with another tray, this time of chocolate shakes with straws.

"You really do have a sweet tooth, don't you?" Lis said.

"One day with us, you're nearly killed, the other you're nearly raped, and as far as I know, that's just a normal April for you. My God, if anyone deserves milkshakes, it's you. I didn't actually ask if you wanted one, though. Do you?"

Lis accepted one of the frosted glasses. After the first thick swallow, she was surprised how good it was and how *much* she wanted one. She shivered from the cold in conjunction with the air-conditioning, since she was used to layering, but she wouldn't have it any other way.

"How come a werewolf can eat chocolate without getting sick?" Lis asked.

Simon snorted into his shake. "It's not a good idea when I'm the wolf. But it seems fine if I drink it while human."

"What if you turn into a wolf before it's through digesting?"

"I've never been sick as a wolf for what I've eaten as a human, and things I eat as a wolf don't seem to bother me as a man. I can eat a coyote as a wolf, then turn into a man and still be hungry for cheesy fries."

By the time Lis finished with her milkshake, Rose had already finished hers. She took the two glasses and set them on the side table with the platter. Then she put her cold hands on Lis' face, stepped close enough for their legs to overlap from the way Lis leaned against the wall, and brushed her lips against Lis' in a soft, almost chaste kiss.

Lis had had tentative before, from people almost as inexperienced as she was, but she'd never had such a soft, sweet kiss, so soft it almost couldn't be called a kiss, not until Lis didn't run or resist and Rose tilted her head to the side to change her angle as she pressed her lips more firmly to Lis'.

"Such a beautiful girl," Rose whispered before tilting Lis' head up and parting her lips.

Lis stayed stiff for a few moments, then let her eyes flutter closed and deepened the kiss, meeting the almost shy caress of tongue with her own. Although she sometimes licked teeth, none were sharp. Everything stayed slow, gentle, unbearably intimate. Arousal that seemed her own rather than external simmered hotter and hotter between her hips. When she balanced herself with her hands on Rose's waist, her fingers caressed bare skin, and Rose caught her gasp with a tender delve of her tongue that made Lis feel like she would melt down the wall.

She was shaking when Rose lifted away from her to stare down, dark eyes blackened with pupils deep and wide. As she smiled, her fangs slid from their sheaths. Lis couldn't feel it, of course, but something about their slow emergence made her bite her lip and press herself harder against the wall to compensate for the weakness in her legs. What had been merely simmering bubbled in an abrupt boil before calming again.

"So you *can* kiss." Rose brushed Lis' cheeks with the backs of her hands, then the soft, cool tips of her fingers, as though comforting the scars, but there was a quiver in her touch, too.

"I've never been with... I mean, I don't think I... I've only with..."

Rose kissed her forehead. "Orientation tends not to mean as much to vampires. Blood is blood, and a heartbeat is a heartbeat. We sometimes have preferences, but we're better served by flexibility. It's okay." She kissed Lis' cheek, then the corner of her mouth, licking lightly, and careful not to let her teeth brush skin.

Then she moved to Lis' ear, breath cold and lips wet, and murmured, "He wakes up hard from dreams where you're hunting him. He wants you, too."

He had to hear, but Lis was nervous to peer around Rose to where Simon watched, still finishing his shake. He appeared nervous, too, although she suspected for different reasons.

"You don't have to do anything tonight," Rose said. "Or I can help, if you want. Like a little alcohol, it can smooth the way."

"*No.* No thrall."

"Okay," Rose whispered. She stepped out of Lis' hold, opening her up to Simon. He swallowed, but with his loose clothes and the way he leaned, his interest was abundantly clear.

Lis unstrapped the blades from her arms. Simon's stiff shoulders loosened as she let them fall to the floor. She had others, of course, but those were the ones exposed after she removed her hoodie and armor.

Simon handed his glass to Rose and straightened just as Lis reached him. He bent down to meet her.

Kissing was different with him than with Rose. Their heights were so disparate, Simon had to wrap his arms around her waist and bend over her, which made Lis feel surrounded and out of control, but she whimpered as she stroked over the corrugation of his ribs up his sides to his back, making him laugh a little from ticklishness. That shifted to a moan as she pressed closer to his erection.

Already it was better than anything that had ever happened to her outside this church. Lis felt like she was being destroyed, one heated cell at a time, but she didn't want to pull away, didn't want to just *get* to it, get it *over* with, *relieved*. Neither Rose nor Simon kissed her like they were only taking what they wanted. There was a rhythm, a consensus. The kiss was shared, as was his body against hers, the slide of his big hands over her knife-strapped back and over her ass to move her against him, to move himself against her. She was participant, not tool, and when she opened her mouth to take him in, to chase him, hunt him into his own sharp-toothed mouth, he tasted and yielded in turn, the coolness of the ice cream quickly melting, although they still both tasted of chocolate.

Lis broke away from the kiss, panting, the waves of her arousal so intense it felt like her slight body couldn't contain them anymore, between the deeply physical ache of hollow need and the dense smoke of desire in her mind.

Simon shifted to her neck, catching flesh between his teeth—sharp, yes, but not so much so that they tore through. She gasped at the harmless threat, then again at the hot slither of his tongue over her skin and the pressure of suction as his hands over her clutched with desperation. For her. Because of her. Not because of a drive for satiation alone. He wanted more than sex, although that was undeniable for both of them. He wanted her. And God save her, she wanted him. She wanted his sharpened werewolf teeth on her shoulder and his cock against her abdomen, wanted his long hair surrounding her, tangling with her own as he snapped the band holding the ponytail and buried his face in it, breathing deeply.

Then he slid his hands back down her body again, grabbed her thighs and lifted her up as though she weighed nothing to wrap her legs around his waist, bringing the intimidating press of his cock against where she'd dampened the fabric of the flared yoga pants she often wore to patrol.

They didn't kiss again, although their lips brushed. A growl rumbled through him seemingly independent of his human throat, rolling through her like continuous thunder. Fitting, because the rest of her seemed a storm.

She was fascinated by his hair, dark blond that was awfully sun-kissed for a night runner, and much longer than hers. Patches of gray tried to camouflage their way through, and this close to him, clean-shaven tonight, more evidences of age were apparent. He looked younger than Archie, but with werewolves, it was harder to tell. He could have been the same age or older, too. Yet there was youthfulness about him — not in lack of wisdom or maturity, but perhaps in his optimism, the prominence of smile lines.

"Are you doing something to me?" Lis asked.

"Werewolves don't thrall, but we do have pheromones that tend to come on really strong when we're running. Or turned the fuck on." He nipped her lower lip, licked it lightly, then kissed her again as though drawn to her by magnetic force. "Some of it even you should be able to smell. But you have pheromones, too, and you might have experienced their effect with other humans — a fresh sweat that can smell sour or so fucking good you want to rub yourself against their whole body. It's animal, darling, signifies an acceptable mate, whether the beast is close to the surface like mine or buried deep like yours." He pressed his nose in her hair again and inhaled deeply. "I enjoy yours, too."

Lis tentatively pushed his hair back so that she could breathe him in, too. She thought of the dusty, dirty, abandoned places where she and others had taken quick moments. She thought of unwashed skin, but given how hot and sweaty she was by the end of most patrols, she could hardly demand better of them than she could offer herself. She thought of the sourness that Simon had described, or the scent of shit that went beyond mere unwashed to unclean. And she thought of the times that what she'd smelled hadn't offended, the ones she'd wanted to cling closer to, who she'd kissed a little harder or longer. Who she'd wanted so much more from.

Inhaling Simon's neck and hair brought her to those rarer moments, but stronger, more aggressively pleasant, and she curled her toes as she rocked her hips against him.

But she did this all the time. Her body got a look or whiff or touch of something she wanted, and it begged — in action and in the small sound that escaped her throat as Simon worshipped hers with his own hunger. Then when it came to what happened when they took off their clothes, usually just enough to get the deed done...

Simon abruptly spun them around to push her against the wall he'd been leaning on. He used his body and the building to hold her up while he cradled her cheek and pulled her leg tighter around him, aligning his cock in almost embarrassing relief to her folds. He rubbed against her clit as he thrust, his growl still deep but harsher now.

Yet he made no move to pull off her clothes, even just to cup her breasts or squeeze them, pinch the nipples hard enough to make her wrench away. Not trying to get under her shirt made some practical sense — that was where she kept the rest of the silver — but what sent her desire into a confused frenzy was that he didn't seem in any hurry, despite his own urgency as the little whimpers he coaxed out of her from kissing her neck galvanized him back to her mouth, where they merged like the mutually starving.

"Fuck, you're shaking," he murmured, his forehead against hers as he, too, caught his breath. "Tight as a string. When was the last time you came?"

Lis started to answer, then shut her mouth.

"No." Simon eased her back to the ground but didn't retreat as though she had some sort of disease. He combed his fingers through her hair. "They never... Not even with yourself?"

"I'm working or living in one room with my mentor. I just never really figured out...how. Sometimes I wake up to it, but I can't think of any one time."

"Which means not nearly enough," Simon replied. "My God. No wonder you're so damn frustrated. You're about ready to snap. Hunter, you're worth demanding satisfaction. If they can satisfy themselves with you, you can satisfy yourself with them. Why should they frighten you more than a demon?"

Rose intertwined her fingers with Simon's through Lis' hair. "I suppose the motel chains you frequent probably don't have detachable showerheads. But there are other ways to take care of yourself on your own, too. We'll discuss that another night. In the meantime, we should address this gross oversight by such ungrateful, unworthy boys. I want to show you something. Let's go, puppy."

Rose playfully tugged on the erection tenting his sweatpants, then guided Lis toward the chancel.

Lis expected to be led to the bedroom where the altar had once been, but Rose took her by the hand toward the stairs, which wound up beyond Lis' sight. She followed anyway, although her folds were sensitive and swollen and just walking felt more uncomfortable than she was used to.

The steeple landing was a small room covered in what looked like repurposed cushions, throw pillows, and blankets. The nest took up most of the room, other than a lamp, an armchair, and small pile of books beside them. The room itself was surrounded by circular stained-glass hinged windows. They could open to let in a breeze or provide a view of Cemetery

Grove, but while closed, they filtered in deep, unreal colors from the external steeple lights.

"Sometimes I sleep here. The colors protect me from the sun, but if it's too directly on me, I can just roll closer to the wall. And I read, obviously. I hadn't brought Simon here yet. It's been my little secret. But I wanted to share it with you. Both of you."

Rose toed off her shoes and left them on the staircase, then released Lis' hand to crawl onto the cushions close to the armchair, where she crossed her legs and beckoned.

Simon left his shoes and socks on the staircase as well, then pulled off his shirt before crawling onto the cushions with her. When he flipped around, holding himself up with his arm hooked around his knee, he was splashed with red and yellow, solemn as he stared up at Lis with blue eyes that resisted color mix.

"You don't have to do this, Lis," he reassured her again. "You don't have to do anything. We can call it a night and just rest. I can hold you, if you want. Or we can both hold you. After tonight—and what you implied about everything before—I don't want to do anything to you that you wouldn't relish. But if you join us here for anything more than an embrace, you'll need to remove your clothes. All of them. You need to let the silver go. You should never climb into bed with someone you don't trust."

"I know we're asking a lot of you," Rose said. "If you remove your clothes, we'll remove ours, and in that respect, we'll be even. But we're never completely vulnerable. We can't strip our weapons away. And that's what we're asking from you. I can promise that we'll make it well worth your while, revenge against everyone who has ever let you down. We can promise that this will be as good for you as your body swears it can be."

She held out her hand to Lis. Regardless of whether they were as turned on as Lis was, neither of them touched themselves or each other, and they didn't look away from her.

Lis unlaced her boots and left them on the staircase with her socks and the blades she kept near her ankles. Then she pulled off her tank top.

Underneath, she wore a sports bra and straps with blades across her stomach and back. Even in the colored light, scars from countless claws and falls and training accidents and weapons mistakes were abundantly evident on her night-pale skin. Nothing she could do about them except moisturize and take her supplements. Neither Simon nor Rose said anything, but she sensed their regard. She didn't heal like they did, although a few raised scars striped over Simon's chest and abdomen, maybe from before he was turned.

Rose pulled off her shirt as well, to match the other two. Because she hadn't been wearing a bra, Lis was briefly captivated, caught between envy and fascination. She'd lived with a man most of her life — and the accidental exposures that entailed. She'd mostly fought men. Hers was the only woman's body she'd ever known with any kind of familiarity.

Lis unbuckled the straps from her belly and back to discard them on the ground, which somehow made her feel even more naked than removing her shirt. Her nipples pressed against the cotton material of the bra with embarrassing proof of her own interest, because it wasn't particularly cold up in the tower, although a draft came up the staircase to keep it from overheating.

She pushed her pants down, then removed the knives strapped to her outer thighs and one to her right calf. The ones on her thighs weren't easy to get to unless someone tried to take her pants off, which was the reason they were there.

When she set them down, that left her completely without defenses beyond her training.

Rose removed her pants as well, and with them her underwear, leaving her exquisite, like a burlesque mural in her secret retreat. Simon removed his sweatpants as well. He wasn't wearing anything underneath. Then they were both naked and waiting. Simon was erect, prominent, jutting with male confidence that left Lis' mouth somehow both dry and watering. He splayed his legs, as though offering himself.

Lis pushed her underwear down, then worked her sports bra off. She stored her spare cash in a pocket, then stood, self-conscious and feeling both young and voluptuous at the same time — on the inside more than the outside, although she had some weight to her breasts and curve to her hips.

She stepped onto the cushions with Rose's help to steady her. Even so, at the first rasp of Simon's leg hair against her leg, she lost her balance and fell to her knees straddling his thighs, closer to his cock than she'd intended.

Almost afraid to touch him, she gasped air that seemed too thin. But she grabbed his shoulders and pulled herself in to kiss him again, his erection caught between them as he groaned his delayed desire into her.

Skin on skin, the twist and tangle of hair, the rasp of his over her... She had never been completely naked with anyone but herself in the shower, and that solely functional. Arousal maddened her nipples with hypersensitivity against his chest, and his breath and body was a furnace to hers.

Her knees dug into a strange patchwork of textures from the nest Rose had created for herself. Lis had hands on her in places where she didn't think anything but soap had ever touched while she was still awake and not in a hospital.

Simon's growls had resumed as soon as his erection had made contact with her, smearing pre-cum in its wake as she pressed herself against him, relishing the not-quite-enough friction.

"Not yet," he murmured.

He wound her hair around his hand and used his control of her head to whip them around so that he was a color-wreathed shadow over her, holding his body away from hers as he kissed her silly into the cushions.

She felt on the edge of something vast and high, but instead of falling over the edge, it kept jutting higher and higher, like unsettled ground. Just when she thought she'd never known it could get this high, he pulled her head back to bite and kiss down to her breast, which brought her even higher. Sounds she'd never heard herself make keened from her throat as he closed his mouth over one nipple and caressed her other just as taut between practiced fingers.

Embarrassment distant but still present in her inundated mind, she covered her mouth with her arm, muffling her shouts as Simon switched sides. He used teeth to surprise her, pulling her breast up as he lashed the nub of flesh with his tongue while caressing her other more gently. She arched up to follow, but he loosened his teeth only to suck her in and press her back to the cushions.

Then he kissed and licked his way down.

"What are you—?"

Lis didn't even have time to be self-conscious before he parted her legs and kissed up her thigh to the fragrant dampness between her legs. The swipe of his tongue through her folds left her gasping. He stroked back her dark curly hair to find her clit, then closed his mouth over it.

She jerked upright, almost screaming, but he hooked his long arms under her legs to rock her onto her back again, and none of her squirming deterred him from the feast he made of her. He groaned with every delve of his tongue back to her cunt, proof of her need and his single-minded skill.

Too high, too high, I'm going to fucking fall if I don't…

But he wouldn't let her. Just when she thought she would, he'd pull back to the entrance and feed from her, the insinuation of his tongue its own obscenity, but not the same. She pressed her thighs to his ears, locked her legs around his head as though she would snap his neck—because she could, but she didn't. She just held him against her, tried to tell him without words what she wanted, because she had no words but *please* left in her lexicon.

Then he slithered his tongue back up to her clit and its hood, humming with pleasure, and this time he didn't stop. She made fists and knots in his hair, holding him to her, and he didn't deny her again, locked onto her as she was to him. When he brought her to the edge, he finally shoved her over into the dangerous fall. She hoped she'd never hit the ground.

Why did no one tell me?

That was one of the few things left in her head among bursts of delight in concert with the ones between her legs, where she seemed to squeeze more wetness out than she ever had during her one-offs with strangers or waking up dead noon with her sheets kicked off and her face pressed into her pillow until she could control her breathing.

But who would have told her? The boys who just wanted to get off? Archie, who'd given her books when he hadn't known how to explain things? He'd only answered her questions like a hunter to a hunter, explaining that relationships were dangerous distractions, hormones tricking you into thinking and feeling things that distorted reality, and she had to stay focused for her own survival. She'd learned to read those supplemental books without her face flushing bright red. Just anatomy. Just bodies. Just things that happened because she was an animal. Once a month she bled and cramped, and pregnancy, disease, and sex itself would make her vulnerable, so why take the risk?

Focus on the mission.

At that moment, as her orgasm tensed into harsher clenching and she finally felt the blanketed cushions under her back again, the only mission she could think of was having that again.

Chapter Eleven

Lis didn't let Simon go, kept her legs wrapped around his neck and her pussy plastered against his mouth, and he didn't seem to mind in the least, laving her with slow, broad licks. She twitched with every aftershock until they weren't aftershocks anymore and she arched on the cushions.

"God, again?" she moaned, sliding her arm from her mouth to the dark burst of her hair over the rumpled blankets.

"Oh yes. Even without supernatural help you could go all night, with a little downtime between," Rose said, legs spread. She wasn't stroking herself, just idly caressing her breasts in soft stimulation, but her fangs were fully extended and her exposed folds glistened. "With supernatural help...I couldn't tell you how long you'd last, how many times you could come, before you collapsed or had a psychotic break. I've never tested the full endurance of a human woman in thrall. We tend to lose track of time. And count."

"Oh my God..." Lis finally unwound her legs from Simon's neck and curled her toes into the blankets.

Simon, however, didn't let go of her legs, and he guided her over him as he rolled onto his back. She adjusted onto her knees, riding his face as he started applying suction, until his chin was wet with her arousal and she felt feral over him, grinding down over his tongue, her fists in the blankets and his hair.

But she pushed herself up, away from his mouth, and tugged at his fingers around her thighs to free herself. When he relinquished her, she didn't clamber away or fall to the side to rest or breathe. She crawled back over his chest to his abdomen and dove down to kiss him as thoroughly as he had gone down on her.

He smelled like her. It wasn't her favorite smell, but mixed with his, it struck a primal chord that had her groaning almost from the same place as his growls, licking his mouth and his tongue and over his chin before taking him again. They consumed each other until his hips seemed to lift of their own accord and his cock pressed bluntly against her cunt.

That, at least, she knew what to do with. She rose up again, hand on his chest, feeling full and sexual and different than she had been with any other man — perhaps because Simon *was* a man, older and more mature rather than stunted by circumstance, and because this wasn't just sex. Not really. It wasn't kiss-until-hard and pump-until-sticky, the basic mechanics of getting off that centered almost solely on the man's orgasm rather than her own. That urge that had brought her to strangers had always been left unfulfilled. Now she knew what it had been striving for and how woefully short they'd fallen. And she hadn't even taken his cock into her, although the lush, thickened hollow of her demanded it.

She didn't know if this would be the same disappointment, desire to reality. But even though she couldn't anticipate what it would be like, she doubted it. Because her skin was singing and he looked at her like she was steak to the starving, and he wasn't throwing her to the cushions to stick himself inside, but letting her reach down between them to massage the head and bring it to her entrance. She probably wasn't as expert as Rose, but it didn't soften him one bit.

He clenched his sharp teeth and caught her wrist. "It was an honor, Elisabet," he said, nearly hoarse with desire. "You gave me an honor. You should accept no less."

"A gentleman should make his lady come first," Rose agreed. "It makes you so much more ready for this. Kiss her while she takes you in, puppy. Kiss her anywhere but make the connection. Make her cry out, make her need. *Yes*."

Simon kissed Lis' breast, sucked gently on her nipple in the same rhythm he'd sucked on her clit to bring her off. The nerve connection between the two shuddered a moan from her as she pushed back on his cock and took him in.

He was longer but not thicker than she'd taken in the past, but no matter size or shape, it had always felt awkward, like stuffing a pillow with fistfuls of cotton batting. Now, with his mouth on her breast, sensation shooting to her clit, her cunt twitching and clenching inside around him as he entered her, became *part* of her, stretched her thin and was embraced by her...

She reared up over him, sliding down further, and held him to her breast as she moved her hips to take him in again and again and again. The inside didn't *feel* things the way her clit did, and she felt the stretch more than the length, but knowing that she was taking him in, feeling the tension in his chest and neck as his hips canted up to meet hers...

Tears raced down her cheeks as she clenched her eyes shut and rode him again, this time with him long and hard and inside, as he groaned and growled in time to her rhythm.

Is this what it was supposed to be like the whole damn time?

"There it is," Rose muttered. She ran her long tongue over the length of her fangs and slid her hands down to her folds, stroking her clit with one and pushing two fingers into herself with the other. "When you're ready, touch yourself. If you haven't already tried, you'll discover what you like. And if he doesn't find the place inside now, I promise he'll find it with his fingers later. God, yes, just like that." She seemed to have found her own spot and arched, bracing her head on the armchair cushion. "He can hold back until you're coming. Can't you, puppy?"

"Yes. Oh... I'll try."

Lis braced herself on Simon's chest with one hand while she reached between them, this time to stroke her fingers over her folds where they parted around him, up to her hypersensitive clit. She jumped a little at touching herself directly, but when she pressed on either side, plumping her clit and the lips, or rubbed over and around the hood, using it as a barrier that was sensitive all on its own, and when she pressed beneath to bone, she sparked over and over around him. With Rose and Simon watching her rub herself sticky and work herself over his cock, those sensations reached not just her head but all the way down to fingers and toes. Her body felt like highly charged static electricity, her mind like old television snow. All of it together was a gunpowder factory, one thing setting off another, hair-trigger sensitive and explosive. It was hard to believe at that moment that she could ever tire of this.

Especially as Simon sat up, angling his legs so that she had something to push back against that also shallowed how deep she took him in. He held himself up while he pulled her back into a hungry, wicked kiss, wild and wet and messy, her hair sticking to her forehead with sweat the air-conditioning downstairs couldn't combat. Condensation built on the windows from their panting and the heat between them, particularly from Simon, who burned with fever.

He brushed her hair back from her forehead and caressed his lips against hers as he spoke. "Lean back. The angle is easier to find when I take you from behind, but let's give this a shot." He guided her with his palm between her breasts to lean back against his legs as she kept riding him. Then he slowly slid his heels forward, sliding his palm down to press against her abdomen.

"*There*," Lis cried when she realized what they were talking about when they said 'finding the spot.' It wasn't so much about hitting it but rubbing against it at this angle, and she pushed his legs down to hold his thighs and cant her hips to do exactly that, her vision going gray with breathlessness and fireworks. She pushed down and he pushed up, and they were groaning at the same time now. Simon looked like he was in pain. She didn't think she looked much better. She rubbed furiously around her clit and climbed that quaking shift again, bearing down on him, wetness smearing halfway down her thighs as she came again with a surprised shout.

"Yes...oh...yes...so fucking good...*oh*..." Simon stroked over her hair, her neck, her breast, the scars on her abdomen as she continued to use his body and her fingers to extend the orgasm. He came at the tail end of her climax, jerking up into her, moaning like she was killing him and he was happy to die in service.

For a moment, she panicked, the way she always panicked, but only demons could impregnate a human woman. Hybrids were made rather than born, and neither vampires nor werewolves caught or spread the same diseases as humans. She couldn't say she'd been so safe with other men of her own choosing. She couldn't say she'd been safe here, but those weren't things she had to worry about with them.

She had to worry that hunger still gnawed hollow within her and tried to keep him inside, but he eased her off him and kissed her again, claws against her back and his teeth even sharper as his seed dripped from her onto him.

Rose had told Lis that he'd dreamed of her, of having her like this. Lis wondered if the experience had lived up to the dream and if steel concerned him nearly as much as silver.

Lips that were especially cool on her heated skin pressed against her shoulder. Rose pulled back her hair to lightly kiss her neck. Lis broke from her kiss with Simon as Rose brought determined, dexterous fingers to Lis' folds, squeezing them between her cold fingers, plumping the flesh around her clit before working the hood over it with gentle, implacable relish. Lis twitched and gasped, then twitched again as Rose slid two fingers inside her and curled — knowing almost exactly where to stroke.

Lis leaned back, encouraging Rose's curvier body against hers. The motion pushed Rose's lips past her fangs and pressed the teeth upon Lis' skin.

Lis bucked, eyes flying open to the trippy color surrounding them that just added to the singular strangeness of the night. She hadn't thought she could get this high again so fast, but a mere brush of fang was enough to make the deliberate rubbing of Rose's fingers inside her squish as she moved. She gripped Rose's wrist but not to pull her out.

Simon was pinned where he was by Lis still straddling his thighs, but he didn't seem put out as he stroked himself with their spending over his cock, reawakened by the sight of Rose finger-fucking Lis and the involuntary thrall that wrapped around them like translucent cotton and made it even more difficult to breathe — but Lis understood better now why Simon happily smothered himself with her.

Lis reached behind her to stroke over the soft short hair on Rose's scalp, to keep her kiss and her fangs against Lis' neck.

"Bite me." She'd been bitten before. She remembered the manufactured lust. It didn't hold a candle to what she was feeling now all on her own, but she craved knowing what it felt like in conjunction with hers.

Rose raised her head and paused her fingers inside Lis. "Are you sure?" She was quiet, uncertain, but her fangs continued to slur her words at full extension.

"Yes." Maybe this had been the endgame the whole time, but by now, Lis didn't care, because parts of her were awake that she'd thought had died or that she couldn't have known she had. If her death was the inevitable conclusion, it would have been well-played and well-earned.

Trust left her a raw-nerve body, shaking as she leaned her head to the side to expose her length of neck.

Rose sank her teeth into the base.

Lis seized, her blunter nails scratching Rose's scalp, as she came again, and again. Rose moaned her own climax while buried deep inside her, until they seemed like the same raw nerve, or perhaps two entwined into one. And when Rose sank her thrall into Simon, too, their twisted nerves braided into three, into tangled limbs and mouths on skin, Rose growing warmer and warmer with Lis' blood, their heat radiant between them. Their cries trembled the stained glass as the small room filled with the mist of sex, sweat, and coppery blood.

* * * *

Even in the industrial district, there were utterly rather than nominally abandoned buildings. Archie had commandeered one of them and reinforced his chains so the werewolves bound with silver-coated shackles around their wrists and neck couldn't pull them out of the ground, even at full strength, which they weren't. Archie went through a lot of tranquilizers while testing, and the silver on the shackles meant that the werewolves couldn't just phase into their bigger forms, not without decapitating themselves. The vampires couldn't even do that. Surrounding them with religious symbols, granted power by conviction, kept them weakened enough that they couldn't break free of the burning silver, even if it wouldn't quite kill them the same way it did their werewolf counterparts.

Ars Cruor lay open on a table in front of him. He'd finally found what he'd been looking for.

And not a moment too soon. After his and Lis' argument, he'd known that they only had a little time. Doubt was like cockroaches. One was bad enough. Once you encountered two, you already had an infestation. At that point you had to completely exterminate the entire mass. Brutally, if necessary.

He'd thought he'd exterminated it when she was fifteen and going through her albeit predictable rebellion. Forcing a quota made her too tired to fight anything other than monsters, and she'd always had a sense of personal responsibility for what she could do that others couldn't. He'd been proud of her for that since day one, more and more every day after.

This is all for you.

It was only appropriate that her blood would be the key.

Although it had lost some of its efficacy since she'd turned sixteen, she was still young, and purity and innocence were funny things by blood magic standards, more complicated to define than the state of a hymen. One might argue that watching her father die by a vampire's teeth had stolen innocence from the beginning, and every way she'd had to become hard, control her feelings by shutting them away, had contributed to the erosion of that innocence.

Sex was another part of it, but he suspected the sex itself hadn't been very good, which was why he could still use her blood in spells that demanded purity, like his analgesic potions. His spine calcified whenever he thought of exactly how the sex might have been bad, but even when she'd told him she needed to go to the hospital for something he couldn't see, she'd refused to discuss it and had gone back to hunting in a few nights.

As proud as he was, his heart broke for her, too — every night she went out, every morning she came home, every injury, every bandage, every stitch, every hospital visit. What he wanted to do now wouldn't necessarily make that part of her job easier, but doubt was more dangerous than any monster she'd faced. Doubt led to hesitation. Hesitation was all a demon needed to cut a hunter's throat.

And what if she decided she didn't want to be a hunter anymore? She wasn't made for anything else. She'd end up on the very streets she'd protected, with no other choice but to bite and claw for survival in a way she didn't have to under his supervision.

No, this would allow her to keep her job security, but more importantly, clarity.

Archie mixed werewolf blood, Lis' blood from her most recent blood draw, and the other ingredients listed in the book. Most of them he'd already purchased from the witch, but he'd had to go back for more, plus slaughter several pestilence demons for their pituitary glands, the catalyst for the magic, even before the words he spoke over the redolent mixture.

He poured the resultant liquid into an aerosol can. Because he couldn't fight the way he used to, magic aerosols had become as much a part of his repertoire as Lis' knives. He could spray a spell from ten to fifteen feet away, and they were often bound to specific targets, so it didn't matter if anyone or anything else got the mixture on them, including him. He had to be more careful with general paralyzing agents in a crosswind, though. His hand almost always went stiff and numb when he used them. Between aerosols and the blood potions he used to help with pain management, he could still be an effective hunter. He didn't have Lis' numbers, but most hunters didn't — the difference between hunting big game and small, as well as the difference between being fifty-two and twenty-two.

Archie shook the aerosol can, then stepped across the large room to the naked, dirty man in chains. Silver had raised contact rashes over his skin. His eyes rolled as he followed Archie's progress. He bared his teeth and pushed himself up onto his hands and knees, but he tilted to the side whenever he tried to climb onto his toes.

"You perverted bastard." The werewolf spat foamy saliva on the floor as he spoke. The tranquilizer sometimes had that effect. "This how you get your rocks off? Why don't you just kill me?"

"All in good time." Archie brought his chair close to the edge of the werewolf's reach at the end of his chains — not that the wolf could do much more right now than crawl. "And yes, this is exactly how I get my rocks off. It's satisfying seeing a beast in its place."

The werewolf laughed, wiping more saliva from his chin. "You don't even know what the beast can do."

"No, of course not. I captured an urban werewolf in his own environment and kept him contained and sedated because I'm an amateur."

"I see a worn-out dinosaur trying to take shortcuts 'cause he can't get it up anymore," the werewolf retorted.

"No shame in finding the shortest path between two points. No reason to make the work harder than it already is."

"You homicidal *hack*—"

"You're part of something important. I know you can't appreciate that, low animal that you are." Archie bent forward to rest his elbows on his knees. There had been a time when he couldn't hear the gravelly popping of his neck or back, when he didn't grunt or groan when he sat down or stood up. It seemed like seven lifetimes ago. "Even if this doesn't work, you're a piece of the puzzle, and the final picture will be glorious. Enough with these dirty mirrors. I'm getting the goddamn Windex and elbow-greasing that glass clean, pure and sharp as new."

"Oh my God, you're actually crazy, aren't you?"

"Things have never been clearer," Archie said calmly. The only reason why he was even talking to the wolf and letting the wolf talk back was because nothing said would make a difference, regardless of speech, carriage, clothes, or artful pleading. "Now to make it clearer for everyone else."

Archie sprayed the spell in a bear-mace stream at the werewolf's face.

The werewolf sputtered, spattered in blood, organ, powder, and herb. It didn't matter whether it got in his mouth or not. The smallest droplets, invisible even to werewolf sight, would enter the wolf's eyes, his nose, absorb into the mucus membranes of his inner lips, into his skin. What didn't happen naturally would be accelerated supernaturally. The werewolf had been doomed from the moment Archie depressed the button. Holding his breath or wiping his face would only make it worse.

The vampire sat up, bleary but awake and visibly braced to be horrified, because he'd already know this wouldn't be a supposed 'cure', which apothecarists, alchemists, and hunters had been working on for centuries. 'Cures' were hard to come by. Poisons, on the other hand, were embarrassingly easy, and what was a pesticide but a more specific poison?

The effect wasn't instantaneous, but once it started, it moved quickly.

The salivation intensified to a true foaming of the mouth, mixed with the blood of the aerosol and minor hemorrhages of the same mucus membranes the spell used to enter the bloodstream. The whites of the werewolf's eyes went red as well. But the hemorrhagic effect was short-lived, part and parcel to the spell binding blood to blood, and in doing so, diminishing the impure humanity and enhancing the beast — erasing the lie to leave only the truth, which was not the 'were' but the 'wolf'.

The werewolf's teeth emerged, large and curved and interlocked, as the transformation was forced upon him — not enough of the man left anymore to hide behind. The silver shackles forced him to stay bipedal and kept him from reaching full-grown, but in looking into the creature's eye, there was no mistaking that the man was utterly obliterated.

"My God. What did you do?" the vampire muttered.

The werewolf lunged against the chains despite the tranquilizers. Archie wasn't concerned. Burning fur told him that the silver would do its work before the beast could break out.

"Just making sure the spell works," Archie said, returning to his table to do the same spell with vampire blood. "If it works on one, it's just a matter of binding on a much larger scale."

"You can't do this." The vampire's ear cuff glinted as he tried to pull himself forward without touching any of the dried holy water or crosses that Archie had cut into the concrete. "We weren't doing anything to you."

"I obviously can do this. I'm doing it now." Archie poured the vampire blood batch into a new aerosol can. "And I don't kill demons based on what they're doing to *me*. That's the whole point of hunting—to protect others."

"I don't hurt anyone. I took an oath. Please. I would never—"

"I took an oath, too. Honoring your oath would break mine. You're a monster. I'm a hunter. It's all so very simple. You'll see in a minute."

The werewolf lunged, tearing through his own skin and exposing his insides to the silver from the shackles. Either the wolf would cauterize off its own head or the silver would bring it down. It wasn't a concern anymore, although Archie had his gun at the ready, just in case.

"Please, don't do this to me!"

Archie approached the vampire with the new aerosol can and shook it, like cocking a rifle. "Now, let's see what you really are."

* * * *

When Lis knocked on the motel door in the morning, she tried to look contrite as Archie opened the door, his gun aimed at center mass but ready at a moment's notice to target her heart instead.

Archie let her in after she gave him the password and displayed the gleam of sunlight on her clothes and the back of her neck with her hood down.

She put a single heart, the cash, and single set of vampire fangs on the small table.

"Not much of a haul," Archie said.

She leaned back in the uncomfortable chair and pulled off her hoodie for a blood draw, since it had been a week since the last. "Lean night. And a bunch of guys harassed me. Human."

She suffered a strange moment of panic that what she'd done with the vampire and werewolf almost all night—with a fever-dream break to rest in the middle—would be as visible as indelible ink on her skin. But Rose's bitemarks had already mostly closed and healed over, and the scratch marks from nails and claws were all under her shirt where Archie wouldn't see them unless she showed him, and she certainly wasn't going to do that.

Lis honestly wasn't sure how she was going to just be able to go along with her usual life and routine while knowing what a human body was capable of feeling. Even now, she couldn't stop thinking about Simon holding her down, like countless other men had done to her, but none of them had ever made her feel the way he had. She ached everywhere from using her muscles in totally different ways than during patrol and training, and she felt vaguely raw and bruised inside, as though she'd been scraped extra hollow, although Rose had told her she'd feel better in a few hours.

As after the first time she'd had sex—inadequate though it had been—she felt different, like everyone should be able to see that difference, especially Archie, who sometimes seemed to see right through her.

He didn't say anything. She wasn't even sure he noticed. He looked tired, drained, the dark circles under his eyes purple and his gait stiffer than usual. His nails were filthy, his eyes red. Most of the time, he spent the nights reading and researching, experimenting with his spells. She knew he was looking for a better analgesic, and he was always looking for ways to improve her strength or the general hunting experience. He figured if he could perfect some of his spells, he could then sell them within the hunter network. There would always be a market for good nonaddictive painkillers, and if there were a repellent for demons that worked better than the intermittent effectiveness of holy water, they might be able to get a proper revenue stream in. Maybe then they could upgrade their motels to ones where Archie didn't have to fix the air-conditioning and plumbing.

Lis dreamed of room service and an indoor pool. She wasn't even sure if those things were real, but they sounded nice.

Whatever Archie had been doing overnight must have aggravated his injuries, and he looked so exhausted that she planned to stay out of his way today. She just hoped he couldn't smell the kind of sex she'd been having. She hadn't showered, because she usually showered after a blood draw and to change her routine would be suspicious, but she'd managed a quick sink bath in Rose's obscenely nice bathroom, which had once been two Sunday school classes. Rose had also shown Lis a place where she could rest alone if she ever wanted, a guest room constructed in another old classroom, as luxurious as Rose's open bedroom, but private.

Archie passed her the usual orange juice box while he cleaned her elbow and inserted the needle. He didn't cast surreptitious glances in her direction or anything, just sat across from her and closed his eyes until he had to replace a full vial with an empty one. After he nodded her toward the shower, she grabbed some clean clothes and went to hide in the bathroom, relieved.

She stripped bare once more, for her own benefit this time, and in the mirror — of which Rose had none, for obvious reasons — she stared at herself. She was used to seeing the cut and line of muscle, her scars, all the ways she'd become a woman, wondering whether she looked more like her mother or father.

She touched where she'd exposed lingering bites, claw marks, bruises from powerful grip but also from kisses. The most profound of her aches and pains were internal, though, and when she searched her expression, she couldn't discern arousal, desire, hunger, or satiation there, except for a light flush on her cheeks, which was normal as the weather warmed.

But in her reflection, she saw someone who two people — albeit monsters — had been so enamored of that they'd made her come at least seven times. Beyond that, she'd been so lost in thrall that she couldn't keep count. Then they'd snuggled up against her by morning. She didn't understand it, but in their hands, she'd been a desirable thing, and they hadn't once treated her as delicate because she was small. They'd treated her like a hunter in bed with a werewolf and a vampire, although they'd been more intrigued by the dearth of pleasure in her life than her mortality.

Lis had thought she'd wiped off all the scent, but freed from her clothes, she smelled it again, as though she'd been rubbed all over with cum, not to mention what Simon had called pheromone. She didn't know how Archie hadn't smelled something.

She couldn't believe it, but inhaling it turned her on all over again. She stroked through the hair between her legs to her folds, which appeared more flushed than usual, not that she'd looked at herself often enough to make the comparison.

But every last ache in her body was finally catching up to her. She usually spent her nights walking, with brief stints of battles. She'd never had this kind of sustained exercise, hyperventilation, racing heartbeat... The high from all the sex was rapidly crashing. After this shower, she was going to sleep so hard.

* * * *

Archie mixed diluted water and Lis' fresh blood with the same herbs and powders that he'd used for years now. For the analgesic, the blood had to be fresh.

Lis had made it clear early on that she welcomed the use of her blood to ease Archie's pain, especially since she reaped the benefits, too, after early evening training sessions or when she returned from an especially brutal fight. At the time he'd asked, he hadn't explained just how many things he used her blood for required virgin blood. It wasn't *why* he'd taken on a child as a hunter, but as he'd explored spell options, having such a ready supply hadn't hurt. The efficacy had waned since her mid-teens, yes, but they still worked enough that he didn't have to lean on pain pills. He needed to stay sharp. The potion he'd been making for ten years allowed him to do that.

He didn't know why he was so tired today. A tranquilizer gun, a plastic tarp, and a dolly had done most of the hard work for him. But the skin of his hands seemed strangely loose in the cold air, the veins prominent, and he felt particularly old, like he'd had one drink past his limit, although he hadn't touched a drop of alcohol in months. Along with the exhaustion came pain, worse than it had been just a day ago, as though he'd stepped on his bad leg wrong and wrenched other muscles in the process. He was ready for some relief as he injected the potion solution into his leg muscle.

He drank some orange juice, too, as he waited for the potion to take effect. It used to be instantaneous. Now it could take around five minutes.

He leaned his forehead into his hand, dry eyes closed, and listened to the rumble of the air-conditioning. He nodded off a few times. He didn't want to go out for a meal or cook anything on the hot plate today. Chinese delivery — if he could just sit up and call.

When he looked up again, it was twenty minutes later, and he'd awakened from unsettling images more hallucination than dream.

His leg and back still hurt.

He stared at the empty syringe, his half-drunk orange juice, his leg, then at the wall separating the main room from the bathroom. She was still showering. She liked long showers after long nights.

He accounted for every step in making the potion and found nothing wanting. Which meant it was the blood-binding ingredient that had gone bad.

Her blood was completely useless for his analgesic potions and therefore for the purification spell, which required a pure soul — pure of action and of intent. He'd already known she had doubts, a lack of conviction that muddied her intent, but if her blood didn't work for the analgesic spell, her actions had also betrayed him. Her blood no longer met the criteria of virginity, by any measure. Every vial in the fridge could only be used scientifically, biologically, medically, not magically.

He was already too late.

Now he just had to contain the damage. Then he and Lis could talk about what had happened. She didn't know how selfish she'd been to compromise her blood, since she hadn't known purity was a vital component. He couldn't blame her much for that.

Mostly he blamed himself. He'd lowered his guard, assumed she was grown up enough to make the right decisions. He'd trusted her too much with little to no oversight, accepting what she'd *said* happened. Trusting without verifying. She'd become drunk on freedom in a new city, with its unique challenges.

He laid the rest of the responsibility squarely on the Alliance. This was why these filthy waters needed to be cleansed. Purified, as she could never be again. There was no regaining innocence. He knew that as well as any hunter. But at least he had purity of intent, greater than that of any hunter in Meridian — the very last true warrior of good against evil. His blood would be enough for the *Ars Cruor* spell, if not for the potion that banished pain from his weary bones.

His girl had been a rare thing indeed. He wanted to destroy whoever was responsible for breaking her.

I'll fix it, Lis. I'll fix everything. I promise.

Chapter Twelve

After their training session in the motel alley — often witnessed by a somewhat bemused and possibly perverted building manager — Archie gave Lis a three-minute head start, then followed her, which he hadn't done in years.

He'd never taught her to catch a tail. If she'd learned anything on her own about that, she didn't seem to notice him as he kept his distance and ducked into any shadow he could find on the way. She was either careless or his boots were that good at concealing his footfalls. Possibly a combination of the two.

But one thing he was sure of — she wasn't going into the Wastelands to patrol.

He tried to tell himself it was nothing, that she was just starting her night in Cemetery Grove. Since it was within walking distance and riddled with wickedness, it was an acceptable alternative.

However, his hunter gut — his *father* gut — whispered that she wasn't doing what she should. But if he were to interfere now and put her back on her path, she would only deny it, because she hadn't yet done anything wrong.

Part of him wanted to do it, wanted to run up to her and shake her by the shoulders and ask her how long she'd been shirking her duties, ask when in the last week she'd lost the last of her innocence, and how was he ever supposed to trust her again? All just to play hooky with some handsome drifter who was probably conning her out of her foraged money to buy weed.

She passed a graveyard and more storefronts, crossed an intersection, then made a beeline for a church.

That...was not what I expected.

He'd taken her to church now and then, especially during Advent and Lent, but more often than not, they addressed religious matters in whatever motel they were staying at. Religious texts and commentary were part of her unofficial curriculum, and it was difficult to pretend God didn't exist when angels and demons did—the existence of atheist hunters was more mysterious to him than God Himself. If all Lis was doing was attending an evening service or class... There were worse things to play hooky with, and frankly worse places to lose one's virginity.

He toyed with the idea that there was a Bible study or anonymous support group within—although he couldn't think of one that would address her life situation, unless it was for hunters, which wouldn't necessarily surprise him.

She climbed the steps and knocked on the door.

Maybe the support group kept the doors locked for safety.

Someone opened the door and let her in.

Archie waited a few minutes, then approached the church. He was careful turning the knob so he wouldn't be heard, but the door was locked. Far be it from him to compromise the anonymity of anonymous support groups, but there was no signage on church property, no paper on the door letting visitors know what they were getting into, and his gut still writhed like an octopus.

He cupped his hands to the door and pressed his ear between. He heard distant talking, but it was just a series of nonsensical sounds, not clear enough for words. He discerned at least two voices other than Lis'.

He crept to the windows, hoping the thinner material might help him hear better, but the group was still out of range.

About twenty minutes later, the front doors opened again. Archie crouched—wincing against the protest in his leg and back—then crept forward when he determined no one had seen or heard him.

Lis was leaving with a man and a woman.

His night vision had never been as good as Lis' and had only gotten worse with age. But even he could tell, clear as day, that Lis had changed from her patrolling uniform to a dress that couldn't hide nearly as many knives and certainly didn't protect as many critical blood vessels and organs as what she was supposed to be wearing. The only reason why she would wear something like this to patrol would be if she were playing bait. The people with her dressed in similar styles and were emphatically *not* hunters. He doubted they were all supposed to be bait.

The woman's hair was brutally short, although she had the profile of a queen the way she carried it. In a gender swap for the ages, the man wore his hair to his waist, tied back in a tail. Archie might have been able to convince himself that these were just beautiful people luring his Lis away with a good time if it weren't for the titanium cuffs—large for the man, who was undoubtedly a werewolf, and more delicate for the woman. Her wrist tattoo clinched it.

Alliance monsters. Demon hybrids. Creatures Lis was supposed to kill, not step out with in a slip of a dress showing too much of her breasts and her legs, powerful but uncertain in heels Archie knew weren't part of her wardrobe. She kept nothing frivolous, formal, or even colorful in her dresser, with the exception of some of the secondhand T-shirts she slept in. Color drew attention. That deep red especially did against her dramatic coloring, and her eyes and lips had never been so emphasized on their own. She looked pretty, grown-up, disconcertingly like the prostitutes who Archie sometimes patronized to take the edge off after he had unfortunate interactions with sex demons, which were not and had never been his specialty. Vampires were bad enough.

Damn it, Lis. Have you learned nothing over all these years? Do you listen to a single word I say?

The vampire woman wore a tight beaded gold dress with flowing flapper skirt, and the werewolf man wore pinstriped pewter with a vest. The three were all so elegant and put together that Archie guessed the woman had arranged the wardrobes.

Can't you see what they're doing? They've planned this down to color coordination. How could you fall for such an obvious scheme?

Archie tailed them to a car, a beautiful black Mustang. Lis climbed into the back, exposing way too much of her thigh. The werewolf stroked along her leg in appreciation.

Damn it.

Breaking and entering were skills most underworld hunters had to learn, and hotwiring cars had been part of the training he'd been given in his early days, because cars were both quick shelter and a way to follow something that could run much faster.

Useful skills, but he had to be much more careful using them than the white man who'd taught him.

He didn't want to lose her, so he bit the bullet and broke into a much less impressive car parked near the cemetery. Then he followed the Mustang north to historical downtown.

It was a beautiful part of the city, although 'historical' wasn't entirely accurate, given that most of Meridian had arisen in the eighties. Archie refused to believe that the nineteen-eighties were 'history'. But between renovations and recreation, the historical district had become a lively extension of the city's central nightlife.

He used to hunt in places like this but hadn't in so long that he struggled to find a place to park and was briefly bewildered by the number of people still talking and laughing and playing music in the darkness. He wanted to tell all of them to go home and go to bed like normal people. It was too late for this kind of awake.

But he forced himself to ignore the pulse and flow of people—human and demon, difficult to tell in the dark—and focus on the blood red of the ribbon-corseted dress Lis wore while she hooked her arm with the vampire, who led her companions to an alley. Archie's abdomen and spine stiffened, but they weren't the only ones headed into that alley, so it probably wouldn't become the site of secret murder.

Yes, there was a whole line leading to a set of steps down into someone's basement. No sign, but everyone else was dressed in the same fancy clothes — either just a notch over club clothes or bordering on costume. He'd read articles about this kind of thing, a revival of speakeasies without the accompanying risk of Prohibition.

Unless…

Painted by the opening down to the door was a crest of inverted W and V, wrapped with an oath in a circle around it in Latin. An Alliance establishment. And there was a scent in the air that most of these young people would never have occasion to recognize — the smell of fresh blood.

It was all Archie could do not to shout at everyone in line that they were opening the door to much darker forces taking advantage of them outside these so-called safe spaces. Based on the smell, this was not a neutral space, like the twenty-four-hour bars and coffee shops. This space favored the demons, and they invited lambs in to give their blood of their own accord — all for the sake of some gothic affectation.

Sickening that such a place even existed, and more so that his Elisabet was walking straight into one without having to go through the line as the bouncer shared a nod with the vampire woman.

Archie waited a few minutes after Lis and the two demons descended into whatever lovely hell they'd created in the building's basement. Then he went up to the bouncer.

As anticipated, the bouncer put up his hand to stop Archie from entering. "No jumping the line, Pops. You gotta start at the end like everyone else."

"You let my daughter in without checking ID." Archie pulled out his wallet to display a picture of him and Lis that they'd taken a few years ago on a rare day off around her eighteenth birthday. They'd been in Dallas then and visited the State Fair at Fair Park. It was one of the few times he'd ever used his camera for anything other than surveillance—a whole day of Lis, in goggle-like sunglasses to protect her vision, but cracking a smile and even laughing, between the funhouse, Ferris wheel, car shows, and food they'd tried. Since she was ten, he'd made sure to get pictures of them printed for occasions like this, when he needed to prove to hospitals and potentially police that a Korean girl was his responsibility.

The picture he showed was of him and Lis grinning while they ate corndogs.

"She's sixteen years old," Archie continued. He could probably push it down to fourteen or fifteen in the dark. "You allowed a minor in without verifying."

"Shit, man. I'm sorry." The bouncer opened the rope. "Do you know what kind of place this is? It's hard to tell with some of our clientele, and there are so many good fake IDs."

"That's no excuse for not at least pretending to check. I'm sure if I let the MPD know about your lax policy here, you'll be able to recreate a genuine speakeasy experience for your underage clientele."

"Hey, I'm letting you go look for your daughter. Get her out of here as soon as you can and we can pretend this never happened. Start talking about bringing police here and we're going to have an issue."

"I just want to find her."

Archie held the railing to descend the steep steps. They had to be murder in heels and were definitely not made for anyone but the young and able.

In the annex, he tried to be inconspicuous, but there was only so much an older, mortal, tall black man in police drab could blend among the goth and Gatsby crowd, so he mostly stuck to shadows while he skimmed the crowd to find Lis—not easy, when her head would be *lower* than most everyone else's.

He finally found her at the bar, getting a sangria while her vampire companion accepted a glass of actual blood in a red wine glass and her werewolf companion asked for a dark beer and ordered several things off the menu. The bartender didn't card Lis, either.

He understood the unique dilemma of an establishment that catered to vampires who didn't age and whose IDs often had to be changed. Vampires didn't generally turn children, but adolescence had been a murkier area a hundred years ago, and the last thing an immortal teenager wanted was to be perpetually regarded as a teenager.

Archie understood but was unsympathetic, because his ward was being led from the bar to one of the private booths on the edge of the room, and the music from dueling string instruments on stage didn't drown out the kind of activity that preferred that kind of privacy.

Lis, so help me God...

The vampire closed the curtain. Archie clenched his fists.

* * * *

Lis couldn't remember the last time she'd worn a dress. It was entirely possible she hadn't worn one since her father had died. Some hunters lured with the 'helpless, vulnerable damsel in distress' disguise, but Lis didn't have to work that hard to look helpless and vulnerable without adding feminine to the list.

She felt like there was too much air on her. And as little as she'd recognized herself in the motel mirror, she recognized herself even less looking down now. The cut of the V-neck was too low for a bra — or to hide a pocketknife. Her breasts over the neckline moved when she walked. The bodice beneath was by and large structured like a corset, which at least gave her somewhere to strap her knives, but they wouldn't be very accessible unless someone ripped the dress off.

She was smaller than Rose, so the dress she'd offered Lis had to have been bought *for* her, a concept she couldn't wrap her head around.

And her feet were smaller than Rose's, so Rose had also bought shoes based on the size of her boots. Despite all the balance Lis used scaling roof edges and fences and fighting in a crouch, she struggled getting used to a two-and-a-half-inch heel, although Rose walked in over three inches without effort.

Constriction in her clothes was nothing new — between straps, body armor, and spandex — but tonight she'd pared down from three layers to one and didn't know how to walk, stand, or sit with a skirt that ended so far up her thigh that the blade on the outside of her left thigh was visible. Other women's skirts were even shorter, but Lis wore long pants year-round. Anything above her knee was too short, too exposed, and too dangerous in her line of work.

She was so used to being confused for a child — and encouraging the confusion — but whenever she caught sight of herself tonight, she saw an adult's body, the bodice calling attention to the fact that she had breasts, that she had a small waist, and broad hips, thighs, and calves thick with muscle on her comparatively small frame. Her bare arms — no blades on her forearms — showed off muscle there, too.

Rose had expressed admiration at how she'd worked so much harder to look the way she did in comparison to Rose's or Simon's supernatural enhancements. Lis had countered that she didn't work hard to look good. She worked hard not to die.

"And that's something most people will never understand. But that doesn't mean you shouldn't be proud of the results," Rose had replied.

Simon had kissed her strong thighs while Rose had completed the look with basic makeup and simple hair. By the time Rose had finished, Lis' underwear had born the telltale dampness of her arousal. Simon had breathed her in but withdrawn to pull on the last of his ensemble while Rose went through her own makeup routine.

Now, Lis fought not to pull down the hem of the clinging skirt as she sat in the booth. Shadows alone would obscure what keeping her thighs pressed together didn't, but the sangria was already making her relax, which she worried might translate to letting her legs part in a position more natural to her.

Simon nudged her playfully with his shoulder. "Is it the drink, the dress, the crowd, or the music that's got you so uptight?"

"Yes."

Rose slipped in closer on her other side. "This is supposed to be fun. And private."

But Lis heard what was happening in other so-called private booths, and she flushed at the thought of being heard, too. That Rose and Simon had heard her multiple times the previous night was already enough to leave her in a fever without adding perfect strangers to the mix.

"That other people know what's happening is half the pleasure," Rose explained. "But no one cares, Lis. This place was made for people to enjoy sharing their space with vampires and werewolves. A certain amount of horniness is expected and encouraged. If you get really uncomfortable, there are small rooms in back. Small rooms, with one small bed, the three of us cozy and making the mattress springs creak. You can be as loud as you need to be."

Simon kissed her neck under her ear, curling his fingers under her knee to tickle her, then sliding his way up her thigh, under her skirt. He paused at the garter strap, but the knife was on the outside of her thigh and not dangerous to him — yet.

"A new experience," Simon whispered. "Enjoy the music, the drink, the food, and later we'll dance, and I think you'll have such a nice time. You can relax. It's safe here. The blood-letting and sex is entirely consensual, no one gets hunted, no one gets hurt — more than they ask for." He bit her jaw, then licked the dents left by his sharper teeth. "Just like when you're with us."

"You can do what you want." Rose sipped on her drink, making her lips redder than usual. "Your whole life doesn't have to just be about *need*, yours or others'. What do you *want*?"

Lis lowered Rose's forearm to convince her to set the wine glass on the table, then drew her closer for a kiss. Most of the blood was gone—a vampire wouldn't let good blood congeal on her lips—but Lis still recognized it on her tongue, salty and gamey. Although it wasn't her preferred beverage, she didn't mind. She associated the taste with a fight, with aggression, with righteous battle and war wounds.

Rose moaned into her mouth in surprise but closed her eyes and leaned into the kiss, deepening it.

As Lis held Simon's mouth against her neck, she reached down to convince him to stroke her over her underwear, then underneath.

It was amazing how quickly her body responded, which confirmed how much she'd been craving them since she'd woken up that early afternoon, vaguely remembering hot dreams that had soaked her sheets despite the air-conditioning.

After the night before, she couldn't understand how she could still yearn for more, just as intensely as before, her whole head swimming with memory and desire for contact, within and without. So much so that she would agree to any of this—*again*.

When Rose kissed away from Lis' mouth, Simon took over, as though he'd been impatiently waiting for his turn. Kissing him only made her hungrier. She whimpered helplessly into his mouth as he stroked in firm circles over her clit—designed to tantalize, not make her come, although she wanted to, panted for it, tried to cant her hips to encourage him faster, but he groaned and growled into her body and forced her to sink back into the sensations.

Then Rose pushed one of Lis' dress straps down, baring her breast, and closed her blood-warmed mouth over Lis' nipple while her fangs slid out on either side. When they pricked the skin, Lis surged up against them, and Rose sucked fresher blood, albeit a thinner stream than she could swallow from the glass.

Lis didn't come immediately, but she nearly sobbed into Simon's kiss as he quickened his fingers over her.

"May I enter?" a young man called from the other side of the curtain.

Rose withdrew from Lis' breast, new blood on her lips and seeping into the wells left by her teeth. The shallow wounds stung without the thrall turning pain to pleasure. Lis gripped Rose's arm as she pushed herself to the end of the booth bench, but Rose slipped out of reach to part the curtain, leaving Lis exposed, her legs parted, her bleeding breast bare to the server's gaze, and Simon still stroking her, although he'd paused their kiss.

The server looked, registered what he saw, and maintained an even demeanor, but he did look again, his tray teetering slightly. However, such sights were probably so common that it barely interrupted his day. He set the tray on their table to dole out the dishes of sushi, sashimi, beef tartare, and fried okra.

"Thank you," Rose said politely, as though nothing were strange or supernatural about the tableau.

The server withdrew with the tray. Rose closed the curtain behind him.

"No one cares," she repeated as she pushed herself back over the vinyl to eagerly feed once more from Lis' breast.

Pleasure rushed in over pain before she was ready, and she came before Simon could kiss her again.

He kissed her through her aftershocks instead, stroking steadily until she shuddered from over-stimulation. Then he gathered her arousal and tasted *her*, sucking his fingers into his mouth until they glistened. Rose licked the wounds on Lis' breast closed, her skin otherwise clean enough to replace the dress fabric to cover her.

All at once, Lis was in the same state she'd been before they'd entered the booth, but she felt like a hot, melted mess. She adjusted herself into something approaching appropriate as Simon gathered tartare onto a toast point and enjoyed some of the fried okra.

"Have you ever had sushi?" he asked.

"Never had raw meat. I've always been told it's not safe unless it's cooked."

"Sushi and sashimi are perfectly safe if prepared properly." He arranged some of the raw fish on her dish with soy sauce, then added some fried okra as well, which had been Lis' contribution to the order. "In the interest of your adventure into new experiences. I prefer the tartare to seafood, but the kitchen is limited in the kinds of raw meat they can provide. They're already pushing it by serving real blood on the premises."

Lis bent down to sniff her sushi. "It doesn't smell much like fish."

"If it's good, it shouldn't," Rose said, serving herself a selection of raw meat as well.

Lis opened her chopsticks, removed the splinters, then poised to pick up a roll when she noticed Rose and Simon both a tad surprised.

"My mentor and I eat a lot of Chinese and Thai. He just doesn't trust sushi in the places where we live," Lis explained.

Rose nodded. "Fair."

"But I knew how to use chopsticks before he started training me." She dipped a tuna roll in the soy sauce. "To adventure."

* * * *

Lis decided she liked sangria, sushi, and sashimi but not beef tartare. She also learned that, though she trained for fighting to an eight count, she didn't know how to dance. She rarely moved to music when listening to it, and she hadn't gone to school since she was seven, so there'd been no school dances, no sense of what music was popular, no dance lessons, not so much as marching band. Her hips simply couldn't sway. Rose tsked as she tried to teach. Eventually, Simon made Rose give up and told Lis to take things one day at a time. He showed her how to slow dance instead, which demanded much less sinuous movement.

While Lis pressed against Simon, her head against his chest and her arms around his waist, she could watch Rose sway near them to the trance-like music of the string players. The viola player was Chinese, the cello player Japanese, and the cello player sang, too, sometimes with lyrics and sometimes just startlingly evocative notes. Rose closed her eyes and seemed like their music made flesh. The golden stage light turned all of her to gold, not just her dress, like a Midas statue.

Lis still wasn't sure how she felt about Rose or even Simon, but to be fair, she didn't know how to feel about a lot of things, including how she liked raw fish, so she decided to focus instead on letting herself feel at all.

Although she enjoyed non-hunting activities during the day, they always had *purpose*. Reading was for enrichment and education, watching TV or movies was for unwinding, sleep was restorative, the food she ate was to strengthen her body, and the training was for warming up before she went out to do what she oriented her entire life around.

Nothing she did with Simon and Rose had anything to do with being a hunter. It was as though she'd spent most of her life walking along a solid pier, then stepped out onto the water to find it holding her, too.

They ate, they danced, they drank. Lis just had the one sangria. After the glass of blood and the drink from Lis' breast, Rose had a sangria of her own. Simon caved to peer pressure. Then they danced some more, with a few members of Simon's pack joining after they recognized him. He introduced them to her and to Rose. Although they were effusive with Simon, using their whole bodies in affection and enthusiasm, they were respectful of Rose and Lis, particularly Lis when she showed no sign of wanting to shake hands or hug, although Rose did.

They stayed until two in the morning, when the string duo took their second break. The speakeasy closed at four, but Lis was tired, less from dancing and more from the *muchness* of everything. Most nights, she was a machine. Tonight, she'd been human, and as it turned out, that whole part of her was rusty.

And she didn't know how to feel about that either.

But she simmered with the same anger and frustration that came to Rose so easily when she talked or was clearly thinking about Archie.

Lis had assumed that Archie had made a great number of concessions back when she'd first resisted to bending over backward to save the world every night without enough ways to relieve some of the pressure.

Now she'd experienced a *tiny* fraction of what else was out there in the world. She supposed she'd known some of it, but that had been from books or on television screens, to the point where it all had seemed like escapist fiction, not easily accessible in real life. But here she was, wearing a costume and eating new things and spending time around people Archie wanted her to kill.

She knew what he would say — that she'd been blinded by hormones. But it wasn't just Rose and Simon. *All* the people here were perfectly nice, and enough of them kind. They didn't seem to go through their lives looking over their shoulders or peering into corners expecting something dangerous in the shadows there, and it wasn't because they were the dangerous ones.

They were from a completely different world than the one she lived in — not just the difference between an abandoned neighborhood and a supported one. A whole different mentality. Lis didn't know if she'd ever seen so many smiles in one place.

That was why Archie hadn't let her into this world and had instead kept her separate, alienated, isolated, focused.

In training a soldier in a spiritual war, his decision made perfect sense. Everything he did was to make her a better hunter, and the last thing she needed to do while patrolling was wish she were somewhere else, think about what she was going to do with friends next evening while her mind needed to be absolutely present against the immediate, fatal threat around her.

Better for her to have no ambition or aspiration, for the motels and long walks and blood draws and roach motels to be just part of cold, hard life, so she would never strive for better.

She was a hunter, a remedy for evil, and that meant sacrifice. She understood that. And most nights, she'd accepted it as the price of keeping people safe.

But now, despite dancing in a basement, she had the high ground to look back at her life and see how much of what she'd lost had, in fact, been taken from her. She'd agreed to go with Archie after her dad had died because she'd been seven fucking years old and he'd been a fucking grown-up willing to take care of her when she'd been afraid to go home to her mother after what had happened. She'd done the training because he'd told her to do it. She'd fought her way through alleys at ten to survive the scenario that Archie had put her into. And she'd committed to a hunter's life at twelve because she'd been solemn and serious and submerged in the life for so long that she'd thought she was mature enough to make that decision. She *had* been responsible, and strong, but she hadn't really understood what she'd been giving up.

She knew why Archie had done what he'd done. He'd wanted to build a better hunter, and he had. But he'd also built a pretty shitty human, made for nothing but dystopia. In just the last week, she'd been shown over and over again that she mattered regardless of what she did for the world. That it was okay to have good sex and enjoy raw salmon and let music go through her body like Simon's growls. That it was okay to want more than rearranging a motel room, with its ancient mattresses and mildew. That it was okay now and then to take off her armor and put on a dress.

Because she wasn't a one-hunter savior in the apocalypse. There were always more demons and monsters to hunt the next night and the next, no matter how many she killed. As much as she wanted to save people, it wasn't her responsibility to save *everyone*.

Now the question was what she was going to do with that information.

She could continue sneaking around at night, but frankly, she was almost twenty-three, a grown-ass woman, and she shouldn't need to sneak around.

Archie wouldn't accept anything less than full commitment. Which meant she had to start thinking about the possibility of leaving him.

And she simply couldn't imagine that.

Archie had been part of her life for fifteen years. He cared for her. He'd put sweat, blood, and tears into training her to be able to protect herself from the world's monsters. True, he used her sweat, blood, and tears in his spells, but those spells were helpful to them both. He'd believed that a child could save herself and others. He'd believed that someone who hadn't grown much taller than when he'd found her could still hold her own against monsters bigger than him. For better or worse, he'd shaped her life more than her own family, who were like a hazy memory of a dream in comparison to the clear reality of her mentor.

She didn't want to leave him. She just wasn't sure, if she pushed back on how he wanted her to do things, she'd have any other choice.

In the parking lot where Rose had left her car, Lis suddenly realized she was walking alone.

Mind in maelstrom, and within the false security of a still-active nightlife, she'd let down her guard, thinking that nothing too dangerous would attack anyone here in plain view of people and cameras.

Lis whirled around, looking for Rose and Simon, who'd been talking and laughing behind her. They were nowhere to be seen, but Rose's Mustang was still in its place about twenty feet away, so they hadn't brought her out here just to ditch her in the middle of historic downtown without money and only heels to walk back home.

Lis lifted her skirt to retrieve the knife. She'd prefer to have two.

"Rose? Simon?"

People were walking down the street to wherever the next club was, but the parking lot itself was nearly empty of people, although still with as many cars as gravestones in a Cemetery Grove cemetery.

Lis crouched, using the cars as shields, but also to change her point of view, searching for shoes or shadows under chasses.

A pair of heels fallen on their side next to a tire caught her attention. Lis recognized them as Rose's, as gold as her dress. Fortunately, the heels still had feet in them, but there was no good reason Lis could come up with why Rose would be lying on dirty, gritty asphalt. There were better places to have rough public sex than between two cars. And the feet weren't moving.

Lis crept forward, still crouched, attuned to all the noise around her and searching for the sound of someone's heels on loose asphalt pebbles.

Crunch, crunch, crunch, crunch...

Behind the cars. Coming closer toward her.

With minimal weaponry, her best course of action was to run and get lost among a crowd rather than cars. But something had incapacitated Rose, possibly Simon. Maybe even killed them. Some*one* had done that, because she hadn't heard their bodies hit the ground, which meant someone had to have caught them, lowered them down, then pulled them almost out of sight, and all nearly indetectable while she'd been distracted.

Her instincts screamed, but she didn't want to believe them, couldn't believe them. Until she reached Rose's unmoving body. A tranquilizer dart stuck out of her shoulder.

"Rose?"

Lis looked up at movement in the shadows and saw wide white eyes and the topography of a face she recognized all too well right before a tranquilizer dart hit her, too. She barely had enough time to worry that he'd used one of the same darts they used for demons and overdosed her before she pitched forward and lost consciousness.

Chapter Thirteen

Lis woke to jangling chains and bright colors, despite the new-moon night. Some artificial light came in through open windows, but, based on the darkness beyond it, they were out of the heart of the city. Then she recognized one of the propped-open stained-glass scenes.

Her hands were duct-taped behind her back, her ankles bound together, shoes off. A strip of tape also kept her from calling out, but she didn't really need to. Rose and Simon were right there, chains attached to their arms by silver-lined shackles. Archie usually added one around the neck for convenient decapitation, but he'd clearly been improvising. Given how awake Rose and Simon were, they'd started gaining consciousness before he could get them to wherever he usually did his experiments on demons. That wasn't something Lis participated in, other than providing demon parts and her own hunter's blood.

She'd only known about the chains because she'd packed them when they'd traveled.

These weren't his usual sets, which he'd probably attached and reinforced in his own facility. These must have been spares he kept in the trunk with his carjack and tire iron, just in case. They were basically just a chain linking two wrist shackles.

Archie had apparently been unable to fasten them to anything in the open sanctuary. So he'd improvised again, winding the chains around the steeple from open window to open window, depending on the brick and beam structure to hold a werewolf and a vampire.

As improvisations went, it wasn't the worst, especially since, with all the stained-glass windows open, sun exposure would also put the vampire at risk.

The cushions and blankets from the tower were gone. Either Rose had removed them for cleaning or Archie had needed to give himself a larger area to work and walk in. The lamp had been switched on so Archie could see. Lis had been arranged as comfortably as possible in the armchair.

Rose and Simon looked up as Lis tried to maneuver her wrists to get one hand out, but the flexibility of the tape worked against her.

"You okay?" Rose asked quietly, almost a whisper.

Lis nodded. Other than being tranquilized by her mentor, then bound and gagged, plus a little dizziness, she was fine.

"All things considered, so are we," Simon said. "Although the silver allergy's a bitch." He held up his wrists, which had broken out in a bright red rash. "I'm a little worried that the hunter *didn't* kill us, though."

"I think he's pissed we corrupted his daughter," Rose said.

"Oh shit. That's her dad?"

Close enough.

"I don't think he's still here. The front door closed, and I can't hear him anymore," Rose said. "Lis, can you get out of that? Because we can't get out of this. Simon tried. That's why he looks like he lost a battle with poison ivy. Turns out they really knew how to construct a clock tower in the seventies."

Lis continued moving her ankles and wrists in a back-and-forth motion, but aside from sweat making some of the adhesive less sticky, it accomplished little. Her breathing quickened with rising panic—not for herself but for Rose and Simon. She had no idea what Archie was going to do with them, if killing wasn't the worst thing he could do.

"Lis, breathe," Rose instructed. "Panicking isn't going to help. If you start breathing properly, you'll get some oxygen to your brain, and then you might be able to think of an alternative. Did he ever give you any training how to get out of duct tape?"

Archie actually hadn't taught her how to get out of bindings, although in retrospect it might have been a good lesson, considering the kinds of humans who harassed her. But she'd read once how to get out of zip ties. It required the friction of shoelaces, and hands tied in front would have been better. Nevertheless...

She twisted her wrists instead of rubbing them back and forth. Then she maneuvered on the chair so that she was curled up like she wanted to sleep. With all her crouching experience, she could bring her knees up to her chest. If she'd still had her shoes on, she could have used the heel as a catch. Instead, she slowly worked her arms under her ass by arching her back, then inched her hands over her buttocks until they finally crossed the point where her shoulders were screaming at her that she couldn't reach, couldn't stretch any more without dislocating. She cried out as something strained, but her bone stayed in socket, and she brought her hands around to the front, where she pulled the duct tape off her mouth, although not off her cheek.

"How long ago did he leave?" Lis asked.

"Maybe twenty minutes," Rose said.

If he was walking, she had another twenty minutes. If he was driving, she didn't have any time left.

"Lis, what's his plan?" Rose said, audibly tense.

"He experiments."

Lis manipulated one of her hands into her bodice. Archie had taken the knife from her thigh holster but left the ones strapped around her middle. Maybe the dress' structure had camouflaged them. Maybe he hadn't thought she'd be able to get into a position to recover them. Or maybe he just hadn't wanted to undress her to retrieve them, although he wouldn't have cared about doing that to a demon.

"The fuck you do mean 'experiments'?" Simon said, rubbing his skin through his shirt to keep from scratching.

"I mean he taught me how to be a hunter because he can't do it the same way anymore, so he experiments on demons and hybrids with whatever magic he's researching. His specialty is blood magic. We came to Meridian hoping to find some specific texts, and I think he recently found one. Or found one better. Gotcha." Lis pulled out one of her silver knives and immediately worked to break through the tape at her wrists.

She managed to cut through the wrist bindings, then started on the part of the bindings behind her ankles.

The double doors below slammed shut.

"Fuck." Lis didn't swear much—Archie had been strict about that—but it seemed to sum up the problem.

"Tell me you can fight him," Rose said.

Lis shrugged while she kept sawing. They trained together, so she knew all his moves and he knew all of hers. He was permanently injured, but she was half his size and without shoes. And she didn't know whether she could actually fight him with the intent to seriously injure him. Nor did she know whether he would hold back, not if he thought she was irreparably compromised.

"Lis…"

"I'm trying," she whispered back. Archie had been more generous with tape around her legs.

The stairs leading up to the tower creaked.

Lis jumped back onto the chair and lay longways across the arms, like she'd toppled over while struggling, so that she could hide where the tape had been cut through. Before she put her arms behind her again, she plastered the duct tape across her mouth, then hid her knife in her clasped hands.

"*The blood is the life, thus sayeth the Lord. And so the breath formed the Word and the Word breathed into flesh and, within flesh, blood flowed to the rhythm of the Word. Where one drop of blood falls, the Word whispers, and so the Word is in all things of flesh, all that must breathe or bleed.*" Archie continued creaking the stairs while he climbed and recited. "*As blood sacrifice wipes clean the slates of sin, so sin can be bound with blood. And as sin binds with blood, so too can all who sin.* Turns out that with the right combination of blood and ritual, I can do what I've been trying to do for years, Lis. And I'd say not a moment too soon, except you and I both know I might be too late."

At the top of the stairs, Archie stared straight at her in the lamplight. He didn't spare the werewolf and vampire even a glance.

Simon strained against his chains to kick out his long leg and catch Archie at his shin. Archie sprawled forward with his bag and the old book he carried, but he recovered quickly, grabbing the baton from his belt and extending it to strike Simon across the face with three brisk, sharp blows that sent Simon back against the wall, eyes unfocused and blood dripping from his nose and mouth.

Lis protested against the duct tape, hating that she had to fake struggling while Simon really suffered. But as a werewolf, he would heal. He would even regrow the teeth he spat out onto the slats.

Archie pulled out a small aerosol can from a custom holster. Lis didn't have to read the label to know it was his standard paralyzing potion, which he sprayed in Simon's bleeding, swelling face.

Then he leaned in, absolutely certain of his safety as Simon froze. "You're lucky I want you alive a little while longer."

He pointed the can at Rose. "You going to cause me more problems than you have already?"

Rose slowly shook her head. Fear wasn't the only emotion in her eyes.

Archie put the baton and aerosol can back in their places and approached Lis. He lifted her chin, then took her by the arms to help her back upright. As soon as she was sitting up, he sighed, then slapped her across her cheek. When she'd recovered from the surprise, he did it again, harder.

"Look what you've made me do." He arranged her back up again, seemingly unaffected by Lis' tears. Just surprised by the sting. She wasn't crying. "I'm not a hundred percent sure this is going to work, but you've not only forced me to discard your blood, I've had to accelerate my timeline. What better subjects, though, to demonstrate the concept than the monsters who told my girl it was okay to be evil?"

He pulled off the tape on Lis' mouth. He didn't seem to notice it was looser than it should have been.

Lis didn't protest, didn't ask what he was doing, didn't beg, didn't weep, didn't say a word. She just glared, her lips thin and tingling from the tape.

Archie tossed the tape aside, then straightened. "What were you thinking, Elisabet? You have *one job*. You're the exterminator. Does an exterminator decide that this cockroach or that cockroach can live, or does it eradicate every vermin in the house? There are no exceptions. There are no alliances. There are humans and there are demons. Any demon that walks this earth is a risk for any human. Do you realize the blood you might have on your hands by letting them live?"

"They don't kill," Lis said.

"So they *say*. For God's sake, you know better than this. You're smarter than them. What, they show you a good time, and suddenly you think they're saints?"

"They don't kill," Lis repeated. "We kill monsters so that they won't kill humans. Well, they don't kill humans. So what the *hell* should I kill them for?"

"It's just a matter of time! My God, I can't believe I have to explain this to you again."

"I'm not going to kill people who promise not to hurt people based on the premise that they *might*," Lis said. "That's ludicrous."

"Do I need to show you pictures of werewolf murders again? Do I need to serve you to a vampire less inclined to play games, just so you understand the stakes?" Archie asked. "Regardless of what they do, regardless of what they say, they're monsters. Killing them is spraying pesticide to prevent the infestation."

"Why don't we just wipe out the whole Wastelands, then, since the police and the city abandoned them to the infestation? But can you imagine if justice was codified by the crime you *might* commit? I can't do this anymore, Archie! I'm fine, just fucking fine, saving people who need to be saved, but you can't sell me this 'humans good, monsters bad' bullshit anymore."

"What did you just say to me?" Archie asked, deathly quiet.

She knew that was a bad sign and didn't give a crap. Her friends were bound and she was bound, and he was the one who'd done that to them. He'd hit her with a tranquilizer gun because he'd known she wouldn't go quietly, because he'd known that was the only way he could control her, and he had no right to do that to her anymore, if he ever had. He was too used to having his way, because his way had usually been her way, too. There hadn't been too much occasion for friction.

But at the first shock of static electricity, he'd resorted to duct tape, and Lis didn't like that at all.

"The demons I kill in the Wastelands, or in whatever shithole you put me in, they're scavenging predators taking advantage of other people's desperation. But about five to ten percent of what I have to fight are human. We've never discussed what sometimes puts me in the hospital. We've never discussed what I sometimes have to do to people with a pulse. You don't want to see it. You don't want to know. But you put me out there as a hunter, knowing there are predators of all kinds. You trusted that you'd given me all the training

I needed. And most of the time, I either started the fight or finished it. But *you* just showed how I can't always fight back. And of the three people in this room, *you're* the only one who attacked me."

Archie knelt in front of her. She could kick out her partially bound legs and perhaps do some damage, but he could just paralyze her in retaliation, and she might call attention to the fact she'd sawn through part of the tape at her ankles.

"If the fact you've blatantly gone against whole tenets of being a hunter wasn't enough, I have proof they've corrupted you. I knew to follow you because I tried to use your blood for the analgesic potion. Imagine my surprise when, from one week to the next, its effectiveness went from decent to nothing. So I follow you, and you're not hunting vampires. You're going to a vampire bar and fucking one. And then you have the teenage-girl audacity to tell me that trying to get you out of that situation is the problem here."

"Wait, wait, wait, wait... You use her blood for your pain relief?" Rose asked in disbelief.

"Stay out of this, demon," Archie snapped.

"His area of research is blood magic," Lis reminded her. "He has a pain potion that requires young blood."

"Oh my God, you're one of those people, the ones who use young blood to make them younger," Rose said. "You know what they like to call them? Vampires."

"The pain potion requires blood as a binding agent for the magic. It's incredibly common," Archie said, clearly annoyed at having to clarify.

"He uses it with my permission, Rose," Lis said.

Archie rolled his eyes, then pulled himself back to his feet with the arm of the chair.

"But it's not just young blood you need, is it?" Rose narrowed her eyes. "It didn't lose its efficacy because she got older. You knew she'd been 'corrupted' because it stopped working between last week and this week, after she'd had sex with us. Which means the potion requires virgin blood. But you didn't tell her that part, did you?"

Lis looked from Rose to Archie, who fought against shame because, given the situation he'd bound her in, he obviously thought he didn't deserve to feel ashamed. She'd given that blood to him willingly. If he'd told her it would only work because she was a virgin rather than because she kept her hunter's spirit pure, she might still have given it to him willingly, then met his eyes in shame of her own after her first time. Except...

"Last night wasn't the first time," Lis said. "I've had sex before. Last night was just the first time I—"

"Apparently, he only takes umbrage when the potion is utterly useless to him," Rose said. "It didn't matter as long as you were having bad sex, incomplete, and the potion still had some effectiveness. It was good sex that crossed the line for him. That was the kind of sex he had to go investigate and castigate you for having."

"It wasn't the sex I was going to castigate her for. I followed her expecting to find some long, lanky emo kid playing Romeo to Lis' Juliet. What warrants all this"—Archie gestured to the steeple tower and the chains—"is you two. Because she's so smitten that she doesn't realize she's walked right into the spider's parlor."

"Of course I knew," Lis replied. "I've been careful the whole way. They've been very kind, very respectful, and not once have they lied to me, which is more than I can say for you. I can't believe you kept information about *my* blood from me. This whole time, you could 'monitor' my sexual status by the effectiveness of your pain potion? How could you put that on my shoulders and not even tell me?"

"You knew how I felt about sex as a distraction, but I didn't tell you because I *didn't* want to put that on you. I knew this was going to happen eventually, that letting you go out on your own at night lends itself to a certain exploration. I didn't talk about it because it's uncomfortable and I'm *not* your father. What I didn't know was that it would be with the very monsters you're supposed to eliminate and that, in a matter of days, you'd spout the bleeding-heart sentiments of the most rank, cynical, money-grubbing hunters for your own convenience. And here I am, having to explain myself because the same enchantress who's been turning your head is muddying the waters, trying to put me on the defensive even while she's in chains. But I'm not going to do that."

He turned toward the vampire and pulled out his paralysis potion.

Rose didn't flinch, despite the fact she was still chained, and despite the fact Simon remained frozen in place, his frightened gaze darting from person to person. "You're absolutely right. I'm a killer. I'm dangerous."

Archie paused with the can poised in her direction.

"But there's not a person in this room that doesn't apply to," she continued. "And of the four of us, you're the only one who wants to do any harm. To you, a monster is a monster. Well, neither Simon nor I started out that way. We were pure human once, and we're only a little demonic now. But we've still got our free will. We can choose what we do. That's what matters — what we *do*, not what we *are*."

Archie put his aerosol can back in its holster, but he still towered over her with disdain. "'A little demonic.' Even a little is as corrosive as acid to the soul. You can pretend you've created this little demon-human utopia in Meridian, but *everything* you do, even when not killing people, acts in the interest of the demonic. If there's one thing you learn in blood magic, it's how what you are is present in a single drop. You can't make yourself less of a vampire by wishing. But I can make you more of one."

"Excuse me?"

Archie backed toward where he had dropped his large leather-bound book, then brought it to a lectern he must have rescued from church storage. He arranged the lectern in front of the one stained glass window he hadn't opened. Then he propped the book open to a page three-quarters of the way through and retrieved from a cardboard box in the corner two glass jars of viscous liquid so dark red it was almost black.

"This potion strips any ill-gotten humanity from a hybrid, leaving behind only the violent animal that you are. If that's all I manage to accomplish tonight, I'll still count it a success, because Lis will have no choice but to kill you. But if *this* works…" He placed his hand on the open pages with reverence. "If this works, the monster in your blood will bind to every other monster of the same kind in the city — maybe not the whole city or its surrounding suburbs, but everything within a certain radius. If I activate this potion with your blood and this potion with his, spray it on you, then complete this invocation, it will render every vampire and werewolf in Meridian exactly what they are — without your pretensions of human decency."

Rose's mouth hung open like she wanted to speak but couldn't find the words. Then she abruptly jangled the chains, scissoring them against the brick and billowing brick dust in the air.

Archie extended his baton again, a syringe in his other hand ready to take blood, then stepped forward.

Lis kicked her still partially bound feet forward on the armchair to rock herself standing. She parted her wrists to jump on Archie's back, arms around his neck to throttle him from behind. However, her inability to break the rest of the tape around her lower legs through sheer will meant she couldn't take some of her own weight while her knees squeezed his hips. That albeit slight weight nevertheless upset his balance and sent both of them slamming against window and wall — not enough to break glass but enough to jostle Lis' brain. Between the sedative and the head blow, she fought not to let go and give Archie the upper hand.

She pressed her mouth to his ear to ensure he could hear her clearly. "*You're* a monster."

She couldn't aim from this angle, but she plunged the knife in her hand into his chest.

Archie shouted, although the stab was shallow. He tried to catch her with his elbow, but she was out of his reach that way. So he grabbed her by her hair and dress and bent to fling her forward over his shoulder. She landed on the floor, her knife jolting loose from the impact.

He grimaced against the strain on his back, but he could stand and level a kick into her abdomen to steal her breath, like when she'd first met Rose in the alley.

And without breath, Lis was helpless as he grabbed her by her arms to lift her up again.

"I hope you understand that I do all of this for you. For your own good."

Then he whirled around and smacked her head on the glass once more.

Chapter Fourteen

Rose hid Lis' silver knife under her skirt while the hunter kneeled next to Lis to check her vitals. Satisfied, he propped her sitting against the wall this time.

"There's no such thing as a safe head wound," Rose said. But when she listened hard enough, Lis' heartbeat was steady and resting.

"I'll take her to the clinic when this is over. Once she understands."

"Once she's on your side again, you mean."

"You've known her for less than a week. I raised her from a child."

"You raised her to be a hunter. No self-respecting hunter father would choose that for their children. Giving them knowledge of the paranormal dangers and how to defend themselves — that, I understand. But how could you take a child of seven and put her out there to do battle in your place? Experimentation on demons...deplorable, but you don't see them as people, so that makes sense. Experimentation on a little girl is beyond the pale."

The hunter moved his lips as he went over the recitation on the pages and double-checked that he had everything he needed for the jar labeled *Vampire*.

"I don't doubt your devotion to her," Rose continued, more gently, "misguided though the execution. But you could have seriously damaged her just now, for the simple crime that she doesn't see from your point of view."

"Between body and soul, I will always be more concerned about the latter. You pretend that everything you've done has been for her, but I know what you and your kind do. You're just a step down from sex demons. You've used sex, the venom of gentleness, the masks of mercy, to make her think you're to be trusted. It's not the demon that's the most dangerous part of you, vampire. You wrap your danger in a pretty, seductive, compelling human package. Meridian is a demon's paradise. No one *sees* you, and because they don't see, they can't protect themselves. This is my fault more than yours, for keeping her in places where the distinction between monster and man is more apparent."

"It stands to logic that if there are men who are monsters, there are monsters who are not," Rose said. "It's true that my blood marks me as a vampire by any measure, and my instincts tell me to make man my prey." She carefully found the handle of the blade. She didn't know how to use it with the experience of a hardened hunter, but she would do something when she could. "We are more than our genetic destiny, hunter. You had to learn to be a killer. You had to teach Lis to become one. And I had to decide not to be a killer.

I'll bet Lis has killed more humans than I have, just in self-defense."

Archie picked up his baton again, and the syringe. He strode toward Rose, his limp and the stiffness in his back more pronounced after the unexpected fight.

Rose tried to throw the knife at him, but the jingling chain telegraphed the throw. Archie knocked it to the side with his thick coat. He kept himself out of her arm's reach so that she couldn't claw or bite as he struck her over the side of her head and her face with the baton, like he had with Simon. While she was stunned, her eyes rolling from vertigo, he stuck the syringe into her neck, drawing out thick, dark blood before she could recover.

"The moral relativism that spews from convincing mouths is more lethal than teeth, you leech," he said quietly.

"And your moral absolutism is reprehensible." Her vehemence lost a little something in the slurring as she recovered from the head injury. "You consider Simon and me evil no matter what we do, even though we choose not to hurt people. But when you fundamentally change hybrids to their most predatory traits, *you're* going to kill innocents. *You're* going to destroy this city. And you think that makes you good."

"I fight demons. That is all that matters."

"At what cost?" Rose asked. "A man does magic and says it's from God, they call it miracles. A woman does magic by her own power, they hang her for a witch. Did you *ever* stop to wonder if the demons you fight even did what you're killing them for, or would that just make your job too complicated?"

"Complicated." He scoffed with a humorless laugh. "The Alliance exists, my dear, not because hunters really think you can be good, but because it lessens how many demons they have to sift through. We'll see how 'convenient' it is to let demons decide to make themselves off-limits when vampires and werewolves are ripping off heads."

"You've completely lost the plot. It's going to be a massacre on both sides."

"Such is war."

"Just because you're a soldier doesn't mean everyone is fighting a war!" Rose pulled on her chains again, trying to ignore the hiss of her skin when she pressed too hard against the silver. "Not everything is a goddamn nail to your hammer. People are going to die! You're going to be responsible for the deaths of thousands, maybe even tens of thousands. And you're going to do this other places, aren't you? How long do you think you can knock Lis out like a caveman for her to stay by your side? How long until a coma is the only way to keep her?"

"Lis is a pragmatist. It's part of the reason you got your hooks into her with the whole Alliance concept," the hunter replied, injecting Rose's blood into the jar. "When vampires and werewolves are killing people as their natures intended, she won't let them keep killing just because she's mad at me. She'll do her duty. She'll have to change some of her methods. She'll have to become more comfortable with guns. But she'll do what is necessary. That's why, after I make what you and your wolf are abundantly clear, she'll be the one to kill you. She won't even hesitate."

The hunter spoke with confidence about everything, comfortable and comforted in his black and white world. But about Lis, Rose had no doubt that he was correct. The only reason Lis had agreed to give the

Alliance a chance was because Rose and Simon were not immediate threats. Make them immediate threats, and Lis would put those threats down. Simple as that.

Which was the point. The hunter wanted to make things as simple as he saw them, even if he had to cast the blood-binding equivalent of a nuclear bomb to accomplish it.

This wasn't just a hunter with a mission. He was a one-man cult with a single wayward follower. And for all her power, for all her choices and changes, Rose could do nothing to stop him. She was utterly thwarted by silver, steel, and solid brick.

The hunter took some blood from Simon as well, while he was just beginning to break free from the paralysis. After injecting Simon's blood into the jar labeled *Werewolf*, the hunter rolled up his sleeve to draw from a vein of his own with a fresh syringe. So virginity had nothing to do with this blood spell, which eliminated that obstacle. Rose tightened her fists helplessly against the onslaught of fresh, dripping human blood—and something she couldn't define, something almost bitter that didn't smell right, not even for age, with which she was intimately familiar, or illness, which often accompanied age. Not degeneration, not cancer, not poison. She couldn't discern its origin or its cause, but it didn't seem to do anything to the potion that Archie didn't expect.

When he was finished, he held his hands over the jars.

Rose's whole body seemed to sink while sitting still.

"From consecrated hands, bind blood to blood, kind to kind. Remove impurity, remove costume, remove seem, until all bound become as they are, soil to star, within my power, and with blood both freely and unfreely given. As blood

coagulates crystalline, make of devoted and impure blood a pall upon God's earth, for the edification of man."

Rose had thought she'd found her haven and someone she could help, someone she could love as something more than what they could give. But all her pursuits for better had led to this — a man refusing to bow to reality and instead using magic to make reality bend to him. And she had accelerated it, by seducing — quite innocently — his ward. Lis hadn't been corrupted. She hadn't lost her innocence. She'd simply taken what the rules of blood magic determined was a final stage of leaving childhood behind.

Lis, wake up. Please. Please, God, don't let him succeed. Don't let us lose ourselves.

"Rose..." Simon managed. Even though they couldn't touch each other, he reached for her and she reached for him.

The hunter poured the liquid from the vampire jar into an aerosol can also labeled *Vampire* and the liquid from the werewolf jar into the *Werewolf* can. Then he pointed each of the cans at their respective monster.

"As within, so without. As above, as below, so between."

Lis' eyes shot open. She whipped forward, locked her arm around Archie's good leg, then put all her weight, power, and training into snapping his ankle to the side.

The hunter screamed like she'd torn the whole thing off and fell like a house of cards, dropping the vampire can, which rolled to the side. The fall, too, was at a bad angle that slammed his hip and made him shout again.

Lis grabbed his wrist and smashed it against the floor, then on his face, breaking fingers to keep him from depressing the button at Simon. That can fell from his grip, too. She threw it toward the stairs to clatter down to the main floor.

"I'm not going to let you do this to them. To everyone. To me. Goddammit, stop. Please."

The hunter reached for another aerosol can in his holster, this one unlabeled. She slammed her elbow into his hand in response.

"Let it go," she insisted. "It's over."

He grabbed her by her hair, wrenched her forward, then punched her on the side of her head that he'd smashed against the wall. She fell over him. He flung her off before using the lectern to pull himself up.

Lis, looking paler and greener than usual, rolled onto her back. Her ankles were still mostly bound together, and she couldn't break free without the knife, so she slammed both feet on Archie's knee above the ankle she'd injured. Another series of cracks had the hunter howling, grasping the lectern for dear life to keep from falling again.

"Ungrateful bitch!"

"Myopic bastard." Lis kicked at his other knee when he tried again to reach for something in his jacket.

He went down with a crash. Lis whipped around onto her knees to shuffle forward toward him.

"You cruel, inhuman zealot." She knocked the paralyzing agent from his hand, but he cracked her cheek before she could punch her clasped fists in his face. "You didn't care who got hurt, who got killed, as long as things became 'obvious'."

The hunter managed to get his hands on his gun and pointed it straight at her head, although his hand trembled from pain.

"Fucking child abductor," she spat coldly, eyes narrowed at him as though he were a stranger. "I gave my life to *you*?"

She spun to the side on the floor. The hunter couldn't adjust fast enough, the gun still angled down to where Lis' head no longer was. Lis slammed her shoulder against Archie's arm as the gun went off, sending the bullet into Rose's gut.

It was Rose's turn to scream. Silver wasn't as immediately fatal to her as Simon, but it would still be more resistant to healing. It ripped through her abdomen and buried into the brick behind her. Small mercies that the silver wouldn't linger inside her, not that it felt merciful right then.

"Rose!" Simon shouted, stumbling to his feet and yanking against his chains.

"I'm okay. Don't hurt yourself," she managed through clenched teeth. "Fuck, that burns."

Lis spun again and planted her knee into the hunter's groin, leaving him as briefly paralyzed as Simon had been. Then she held up the aerosol can with vampire blood and pointed it at him.

"You're the monster. You are *not* a good man. I can't let you do this." Lis' tone remained matter-of-fact, but Rose noticed the strangle in the back of her throat, as though Lis struggled to speak through the stone lodged there. "I can't let you hurt innocent people."

His teeth gritted in a rictus of pain and effort, the hunter turned toward Simon and raised his broken hand. "By the blood of —"

"Rose, don't breathe."

Rose managed to stop the automatic but unnecessary process and pressed her mouth and nose against her arm for good measure as Lis depressed the button and sprayed the potion directly into her mentor's face, catching him in the eyes, nose, and open mouth through whatever spell he'd planned to spew at Simon.

Archie screwed his face against the potion, its ingredients fragrantly foul on their own without magic making them more potent. Lis didn't stop spraying until Archie's hisses and coughs of avoidance turned into a rattling shout and he opened his eyes wide despite the spray. The whites of those eyes were viciously red, not the usual little burst of dark capillaries. His skin had gone dusky and ashen, the flesh beneath leaner and the blood vessels more prominent, as though his blood itself had sucked the vitality from him to surge stronger with a rush of oxygen and nutrients, shaking through him like a focused seizure as he lunged to his knees, then struggled to his feet—despite his injuries and that his legs should have no longer held him. Pain alone had ceased to matter. Only mechanical brokenness limited him.

"Lis, look out!" Simon yelled. "He's going to—"

Archie fell on top of Lis, caring little for the way she scratched her nails over his face and punched at him with the empty aerosol can. He grinned madly, showing as many teeth as physically possible for a man still living, as though he had become a premature skull or some violent parody of a reaper.

"If you aren't going to kill them, I've no more use for you, my dear," he snarled. Even his voice was different, desiccated and deep, as though coming from his gut rather than his throat. "You break the rules, you pay the consequences. And the punishment for sin is death, you vile bitch."

Straddling her to hold her down, he managed to get his hands around her neck. His bony, skeletal fingers were implacable. Lis didn't bother trying to fight his grip after the first few seconds struggling.

"You're killing her!" Simon screamed, yanking against his shackles despite the smoke sizzling from his flesh.

While the aerosolized potion was still possibly in the air, invisible, Rose could only watch in horror as Archie transformed beyond words, left with only a lust for eliminating Lis from the world's equation as effectively as an eraser. His laughter was a coyote's howl as he dug his fingers—broken and otherwise—deeper in Lis' neck, threatening to rupture her vessels as well as obstruct.

Panic rising in her expression the more unfamiliar Archie became, Lis desperately rifled through his jacket and trouser pockets like she did with dead demons. When she came up with another knife, possibly one of her own that he'd taken from her, she plunged the blade into the corner of the hunter's eye like a Victorian doctor with a surgical spike.

The hunter's eye popped, and Archie gave the high-pitched anguished cry of a rabbit with its leg caught in a beartrap. He arched backward, releasing Lis to retrieve the knife, but every jostle just caused him more unignorable pain.

Lis yanked him down onto his back by his jacket and slammed her knee into his groin again, then again—harder—giving whatever creature he'd become too many places of crisis so he could address none adequately except to whimper and grimace at her like a zombie who had lost all memory of the man he had been, childlike betrayal sketched across his bloodshot eyes.

Then Lis grabbed the knife handle, put her other hand over it, and used her whole weight bury it completely.

"Shit."

Rose didn't think Simon meant to say it. His lips were pale, like he was about to faint. That he didn't kept Rose from worrying he'd accidentally poisoned himself with the shackles' silver. But between the aerosol spell and whatever the hunter had planned to cast in his direction, his own helplessness couldn't have been an easy pill to swallow. There wasn't much that could stop a werewolf, but this hunter had known all the tricks and a few more. Which meant Lis probably did, too.

Lis fell to the side, breathing hard and deep, staring up at the wooden interior of the steeple. Then, wincing, she sat up to work the rest of the tape off her ankles.

Rose clutched her bullet wound, but she didn't disturb the girl. She'd been drugged, knocked unconscious, then knocked in the head a few more times, before fighting and killing her father figure. Just because Lis had a dearth of expressions didn't mean she had a dearth of feelings. As long as neither Rose nor Simon were in immediate danger, Rose could afford to give Lis some space. Lis didn't heal as fast as them.

Although if she waited much longer, Rose would have to insist that Lis let Simon out so he could get some respite from the silver.

Finally, Lis rolled to the side and started checking Archie's pants pockets — again, quick and methodical from so much experience. She found the shackle key in less than a minute.

Rose pointed her chin toward Simon.

"I'm not the one shot with a silver bullet," Simon protested.

"You're the one who dies with silver in his bloodstream," Lis said, working open the shackles, then pulling them in from the windows. They thudded to the floorboards.

Then she crawled over to Rose, although she swayed on the way and closed her eyes once. Her pupils were uneven. Rose didn't like it.

"I don't suppose you can use his blood anymore, even though he's fresh," Lis said evenly.

Rose shook her head, then chanced a breath. With fresh air circulating from the open windows, the aerosol had dissipated enough that the only blood she smelled was Archie's. That bitterness, however, had intensified and screamed to her animal brain as *poison*.

"It's spoiled. I wouldn't trust what it would do to me, since the potion was keyed to my blood," Rose replied. "I have blood downstairs. Are you going to be okay?" She inspected Lis' neck, which was swelling alarmingly. "Can *you* breathe?"

Lis neither reassured nor dissuaded Rose from touching the strangulation marks. She stared at Archie's body, but as though she couldn't see anything there at all.

Once Rose was sure Lis' windpipe wouldn't close in the next few minutes, she sat back again, wincing against her wound. Sow's blood wouldn't be good enough against the silver damage. She needed human blood somehow, and with Lis looking even worse than Rose or Simon, she wasn't going to ask her to donate.

"What would you prefer we did with the body?" Rose asked, still gentle. "We can hide it. We can put it in a position to be found. We can burn it in a hunter's funeral."

"He'd prefer the cremation," Lis said. "But that's not convenient."

"My closest butcher does cremation. They're not Alliance-approved, though," Rose said. They also would have the kind of blood she needed, unethical though it would be to purchase it.

Lis shook her head. "Just take it to a gutter. The pestilence demons will handle the rest."

"I can take him," Simon said quietly.

"We need to you remove all his paraphernalia first," Rose said. "Given what we know some of it does, I'm not comfortable handing them off to the pestilence demons."

Lis nodded and crawled back to the body. This time, she systematically went through every pocket, including the extra ones sewn into his coat and pants and removed everything from them, storing most in his hunter bag. She also took his wallet, his keyring, the gold and silver cross he wore, and the diamond stud from his ear. The outside stripped, she then searched under his clothes for spare weapons. She found several more guns and knives.

The last weapon she removed was retrieved from his eye and brain. She wiped the goo on his coat.

"Do you need a minute?" Rose asked Lis as Simon shed his clothes. Although Simon could accomplish the task while in his human form, full werewolf strength would make it easier to carry someone of the hunter's size.

Lis shook her head.

"Lis —" Rose began.

"I've spent almost every day and night with him for over fifteen years," Lis snapped. "I don't need to give another minute to the person who gave me no choice but to do this."

Rose nodded to Simon. "Get back as quickly as you can. She needs to go the clinic and get checked out, but if they tell her to go to a hospital, I can't take her. Can't risk the sun."

Simon shifted into his bipedal werewolf form, then gathered the hunter over his shoulder. The stairs weren't made for something of his size, so he swung over the railings to make it back to ground level.

Rose joined Lis against the wall. The vampire aerosol can was in her view. She moved the armchair to block the sight, although she wouldn't really feel safe until it was far away from her.

She waited until Lis got up on her own. Then she and Lis helped each other down the stairs. Rose went back up to grab Simon's clothes and, after a second thought, the book of blood spells. Lis just stood there in the middle of the sanctuary, blearily staring up at the rose window, until Rose led her to the front door, where Simon met them and pulled on his clothes again to take Lis to the clinic.

* * * *

Simon did most of the explaining, for which Lis was grateful, except the nurses and doctor started looking at Simon as though he was trying to control the narrative to mask abuse, which would have been laughable if anything had been funny.

One of the nurses, however, responded to Simon as though she knew what he was, and as soon as Lis started talking for herself and agreed to get checked out privately, the nurse seemed to accept the story and didn't ask any more questions or insist that they contact the police after Lis refused.

As soon as the nurse finished with her assessment, she pulled off her gloves and rested a hand on Lis' arm. "It looks like you definitely have a concussion, but I don't think it's bad enough to go to the hospital. The old adage is that you shouldn't sleep, but that's outdated. I just don't recommend you be alone tonight."

"We're staying with a friend," Lis said.

"Good. I'm going to have the doctor come in and give the official diagnosis and recommendations, but he knows I'm always right." The nurse winked and removed her hand from Lis' arm. "Are you sure you're okay otherwise? You seem…"

"I'm just shaken. From the attack." It wasn't too far from the truth that Lis absolutely could not share with anyone, especially strangers, and especially when those strangers were officials of some authority.

Hunters knew their deaths would often go unexplained, that they'd likely end up considered missing and only presumed dead, if they hadn't been already. An inexplicable life led to inexplicable death. Archie's had been an undignified end, compounded by the method of body disposal, but the last thing anyone needed was an investigation. Even he wouldn't have wanted that. Hunters were part of the background by design, meant and made to fade away.

Under different circumstances, he would have told her to simply take what she could and move on.

"Okay," the nurse said. "Well, it's over. I know it's hard to convince your body and mind of that, but it *is* over. I'll go get the doctor now. But I just wanted you to know...you're not alone. I've got scars a lot like yours."

Lis straightened as the nurse headed for the door.

"You're going to be fine," the nurse said. "Get some sleep and stay safe 'til dawn. Angels and gargoyles will watch over you."

Lis didn't respond. If that was some kind of Meridian hunter code, she wasn't familiar with it, but she thought it was supposed to be comforting.

By the time the nurse left, Lis' head was already feeling better.

* * * *

Simon still insisted on carrying her into the church, where Rose anxiously met them, appearing almost like normal, which meant she must have imbibed something more potent than whatever animal blood she kept in her fridge, but Lis couldn't find it in herself to ask.

Rose's more dynamic face revealed her relief. "God, you already look so much better."

She led Simon and Lis back to the bathroom, where they stripped from their ruined clothes. There wasn't so much as a scar where Rose had been shot, Simon's face only had a trace of bruising, and Lis could stand and walk and turn without feeling like horizontal went vertical and vice versa.

Part of her wanted to go back to the motel, to be alone with the mildew and scent of shared lotion, with the blinds and blackout curtains, shut away from the world and absolutely no one touching her.

But the shower was warm and had its own pleasant scents, there was enough room that Lis wasn't crowded, and although both Rose and Simon touched her, there was no thrall, not even a hint of pheromone — just utmost care, a collective comfort from broad contact without expectations, and a sense that the night swirled into the drain beneath their feet.

After they were finished, Rose offered Lis one of Simon's shirts to sleep in. Rose pulled on a short cotton nightgown. Simon wore a pair of lounge pants.

Simon carried Lis from the bathroom to the sanctuary. She almost insisted that he put her down because she could walk fine on her own, but she couldn't remember the last time she'd been just held.

He lowered her onto new sheets on the large, tidied bed.

"We'll leave you alone, but we'll be just in here," Rose said, pointing to the casual living area. "If you wake up feeling sick, let us know."

Lis grasped both their forearms. She couldn't say it, couldn't ask, but she squeezed lightly and hoped they understood.

Simon let himself be drawn into bed first, crawling over her. Then Rose climbed in next to her. Again, there was plenty of room for all of them. But when Lis closed her eyes, she held Rose's hand, Simon's leg hooked over hers. Keeping contact. Keeping watch.

I wish I could sleep like this forever.

Epilogue

Lis entered the squat, three-story, cream-brick building that looked like it should house accountants in seventies attire. The interior had been renovated within the last five years, leaning gray rather than beige, but the foyer still felt closed in rather than following the more recent trend of open floor plans.

She immediately clocked cameras pointing at the front door, white-painted beadboard reinforcing the drywall, metal reinforcements on both doors and the elevator. At any moment, someone could push a button and all doors would be blocked off. She also noticed the off-white runes painted in the corners and around the front door.

"Hello. Can I help you?" The receptionist was blandly polite but cautious, perhaps thinking Lis was a child who had wandered in by mistake. There was a training gymnasium across the street that mirrored the one next to this building.

To be fair, Lis might not have gone out of her way to look more adult for the visit. She wasn't wearing a business suit or a pencil skirt. She'd dressed one way her whole life and would probably dress that way the rest of her working nights. But she'd wanted to try wearing new things, colorful things, during the day because she'd never had the opportunity before.

And maybe that looked like dressing her inner child. In her defense, she still fit in the juniors sections of department stores.

"I have an appointment with Thomas Gonzales."

"Name?" The receptionist had a feminine voice and wore lipstick, but neither of those things, nor the purple polish on his fingernails, meant he couldn't throw a punch, and the way he wore his shirt just a little too tight showed off gym-rat muscles. Lis knew better than to underestimate anyone.

"Lis Song."

The receptionist finally warmed to her, his polite smile broadening into something more genuine, now that it was clear Lis was supposed to be there. "He's expecting you. Second floor, office 204."

Lis used the stairs instead of the elevator. She had a phobia of falling elevators.

The second floor was split into two sections. Offices lined the edge and bisected the floor in the middle. The rest were low-wall cubicles and looked to be for as-needed use, with monitors and keyboards but no personalization. The private offices were accessorized, more lived in.

Lis knocked on the door to the fourth office on the left. A trim black man in a business suit looked up from his monitor. He animated at the sight of her and beckoned her in. Although he, too, appeared bemused by her as she entered, he stood and stretched out a hand, which she obliged herself to shake.

"Thomas," he said. "You must be Liz."

"Lis. S sound."

"Sorry. Lis. I like your shirt. Interesting choice."

Lis looked down at her pink shirt. Kittens cavorted over the chest. She wore a denim jacket over it, but at least one kitten was showing. "I think I want a cat."

"Okay."

Based on his facial furrows, Lis didn't think she'd bemused him any less.

"Well, Ms. Song, I must admit, I was intrigued by your application. Certainly one of the youngest applicants into our Unusual Circumstances Division. May I ask how you heard of Lost Until Found?"

"One of my friends recommended it to me."

"Did your friend say why?"

"He said that if I'm this good at what I do, I should be paid for it."

Thomas slowly grinned. "Are you good at finding things that are lost, Ms. Song?"

"I'm good at helping those who are lost and finding those that made them that way, Mr. Gonzales."

"Your application says you have sixteen years of experience, but your date of birth here—"

"Is correct." Lis sat on the edge of her seat, because there was no way to look good in an interview with her feet swinging above the floor. "I was trained from childhood. My handler recently passed away. That has left me in several awkward positions, one of which is financial."

Thomas didn't seem quite as bemused anymore. "I'm sorry for your loss. And your handler, was he responsible for training you as well?"

Lis nodded.

"Any relation?"

She shook her head.

"I see." Thomas sat back in his chair, giving her the same troubled look Rose and Simon had when they'd done the math. "I did notice a dearth of education on the application."

"Thomas, permission to speak freely?"

"Your mentor was military, wasn't he?"

"He was. Sir, my friend recommended this place because it's an Alliance-friendly agency that pays its hunters under the auspices of legitimate business. I work the Wastelands and sometimes Cemetery Grove. Most hunters focus north of those neighborhoods, because that's where high-value demon bodies are, but that leaves people in greater need abandoned. I would rather not leave them vulnerable just because vampire teeth don't pay the bills enough for myself or to justify a collective inducting me in. My friend said that your hunters don't work solely on commission."

"May I ask who your friend is?"

"He's an Alliance werewolf. He doesn't know any agent here personally. He just knows the agency."

"I respect that you respect his privacy," Thomas said. "Your friend is right. Our hunters are paid a salary, plus commission. This way, high-value harvesting can be quite lucrative, but we also support those like you, who simply want to help, and if you need an extra bit of cash, one or two high-value bodies can cover that. We believe, like your friend, that being a demon hunter in a city like this is a thankless, high-risk job, which we want to mitigate as much as we can. We do that by being a legitimate private investigation firm, which takes up the front-facing first-floor offices.

That also provides a transitional job for hunters who've experienced injury or life changes that make hunting less viable. Either way, we provide full health benefits, vision, dental, 401(k), the works. The founders believe that's the least we can do for people who do their part to protect our city."

"Another friend told me to ask about tuition assistance." Lis looked down at her clasped hands. "You noted that my education was lacking. I was…homeschooled. Very little formal education or testing. I'm interested in getting my GED."

Thomas crossed his legs, still studying her like she was a picture with frightening but important images hidden in the shadows. "We don't have a formal program, but I could speak to the founders. We have an arrangement with the University of Texas-Meridian that we might amend to include tuition assistance. I do know that UTM offers GED and ESL night classes as well. It's just that most of our hunters are — "

"Older," Lis finished for him.

"Yes. Most people don't get their calling into the profession until they're well into adulthood. That's why your application intrigued us. We've also been looking into recruiting more women into the agency. Permission to speak freely as well?"

Lis nodded.

"Given your stature, I'm curious as to the secret of your success. I can see from your scars that you prefer hand-to-hand combat, which is difficult even for men bigger and stronger than you. And I can tell from the way you walked in and move that you have great command over your body. If we could learn some of your techniques, we might be able to expand our training modules away from an assumption that bigger is better."

"My mentor developed training modules specifically for me," Lis said. "He even called them that. I could be of some help in that respect."

"We'd compensate you for that additional contribution, of course. I'm afraid our starting salary, sans commission, isn't as high as we'd like for it to be. We're dependent on the smaller but legitimate PI business and our exclusive body brokering to keep the lights on and our hunters supported. That also means that all harvesting for profit goes through us—no exceptions, no matter how small."

"Jewelry?"

Thomas nodded. "It may have mystical relevance, or we just sell the metal and stones."

"Cash?"

"Anything under fifty you can keep, as long as you note it in your daily report."

"Gift cards?"

He grinned. "You can keep those, too. And loyalty punch cards. I got a free pretzel once."

"I work in a less expensive area."

"Yes, you do."

Lis had an eye on a Cemetery Grove apartment building within easy walking distance of Rose's church, a bar, a coffee shop, and a grocery store. Rose had assured Lis that she could stay at the church for as long as she wanted, but with Archie gone and the motel cleaned out of all their things, Lis found herself dreaming of a place that wasn't liminal, where she wasn't kept and she could put down roots. Where she could hang a picture or Christmas lights or leave a pizza box open on a coffee table of her own choosing.

She and Archie had nested wherever they'd lived, whether in motels or abandoned buildings—even a janitor's closet once—but now that she was on her own, she couldn't shake the dream of a home that was just hers to do with as she pleased, like Rose had done to the church. Lis would have a much smaller budget to work with, of course, but because of her time with Archie, her expectations were incredibly low. The apartment she wanted seemed luxurious in comparison.

"What do you like most about working in an area that most hunters avoid?" Thomas asked.

"I like helping people who have enough trouble fighting off all the things sucking them dry without adding vampires into the mix."

"Would you be open to occasionally working with a partner? We have agents who work Cemetery Grove, and we find that partnering our agents protects them and keeps the activity from being too solitary."

Lis nodded. She worked alone, but the Wastelands could only benefit from an extra hunter helping the community.

"We also sometimes enlist our hunters to work on the investigative side, to get a feel for the business. In cases of long-term injury or illness, working for us as a recruiter or private investigator can act as a stop-gap or a new phase. In Meridian, there's more overlap between our investigative branch and the hunting side than you might think. A little more variety, too. I understand you specialize in vampires."

"Only because vampires tend to specialize in the areas I serve."

"I like that. And since you were the one who brought up the Alliance, I trust you're familiar with its policies?"

"No intentionally killing someone who swore not to intentionally kill you."

Thomas' smile broadened. Lis wasn't accustomed to having so many people find her dry, flat delivery of facts so delightful.

"Exactly. The job's already hard. No need to make it harder."

"Are you a hunter?" Lis asked.

"Sometimes. I primarily work as a recruiter these days. My partner — in work and in life — works the streets more than I do."

Lis had already noticed the flash of a gold wedding band on his left hand.

"He and I are also both responsible for the training modules. We've researched and developed a variety of methods to more safely and effectively fight demons. The training gym next door is where I spend my time when I'm not here. I suffered an exsanguination a few years ago that I haven't quite recovered from. Fortunately, LNF doesn't just throw out hunters because they're no longer safe on the front lines."

Part of what had led Archie down his path had been trying to live out his hunter aspirations through her after injury had left him less able. Lis was younger than most hunters, but she wouldn't be young forever, and she put herself at risk every night. So the idea that she could get her GED, maybe a degree, and wouldn't *need* to hunt for the rest of her life definitely appealed to her. When she imagined reaching the other side of thirty and *not* hunting in the same way she always had, it spun her head, but it was also kind of exciting for the future to be longer than one more night.

"Do you think you can use me?" Lis asked.

"Ms. Song, there's no question. What we hope you ask yourself is if you can use us?"

She stood and stretched out her hand. "Absolutely."

Thomas met her with another firm handshake. "I'll get the paperwork together by tomorrow. You'll need to bring some documentation, and we'll go over benefit options. I should have something preliminary from the director regarding tuition assistance at that point. I'll go over expectations and schedules, and you can make your final decision whether to sign on. I think we have a lot of offer each other, though. Would you like to see our training facilities and run through a few of your methods with any hunters who might be there?"

"Do they haze the new girl before she's even hired?"

"They won't go easy on you. But if they really try to hurt you, I'll just shoot them."

"One more thing," Lis said as they left Thomas' office.

"Yes?"

"A hunter agency may say it's Alliance-adherent, but many hunters simply tolerate the agreements. I'm in a relationship with a werewolf and a vampire."

None of them had quite figured out what kind of relationship it was yet, because Lis hadn't figured out who she was or what she wanted. Becoming her own kind of hunter was the first step to getting there.

All she knew was that she liked being with them and they loved to spoil her. At least, it seemed like spoiling to her. Whenever she said that, they just looked at her with that funny expression that told her what they did was standard rather than above and beyond.

"Both are Alliance-marked," Lis continued, "and they've saved my life multiple times. Is that going to be a problem?"

"No, ma'am." Thomas held the door to the stairway open for her. "Our founders were instrumental in the agreement's development. You might hit against some friction at the company Christmas party, but policy is on your side. Me, I don't have a problem with a vampire as long as they're not drinking. I figure if *I* can feel that way, other people can get the hell over themselves."

And Lis felt that if she could continue being a hunter after everything Archie had done to her—mostly because that's all he'd left her able to do—she could work for a hunter agency that gave her the means to do what she wanted and give her what she needed.

Maybe the investigative team could even find out her real name and whether the rest of her family was still alive.

All she really needed to know now, though, was that Thomas was offering her a steady job doing what she'd already been doing for close to free. And after the sun went down that night, the nicest vampire and werewolf she'd ever met would be waiting to take her out on the town to celebrate.

Rose had promised her a chocolate milkshake.

Sign up for our newsletter and find out about all our romance book releases, eBook sales and promotions, sneak peeks and FREE romance books!

Want to see more from this author?
Here's a taster for you to enjoy!

Meridian: Never & Forever
Aurelia T. Evans

Excerpt

Per the invitation's strongly worded request, Heather arrived at the funeral in a rideshare, but there were already cars up and down the street and beyond, clogging up other people's driveways, all for the sake of paying respects to a Meridian institution—Angela Cabrera herself, late at seventy-two and taken far too soon.

Someone like Angela didn't hold with funerals as sad, somber affairs, with black gloves, veils, sheets covering mirrors, and a preserved body on maudlin display in the middle of the parlor. Plenty of the people inside the house attended in traditional sober blacks and charcoal grays, but most of Angela's closest family wore color. Even so, most avoided the faux pas of colors that were too cheerful, instead wearing subdued blues, purples, and greens.

Only Magda, Angela's oldest daughter and Heather's aunt, had chosen a livelier palette of magenta with black accents, a suit she sometimes wore in the courtroom. She was a bright spot in an ocean of dark, but everyone expected that of Magda, who was the neon sheep of the family and one of Heather's many personal inspirations, including but not limited to her grandmother.

Heather would usually defer to her grandmother's wishes more than the plum-colored floral dress she'd chosen for the late afternoon wake, but Heather couldn't find it in herself to fake joy.

Angela Cabrera had died seven days ago—like the beginning of a curse—without any apparent warning. A stroke had struck her during a dinner alone, and she hadn't been found until Heather's mother, Camille, visited her the next morning when Angela didn't show up at her professional studio or answer her phone. Two days later, after showing no signs of improvement or even presence while in her hospital bed, she died, as though everything else gave up at once. No one had had any inkling she'd been sick. The only indication that Angela herself may have had some foreknowledge was that she'd met with her estate lawyer only three months prior, although she'd had end-of-life documents in place for years.

Seven days. Only seven days. But that week had felt like seven years, with the time moving at the most infinitesimal pace for hours, then scurrying like a cockroach along the walls, narrowing actual hours into what felt like minutes.

Heather wanted to honor her grandmother—an even more important figure in her life than her mother—but all she could hold was how she'd never speak to her grandmother again. In trying to cling to every interaction, conversation, and piece of wisdom passed down to her, they kept slipping out like rice between her knuckles, which made her feel like she was already forgetting and therefore dishonoring her grandmother's memory.

She'd taken three days off work, which was two more than they usually allowed after a death in the family, but she couldn't show houses with a smile when grief kept ambushing her like a rabid hyena. She'd cried a flood and didn't know where all the tears had come from or where they'd all gone and why they hadn't left her a dried husk or her apartment soaked halfway up the walls. For the last four days, though, aside from some residual lacrimal leakage, Heather had gone completely numb, and all her colors had disappeared.

The world was duller without Angela Cabrera still in it.

Visually, it was comparable to her ears being stuffed with cotton. Half the time, she mourned that loss with the same intensity as she mourned her grandmother, even though the feelings themselves had been cut off from her as effectively as a hand or foot. The other half, she thought it was fitting tribute, that the world didn't deserve color after taking Angela away. Her aunt's flamboyance was a welcome interjection, though, not quite as intense but evoking the world Heather had known before Angela had died—a reminder that it was still there, waiting, and that eventually the desaturating fog would lift. Hard to believe it ever would.

Heather had only been to four funerals for people she actually knew, one a coworker, one a friend, and both paternal grandparents. She'd never known Angela's husband, who had died of a widowmaker when she'd been a little girl.

Angela's was the hardest hit yet, surpassing the day Heather had had her first cat put down a few years ago, which had been so difficult that she hadn't yet adopted another.

Nevertheless, nothing short of an ER visit would keep her from her grandmother's wake. That was the least Heather could do for her, especially since she was useless to help her mother, aunt, and uncle, who were arguably going through worse, because Angela had been their *mother*. She felt selfish that she'd collapsed when everyone had needed her, but she didn't get to choose what kind of grief she felt, whether low-hanging dark clouds scudding tall buildings or baleful, rain-filled cells threatening rotation.

Right now, her grief and the sky were heavy and gray, through all the dark attempts at color—just an endless stretch of gray.

Her mother was with her brother and sister in Angela Cabrera's foyer, an abundance of white, veined marble accented with black wrought iron. The entire front half of the house was formal and hard and cold as cemetery stone, with examples of some of her more elaborate carvings that had either never found a home or Angela had wanted to keep for herself towering in the twin parlors and the fountain cradled in the curve of the grand staircase. This was where Angela had done most of her more personal business—a showroom of sorts.

The back of the house, however, was dark as caves wherever natural light from the floor-to-ceiling windows didn't reach, but comfortable as a lodge, with matte stone and warm wood making it a retreat. Aside from pieces Angela had bought from Heather, it was free of art, displaying instead photos of family on any given surface—as informal as could be. Even the artwork she'd chosen from Heather's oeuvre was less photorealistic, sketchier in charcoal, pencil, chalk, and watercolor pastel.

The house perched somewhere between large and mansion, because despite Angela's personal preference for cozy, her success had happened quite contrary to her intention and with it had arisen certain expectations—from Meridian, from her family, and most particularly her husband.

The entire interior of the house was full of people, the usually cool air warm and slightly moist, as though grief created its own climate.

Heather wanted to turn around and walk right back out, offended to her core by the crowd, the ambience, the grocery-store charcuterie and canapes, the closed black casket under the marble statue of a seraph in the process of losing her six wings, by the entire sterile spectacle of the wake preceding the early evening funeral.

Instead, she fought a welling of tears disconnected from her surface emotions as she approached her mother, who looked as though she found the circumstances just as distasteful and her eyes just as irrepressibly damp. If Camille had had half the week Heather had, she was probably exhausted—on top of all the planning required to put everything together, even with a comprehensive end-of-life directive.

"Heather, oh sweetheart." Camille embraced her daughter, then laughed a little as she reached into her pocket to pull out a tissue for each of them. "I'm so very tired of blowing my nose, but it just won't stop, and people keep coming in and telling me about all the ways that Mom touched their lives, and it just starts all over again. But how are you doing? You didn't any answer any of my calls or texts, except to say you were coming."

Heather half shrugged, then gestured to generally indicate where they were. There was nothing to say about why she wasn't feeling particularly chatty. "I'm okay."

"You know your grandma loved you *so* much. She was so proud of your art, and your willfulness. It always made her laugh when I'd call her in exasperation that you insisted on having your way *again*. Like Aunt Magda." Camille made a face at her sister, who made a face back, no malice intended either way.

No matter how much of an odd duck Magda or Heather were, that didn't mean either of them had ever been at risk of exile from the family. Angela would never have allowed it.

"She would be so happy you made it," Camille continued.

"Are *you* okay?" Heather didn't want to examine her own feelings on the matter, and without the colors, she could only go by the way her mother looked—the faded red in her eyes, the slight swelling on her eyelids, the carefully curated effort with makeup to cover up her weariness and grief into something more presentable for the Meridian stage.

As much as the family would have preferred to keep their mourning more private, they couldn't deny the entire city a chance to grieve its eccentric mother, who had left her mark almost everywhere in Meridian, with elaborate angels and gargoyles almost anywhere one looked—hundreds of hand-carved statues and even more limited-batch productions and reproductions, not to mention the buildings she'd been commissioned to design, not limited to churches. She'd been a prolific sculptor and architect 'til the day she'd died, her vision and acuity as sharp as the cherub's spear in the other parlor. Wherever Meridian threatened to become too modern or brutalist, Angela had softened the edges— or at least made them more interesting. Without her, the city would never have become known for its particular style, now oft imitated to maintain the Meridian culture.

Angela was Camille's mother, Heather's grandmother, but everyone with Meridian in their blood laid claim to Angela Cabrera as their own, whether they deserved her or not.

"I'm doing all right. Some days are better than others. Your aunt and uncle are handling this better than me, because they don't have to juggle the business and everything," Camille answered, dabbing under her eyes with the tissue to keep from mussing her makeup.

"I'm sorry I haven't returned your calls or come over. I've just…"

Camille shook her head. "I understand. You have your own life. I just don't like to think of you all alone in that apartment, stewing in your grief without anyone to lean on. If not for your dad, I don't know if I'd be upright, much less hosting."

"Can I help with anything?"

Camille bustled her along. "No, no, no, it's not your job, sweetie. It's mine. I know how much she meant to you. Go on. I'm fine. Just need to get through this week, and then it'll be quiet again, and we can all take proper time to deal with this. If I need anything, your dad is waiting in the wings, dealing with the parking logistics. This is why we told people to rideshare here," she muttered, attention diverting from Heather to the many moving parts of managing the funeral of a public figure. At the very least, it would be a distraction. Camille was always happiest when she had a task or five to do.

Heather hugged her uncle, then her aunt, who both expressed that they hadn't seen her in too long. After a girl had grown and gone her own way, family always said that at every last reunion, which was usually the only time she could catch up with everyone.

It was also always so awkward after a divorce, because people didn't know what to talk to her about anymore. When she'd been married, the questions were easy— How was Andy doing at his job? Were they going to move into a house soon? Were they going to be hearing the pitter-patter of little feet in the next year or so? The questions had been easy, even if the answers hadn't been, especially after five years had gone by and certain benchmarks hadn't been met.

But after a divorce, there wasn't a single question that didn't make one or both parties uncomfortable.

And not joining the family business—even Aunt Magda worked with the Cabrera Angels Foundation now and then—meant Heather was always an outsider, estranged by her own normalcy. There wasn't much a realtor who didn't carry the Cabrera name could do for the foundation or the agency, other than pass along a card if a client wanted a decorative statue.

The wake had filled the house with faces either strange or only vaguely familiar, family and close friends dwarfed by the sheer number of other public figures obliged to honor the woman who had helped put Meridian on the map. Between the crush, the warmth, the casket, and the stone, Heather couldn't breathe. She grabbed a plate of cheese, crackers, and fruit and a small plastic cup of cranberry ginger ale and found a windowsill where she could perch, carefully arranging her jacket so she wouldn't inadvertently give anyone a glimpse under her skirt.

She wasn't hungry or thirsty—her appetite had disappeared with the colors—but eating was something to do that wasn't talking with people about her grandmother and how this or that statue or gravestone changed their life or how great her grandmother had been for the city, how cool her style was, how they wished they could be just like her, when none of them really knew who her grandmother had been.

When Heather had eschewed the family business and taken her husband's name — and hadn't changed it back after the divorce — most people couldn't have known she was part of the family. That had given her the opportunity for a front-row seat to any and all speculation about Angela Cabrera, who had been a nearly ubiquitous force in Meridian from its earliest growth but largely absent from public appearances, unlike all the other local muckety-mucks who considered Meridian their little fiefdom. People had called her an angel, saint, psychic, witch, hack, drunk. They'd positioned her as the sometimes-troubled white hat to Meridian's dark forces, a spiritual warrior wielding a self-carved stone sword against a city drowning in demons.

Heather couldn't deny that Meridian seemed to have some pretty unusual crime stats, even for Texas — the sort of thing that, as a realtor, she knew but glossed over in favor of more congratulatory factoids. She also couldn't deny that her grandmother's art had become almost memetic, a running Gothic joke, although Angela had taken every piece seriously — compelled, like many great artists. In Meridian, they were an attraction, photo opportunities for tourists and trendsetters, rather than whatever Angela was desperately trying to give voice to.

But what Heather had always wanted to tell the people sharing ghost stories about her grandmother was that Angela Cabrera was just a woman. Not Joan of Arc, not Teresa of Ávila, not Greta Thunberg... Just a woman with an artistic itch and the financial ability to scratch it. She wasn't fighting the forces of darkness by producing protectors of the city. She was simply carving angels and demons because she had her own that fought inside her every day.

And maybe she'd had a bottle of wine when she should have had a glass, but Angela had never been drunk in front of Heather, and she'd always been there when Heather had been having a hard time — with her mother, with school, with her boyfriends, then with her husband, then with the divorce. She carried the wisdom of years without an ounce of self-righteousness or bullshit that so often accompanied other people's advice. Her grandmother had been *real*, which was more than she could say for so many of those who had come to the wake simply to be seen.

To hell with Meridian. Her parents should have insisted on a private funeral. The city could throw a goddamn parade if they really wanted to celebrate her. Heather wouldn't have cared if the whole house had been filled with balloons at Angela's request, but Angela had never liked crowds like this in life, any more than Heather did. She found it hard to believe that this had been part of Angela's funeral plans, so much as Camille letting the city take its pound of flesh in exchange for the goodwill it would incur for the business and foundation, now that their driving force was dead.

It was an uncharitable view of her mother, but as Heather had noted to herself earlier, it was much simpler for Camille to make decisions on behalf of the business than herself or the rest of the family and what they needed from the funeral, rather than feeding a bunch of parasites with deep pockets.

Maybe Heather simply wasn't feeling very charitable today, her numbness overlaying an undercurrent of rage that threatened to break through.

Knowing it was only another manifestation of mourning didn't make letting it surface any wiser. Angela wouldn't have wanted this crush, least of all in her home, but she certainly wouldn't have wanted her granddaughter making a scene on her behalf.

"*I'm dead, little girl,*" Heather imagined her saying, maybe while cradling a mug of coffee, maybe with something stronger poured in with it. "*I made a plan for my death and after, but all this hullabaloo and whatnot certainly don't affect* me *anymore. It's about what your mother needs right now, even if it's not what you'd prefer.*"

There were some faces in the crowd, though, who were more than just people she'd seen on the news or on fliers and billboards. Some of these people had been in and out of Angela's house when Heather had been over, or in her studio when Heather had visited after school, doing homework when she hadn't had track practice. She recognized some plainclothes police who occasionally played security detail when someone got too hot on the good versus evil concept and decided that they were evil, so Angela must be eradicated. She recognized the owner of the downtown magic shop, which had been one of Heather's favorite places to go in her teens, although she'd since transitioned from geodes and crystal wands to gemstones. She recognized doctors and nurses who worked at the clinics that the foundation supported. She recognized religious leaders from multiple religions and denominations and at least six funeral directors, none of whom were responsible for this particular funeral. Ordinary folks with whom her grandmother interacted on a regular basis. All of these people were here for their own reasons, their little facet of how they knew Angela. They weren't entirely wrong about that facet, but they'd extrapolated upon the entire soul of the woman without enough information.

At least Heather knew her grandmother was something of a mystery. For all that Heather had known and loved her and spent so much time with her, her grandmother still held a lot of herself to her chest, whole angles refracting colors that only Heather could see around and inside her, when she spoke and when she didn't. Heather had interpreted that rainbow the way some people interpreted tongues, but there was a lot of margin for error, like reading tea leaves — more art than science.

Angela Cabrera had lived in this house for all the years Heather could remember her, and she'd had people over almost constantly — for business, for homemade dinners or desserts, for quiet heartfelt talks, for overnights or a week to get back on their feet — but eventually, everyone she'd invited over would leave. Whatever happened in those alone times Heather couldn't fathom, and Angela hadn't shared.

And not all people here for more than a photo op were entirely respected or respectable. Angela had been a single woman of a certain age and mystique and a wide variety of acquaintances and friends.

The funeral was only going to fuel those little rumor fires. Now that she was dead, she'd ascend into the realm of myth or urban legend. Perhaps in a few years' time, people might question if she'd ever really existed, that instead she was some reverse boogeyman or Meridian mascot, as fabled as Johnny Appleseed.

Meridian could make a martyr out of Angela Cabrera all they wanted. Heather just wanted her grandmother back.

Heather had eaten through most of her snacks and drunk most of her ginger ale when an eminently familiar face came through the front door. She closed her eyes and leaned back against the window, which was at least one source of coolness in the thickened room. If she had been less polite, she would have groaned.

She should have known he would turn up. Despite the divorce and having never had children, and despite all the things that had happened between him and Heather, he was still part of the family and had been for over ten years. Angela had never liked him, but she'd always been courteous. He had granted her the same courtesy. Even in the midst of all he'd done to Heather, he'd remained unfailingly polite, even kind, to her family.

When Angela had hurt her arm, he'd been the one to take her to the hospital, then drive her around anywhere she'd needed to go half the time. When Heather's niece and nephew had needed someplace to stay after Heather's sister and brother-in-law had been in a car accident, he'd been the first to suggest that they take the kids in for as long as needed. Heather could talk plenty of trash about her ex-husband, but the way he treated his obligations to everyone else had never been an issue.

Besides, just because they'd divorced didn't mean he'd stopped working at the production company warehouse. That had caused some friction between him and her mother, but given his history of using honey instead of vinegar, it was fairly easy for them to remain cordial, if a bit chilly, for the sake of the business. He was still Cabrera management, so despite the dissolution of the marriage, he was still family, in his own way.

Heather didn't necessarily begrudge him paying his respects to Angela, but she wished he weren't here so she wouldn't have to deal with queasiness from the crowd *and* having the cold fish of him slapping her face at the same time.

She stayed low on the windowsill while he shook her mother's hand. Her mother accepted the condolences with grace. No scene here. Not today. And as long as there wasn't an open bar, hopefully all these strangers with brewing antagonisms — family and friends versus lookie-loos, officials of commerce versus officials of charity, with grief and curiosity fanning flames — would keep their knives to themselves in Angela's honor.

One thing Heather did know from the four funerals she'd attended — They could go smoothly, bland as a sterile wedding, tears and all, or emotions could run high and flare out, grief like a match to natural gas.

Weddings and funerals... Nothing at all could happen, but also *anything* could happen.

Andrew continued into the house without noticing Heather in the parlor. Heather dusted off her hands, then stood to toss the plate and cup.

The thankfully private funeral itself would be in the backyard, which abutted the creek behind them and promised lovely scenery in one of the places Angela had loved the most. Angela would then be returned to the funeral home, who would inter her in the family mausoleum in her church's graveyard.

The body was in that casket, and it would soon be lowered into a stone box instead of humbler ground. One day, Heather could elect to join her family in the same mausoleum, which held Angela's husband and had space for a dozen others — more, if they decided to install a columbarium.

All at once, Heather struggled to breathe. She pushed through the crowd as politely as she could while the aggressive colorlessness of her world intruded on her vision, gray closing in on her in these hard, white rooms. She feared collapsing or exploding or both, like a star, and causing a self-absorbed scene in the middle of her grandmother's wake. The society pages would be buzzing, and her different surname might not save her anymore if enough people knew she was family and so devastated by the loss that she'd passed out in front of everyone. If she could just reach the stairs, she could lie down in one of the upstairs bedrooms and wait for the funeral to start, which was all she'd really come here for, not this…morbid who's who with grocery-store catering.

She ducked under the rope that blocked the stairs — a sign specified only family were allowed beyond. Halfway up the first curve, she paused as the droning hum of conversation fell off like a lapsed teetotaler over the side of a pitching boat.

At first, she assumed — somewhat egotistically — the quiet might be because of her breaking away from the crowd in such a visible way, but everyone was looking away from her, at the front door rather than the stairs.

As soon as she saw him, she understood why almost everything had stopped. She did, too, one foot on the next stair. She gripped the dark wooden railing tighter and tighter with ratcheting tension that joined the tears in the air.

Of all the funerals in the entire city, Bartholomew Vega had decided to waltz into Angela Cabrera's.

About the Author

Aurelia T. Evans is an up-and-coming erotica author with a penchant for horror and the supernatural.

She's the twisted mind behind the werewolf/shifter Sanctuary trilogy, demonic circus series Arcanium, and vampire serial Bloodbound. She's also had short stories featured in various erotic anthologies.

Aurelia presently lives in Dallas, Texas (although she doesn't ride horses or wear hats). She loves cats and enjoys baking as much as she dislikes cooking. She's a walker, not a runner, and she writes outside as often as possible.

Aurelia loves to hear from readers. You can find her contact information, website details and author profile page at https://www.firstforromance.com

ENTWINED PUBLISHING